**Don't miss the first two books in the
Charlie Hernández series!**

Charlie Hernández & the League of Shadows
Charlie Hernández & the Castle of Bones

BOOK 3

CHARLIE HERNÁNDEZ&
THE GOLDEN DOOMS

RYAN CALEJO

Aladdin

New York ✦ London ✦ Toronto ✦ Sydney ✦ New Delhi

ALADDIN
An imprint of Simon & Schuster Children's Publishing Division
1230 Avenue of the Americas, New York, New York 10020
First Aladdin hardcover edition September 2022
Text copyright © 2022 by Ryan Calejo
Jacket illustration copyright © 2022 by Manuel Šumberac
All rights reserved, including the right of reproduction in whole or in part in any form.
ALADDIN and related logo are registered trademarks of Simon & Schuster, Inc.
For information about special discounts for bulk purchases, please contact
Simon & Schuster Special Sales at 1-866-506-1949 or business@simonandschuster.com.
The Simon & Schuster Speakers Bureau can bring authors to your live event.
For more information or to book an event, contact the Simon & Schuster Speakers Bureau
at 1-866-248-3049 or visit our website at www.simonspeakers.com.
Jacket designed by Karin Paprocki
Interior designed by Hilary Zarycky
The text of this book was set in Adobe Jenson Pro.
Manufactured in China 0522 SCP
2 4 6 8 10 9 7 5 3 1
Library of Congress Cataloging-in-Publication Data
Names: Calejo, Ryan, author.
Title: Charlie Hernández & the Golden Dooms / Ryan Calejo.
Other titles: Charlie Hernández and the Golden Dooms
Description: First Aladdin hardcover edition. | New York : Aladdin, 2022. |
Series: Charlie Hernández ; 3 | Audience: Ages 10 to 14. |
Summary: "A young calaca's appearance at school sends Charlie on a quest
to investigate suspicious activity in Miami and learn the truth behind the
Golden Dooms"— Provided by publisher.
Identifiers: LCCN 2021043350 (print) | LCCN 2021043351 (ebook) |
ISBN 9781534484214 (hardcover) | ISBN 9781534484238 (ebook)
Subjects: CYAC: Shapeshifting—Fiction. | Folklore—Latin America—Fiction. | Secret
societies—Fiction. | Good and evil—Fiction. | Dead—Fiction. | Supernatural—Fiction. |
Hispanic Americans—Fiction. | Miami (Fla.)—Fiction. | LCGFT: Novels.
Classification: LCC PZ7.1.C312 Cf 2022 (print) | LCC PZ7.1.C312 (ebook) |
DDC [Fic]—dc23
LC record available at https://lccn.loc.gov/2021043350
LC ebook record available at https://lccn.loc.gov/2021043351

To Ms. Gonzalez and Mrs. Streeter,
because you never forget your favorite librarian
or your favorite teacher, and to Anna Parsons,
for all her hard work and talent

CHARLIE HERNÁNDEZ &
THE GOLDEN DOOMS

CHAPTER ONE

Death came for me at around lunchtime. I was walking out of Ms. Alonso's third-period history, on my way to the cafeteria, and didn't even see it coming. No one usually does. In fact, as I started down the hallway toward the little stairs plastered with prom posters, all I saw was a girl. And she didn't look particularly deadly, either. She was, as a matter of fact, *seriously* pretty. I mean, who would've thought somebody that cute was gonna bring about the end of the world? Definitely not me, or else I wouldn't've stood there like some starry-eyed *goof*, basically just gawking at her as she slipped her way between the streams of hungry middle schoolers and came right up to me.

"¿Perdona, tú eres Charlie Hernández?"

Large hazel eyes blinked up at me from beneath ridiculously long, ridiculously thick lashes, and I think I might've managed a couple of blinks myself. I *think*. . . .

She tried again. "Are you Charlie Hernández?"

And this time I managed a whole nod. (Impressive, I know.) But before I could work up to an "Uh," or a "Huh," or even an "Uh-huh, that's me!" her hands snapped out, quick as a thought, and she was shoving me backward— back, back, back past the broken water fountain, past the row of second-floor lockers, past the little janitor's closet with all the brooms inside, and through a door very clearly marked GIRLS' RESTROOM.

"Hey, what are you *DOING?*" I hissed, watching her flip the dead bolt.

"Locking the door."

"Yeah, *that* I can see. My question is, *WHY?*"

"¿Cuál es el problema?"

"The problem is that this is a *girls'* bathroom!"

"So?"

"So there could've been *A GIRL* in here!"

"There *is* a girl in here."

"WHAT! *Where?*" I whirled, my heart doing its best flippity-floppity, fish-out-of-water impersonation; and a moment later I felt the tap of a cold finger on my shoulder.

"Right *behind* you . . ."

Ah. Her. Right.

As I turned back around, I couldn't help noticing that

she was now staring up at me the same sorta way someone might stare at a three-headed mule.

"You're ... *different* than I expected," she said doubtfully.

"Well, that's kinda your fault for expecting. Most people don't expect much from me. And it usually works out better for everyone that way."

Her dark eyes narrowed. "You seem *tense*."

"That's because I *am* tense! *And* I'm getting outta here before someone catches us and I get even *tenser!*"

I started toward the door, which was definitely a step in the right direction, but not nearly enough. I should've gone running out of that bathroom and not stopped until I'd reached *the North Pole*. (Which, in case you were wondering, was approximately 3,972 miles from South Florida.)

"Wait!" Suddenly, Little Miss Shoves-a-Lot leapt in front of me, flinging her hands out like a traffic cop. "¡Necesito tu ayuda!"

And it was the fear—no, the pleading in those last few words ("I need your help")—that really got me. She sounded alone. And scared. And near tears.

So I stopped. I stared at her, and she stared back. Her hair was thick and dark and wavy, and her skin was smooth and tan and so uniformly flawless that you had to wonder if she'd ever even had a single *zit*.

She was almost too perfect to be real. Which, come

to think of it, should've been my first tip-off.

The second, though—*easily*—should've been her fashion sense. Or, rather, her lack thereof . . . She looked like someone who had been told how middle school kids liked to dress but hadn't actually ever *seen* one. At least not in *a while.* Her hairstyle and bell-bottoms made her look like she'd just stepped out of Austin Powers's groovy time machine, and her colorful purple sweater screamed eighties pop (and actually read, on one sleeve: THE 80S ROCK*!*).

She said, "I'm in trouble."

"*Trouble?*" Confused, I shook my head. "Well, in that case, you should probably find a hall monitor. And those are usually found out in *the halls.* . . ."

"But I don't need a hall monitor," she said pleadingly. "I need *a Morphling!*"

CHAPTER TWO

Had a pair of zombie hands busted out of the floor right then and grabbed me by my big toes, I don't think I would've been any more surprised. Morphling wasn't exactly a word you heard thrown around a lot in school bathrooms. It was, as a matter of fact, an old Latinx myth—stories of kids who could manifest specific animal traits, like wings. Or gills. Or claws. Or even the bony, scaly shell of an armadillo. I knew the stories because my abuelita knew the stories. She'd collected myths like some people collect action figures and had taught me most of them before I could even tie my own shoes.

But it wasn't until about month ago that I discovered two *very* important facts: One, the beings and creatures from those old myths *actually* existed, and two, I, Charlie Hernández, just so happened to be one. There was only a small group of non-sombras (i.e., humans) on the entire planet who knew my secret. And this girl wasn't supposed to be one of them. . . .

I blinked, slowly, and even more slowly, I looked into her strange too-dark eyes. "What'd you say . . . ?"

She stepped toward me, guarded but hopeful. "You're him, aren't you? You're Charlie Hernández. The fifth and final Morphling."

"I, *yeah* . . . But—how do you know that?"

"We all know."

Three little words. Just three. But it was funny how they could make your Panic-o-Meter go all *kinds* of loco. "And who is 'we' exactly . . . ?" I said. "*Who are you?*"

"Mi nombre es Esperanza Sophia Viviana Ramos Delgado de los Huesos."

Whoa. Okay. Now imagine being the poor kid who had to learn to spell all that in kindergarten. . . .

"Mind if I just call you Espe?" I said. And I'm not sure if it was my nerves or the lack of calories or the fact that I was locked in a bathroom with some strange girl who obviously knew a whole heck of a lot more about me than I knew about her, but I began to feel a familiar itch. A familiar tingle. And all of a sudden, I saw an *oh so familiar* sight:

A fat white feather came bursting through the skin of my arm like a fluffy, fuzzy jack-in-the-box!

I guess it wasn't bad enough that I totally *sucked* at morphing. It also seemed to happen at the absolute *WORST* possible times!

Esperanza *clearly* disagreed, though, because her eyes suddenly lit up, and she was practically bouncing up and down on her toes as she whispered, "Is that an ACTUAL feather?"

"Well, it's certainly not an ulcer," I said. (At least not *yet.*)

"How does it feel?!"

"Stings a little, to tell ya the truth."

"That's the most incredible thing I've ever SEEN!"

Just gimme a couple more minutes . . . , I thought.

"Oh, to see a Morphling manifest a feather!" Her voice was high and thin. Her hands clasped together in delight. "My bones are positively *rattling* with excitement!"

"Well, let's try to keep the *rattling* to a minimum," I told her. "We don't want anyone out there to hear you."

My first instinct—*duh*—was to pluck the fluffy little sucker. But in the end I decided that probably wasn't such a hot idea. The last time I started plucking feathers in a school bathroom, I'd nearly drowned the *entire* school. . . .

"By the way, you still haven't told me who that 'we' is," I reminded Esperanza, and she nodded and took a deep breath like she was getting ready to tell. Only instead of telling, she decided to *show.*

And boy, what a show it was. . . .

One moment I was staring at a beautiful, hazel-eyed, rosy-cheeked girl, and the next—¡*Dios mío!*—the girl wasn't even a girl anymore!

Well, I mean, she *was* a girl . . . but a girl without eyes or ears or lips or even a heartbeat!

Heck, without even a *heart*!

No skin stretched over any part of her body.

No muscles pulled on any of her bones.

She was—not only in a manner of speaking but in a manner of literally *BEING*—a skeleton!

A calaca!

One of the undead underworld ferriers of the recently *deceased*!

CHAPTER THREE

O nly . . . Esperanza was a lot *younger* than any calaca I'd ever seen. And a whole lot cooler-looking, too. Her face, whiter and brighter than any snowflake, was decorated in mesmerizing patterns of dots and swirls, hearts and spiderwebs. Her teeth were even and perfect. Huge red and purple rose heads had been painted or carved—or probably both—around the dark hollows of her eyes, and her lips—at least the bones where her lips *would* have been—were dyed a bright blood red and even seemed to pout a little as her eyes dropped shyly to her sneakers, a pair of ancient, moss-encrusted high-tops. Converse, maybe.

"Haven't you seen a calaca before?" she asked in a small, embarrassed voice. "I heard you met the Lady of the Dead."

I took a deep breath, just trying not to pass out from the shock. (Which, not gonna lie, wasn't easy.) "I did meet

La Catrina," I managed. *Barely.* "And I've seen *plenty* of calacas . . . only never had one lock me in a *school bathroom* before." On the bright side, at least that explained how she knew what I was. "So, what are you doing at my middle school?!"

"I thought this was the safest place to meet. You never know who's watching, and I figured I could blend in among the other students."

Smart. Though I wasn't so sure about the *blending in* part . . . "That still doesn't answer my question."

"I've come to beseech you," the calaca said a little anxiously.

Beseech me? "That's, uh, not gonna hurt, is it?"

"No. I've come to beg for help. ¡Tu ayuda!" She got a nervous look on her face. "It's . . . mi hermana. She's made a *terrible* mistake."

"Your sister?"

"Sí. She's always been quite . . . *impetuosa.* Reckless, even. But this time she may have gone too far. And I . . . I'm *scared* for her." You could tell, too. Her expression was tight, worried-looking, and her sneakered feet wouldn't stop making squeaking sounds as she shuffled them on the recently mopped floors.

"So wha-what happened?" I asked.

"Magdalena doesn't confide in me much. That's the

problem. Maybe if I would've learned of her trouble sooner, I could've done something myself, but . . ." Her words trailed off, her face growing sadder, graver. "Magdalena, she's—*well*, she's never really felt at home among the old and lonely graveyards. She's always been more of a . . . *free spirit*. When we were little, she'd make me help her dig tunnels to the surface with silver spoons she'd stolen from some of the older tombs, so that she could play in the rain or watch the sun rise without being caught by the watchmen. She swore to me that one day she'd run away, escape los cementerios for good. Live among the living." Her fingers were trembling. They crushed the straps of her purple JanSport. "I—I know I'm rambling. Perdóname. But what I'm trying to say is that I love mi hermana—la amo—and right now I just . . ." She trailed off again, looking hopeless. "I just feel so *lost*."

I hardly knew what to say to all that. My heart sorta broke for her. It really did. She just looked so sad and small and completely overwhelmed. I wanted to help her. If I even *could*. So what I said was: "Uh, why don't you maybe start by telling me what actually happened. . . . What'd your sister even do?"

"She trusted the wrong people."

"And?"

"I'd rather not say."

"Why not?"

She gave a little shrug. "I'd rather not say."

"So where's your sister now?"

"I . . . I don't know."

"Is she . . . *missing?*"

Esperanza's bony shoulders went up and down again. "I—I don't know. *Maybe.*"

"You realize this isn't an episode of *I've Got a Secret*, right? If you want my help, you're gonna have to tell me *something*. I mean, what kinda trouble is your sister in?"

"The kind that has me risking my life trying to save her."

"Sounds pretty bad," I admitted.

"It's worse. For death stings far more the second time."

And *that* I definitely didn't like the sound of.

Esperanza's fingers, cold as frozen straws, touched my arm. Her voice wavered a little. "She needs my help, Charlie. . . . I'm the only person she can trust, and you are the only person *I* can trust."

"But—you don't even *know* me," I pointed out.

"Oh, but I do! I've heard your stories!"

I blinked, surprised. "You . . . *have?*"

"Yes, and you can never know a person better than through their stories! I really do believe that! And I've heard all of yours. How you defeated La Cuca; how you traveled to the Land of the Dead and back; how you battled your way through las Américas to save your friends and send

La Mano Peluda back to La Tierra de los Muertos." The hollows of her eyes seemed to glow with a blend of hope and admiration. She looked straight at me. "We're all so honored that a Morphling has been born in our time. The entire Sociedad is! You're so brave and selfless and . . . and *maravilloso!*"

Marvelous. Huh. Never been called that before. And I'd been called *plenty*. "Look, uh, I'm not saying that I disagree with you per se. . . . But have you thought about maybe going to La Liga de Sombras with this? I mean, Queen Joanna will probably be able to help you much more than I can."

But the mysterious calaca girl was shaking her head even before I'd finished. "No. No es posible. My sister would never forgive me. Like I said, she can be . . . *difficult.* And please don't tell La Liga that I came to you! That could jeopardize all of us!"

"*What?* How?"

"I—I can say no more. The truth is, I shouldn't even have said what I *have*. It's just that I'm scared, and I'm desperate, and I don't know who else to turn to." Her bony fingers squashed the strap of her backpack again. She stared down at her sneakers and said in a very small voice, "I need you, Charlie. . . . And I know I'm just some stranger who crawled out of a grave somewhere, begging por tu ayuda, but know that I'm only begging for your help because I need it and because there's no one else for me to beg."

Man, talk about pressure. . . . "Listen, it's not that I *don't* wanna help you," I said. "But you haven't really told me *anything*. What do you even want me to do?"

"I wish I could say more, but you don't understand the risks I'm taking by simply talking to you. By coming up to the surface world in broad daylight." Her voice trembled. Her hands trembled. Everything about her was trembling and scared.

"Okay, look, I can *try* to help, but first you gotta help *me*. Gimme . . . *more*. Gimme *anything*."

"All I can give you is this." Unzipping her backpack pocket, she reached inside with shaky fingers and brought out a small rectangle of paper. Something like a business card. It read—

PIERRE D'EXQUIS

—in a big fancy scrawl. And that was all.

The cardstock was smooth and glossy. I looked up from it and into the empty sockets of Esperanza's eyes. "Pierre d'Exquis?"

"Yes, but I have to warn you, Charlie—they're all *villanos*! Dangerous, *awful* villains!" Her long skeleton fingers wrapped tightly around my arm, the bones digging in, and her pale skeleton face darkened like the first thundercloud before a storm. "¡Ten cuidado! If any-thing were to happen to you because of me I'd . . . I'd die. *Again*." Looking away, she quickly added, "I wasn't trying to be funny. I only wanted to say that, para mí, your safety means—well, it means—"

Unfortunately, I never got to find out exactly what my safety meant to her, because right at that moment there came a loud knock. And a moment after, an even louder shout: "*WHY IS THIS DOOR LOCKED?*"

It was an adult's voice.

A *teacher's* voice!

And not just any teacher—

It was Ponce Middle's very own Miss Trunchbull: the one and only Mrs. Kirilenko!

CHAPTER FOUR

Esperanza's wide, frightened eyes found my equally wide, equally frightened ones. "Who is that?" she whispered.

"Someone who's gotta pee! Does it matter?"

More pounding. Harder. Louder. Then the voice behind the fists shouted, "Who is in there? Identify yourself immediately using first and last name or student ID beginning with grade level!"

Yeah, no gracias. Instead, I turned back to Esperanza and hissed, "Put your . . . *your FACE* back on!"

Señorita Pale and Bony looked at me like I'd just asked her to bake a flan blindfolded and with both hands tied to her ankles. "This *is* my face!"

"I mean put your *fleshy face* back on! Your *HUMAN* face! There're people out there! *LIVING* people!"

The pounding grew louder, angrier. Any harder and Mrs. Kirilenko's fist was gonna come Hulk-smashing through the three and a half inches of solid maple.

Esperanza, meanwhile, was concentrating on showing me her "good side." But so far nada. Not even a nice pink *earlobe*!

"¡No puedo!" she said at last. "I can't!"

And the gauge on my Panic-o-Meter finally blew off. "WHAT DO YOU MEAN *YOU CAN'T*?!"

"When I'm too scared or nervous, the glamour becomes impossible to conjure!"

Oh, well, that was just *PERFECTO*, wasn't it?!

But honestly, who was I to judge? I was like 99 percent sure another fistful of feathers had sprouted on my back and probably a couple more in my left armpit, too.

"Then we gotta hide you!" I rasped.

Only one problem: There was nowhere *to* hide her! The garbage can was *waaay* too small, and there were only four stalls; and if anyone thought—even for *a second*—that Mrs. K wasn't gonna go all SWAT team, drop-kicking every single stall door the second she barged in here, then they really didn't know Mrs. K (or about her decade and a half training as a KGB military officer).

But Esperanza was already on the move, already sliding the trash bin aside and peeking under the sinks and stuff.

"Where are those large rectangular cutouts that let you look out of buildings?" she hissed.

"You mean *WINDOWS*?"

"I don't know! *Maybe?*"

"Haven't you ever been in a school bathroom before?! They're no different than *prison* bathrooms! No windows, no accessible air ducts, and always just ONE door!"

BAM—BAM—BAM—BAM!

It was starting to sound like Mrs. K's fist was gonna make its grand appearance, after all. . . .

Feeling fresh stings of pain along my jaw, I turned to the row of mirrors above the sinks—

And froze!

Only at first I wasn't even sure what I was looking at. But then I got a closer look and saw—¡Santo cielo!—that it was *fur*!

Lion fur!

A *MANE*, to be exact!

It grew in tufts and in tangles, all thick and bushy and sprouting out of the sides of my neck and cheeks. The stuff was a little softer than the feathers, a little fluffier at the tips, and a WHOLE heck of a lot more obvious for the whole world to see.

Not a bad look, though . . .

Like a Tween Wolf or something.

Definitely Halloween material.

Focus, Charlie!

I realized Esperanza was staring at me from across the

bathroom. Her jaw was hanging down around her collarbone, her bony skeleton face giving me the kind of look usually reserved for flying pigs. My guess was that she was probably trying to decide which one of us would've made the better circus sideshow. And I'm pretty sure I knew the answer, too, but it didn't exactly make me feel that great about myself. . . .

Dios mío, where am I supposed to hide this girl? I thought. *Where am I supposed to hide ME?*

"I have an idea!" Esperanza said suddenly. She hurried over to a stall and—this part I could hardly believe—started wiggling out of her clothes!

"WHAT ARE YOU DOING?" I screeched—quickly turning around, of course. . . . Y'know, to give the girl some privacy or whatever.

But she flung her hoodie at the back of my head, whispering, "Put that on to cover your feathers and mane! And what in *the tombs* are you staring at the wall for?"

"Because you're getting *naked*! That's why!"

"*So?* You've never seen *bones* before?"

What? "Of course I've seen *BONES* before, but—"

Bah, she was right! I mean, let's be honest . . . she didn't *exactly* have a whole lot for me to "see."

But just as I turned back around again, things got even *weirder*. Because just as I turned back around again—no joke—Esperanza began *disassembling* herself!

CHAPTER FIVE

I gaped as she jerked loose a rib.

I gulped as she pulled free a collarbone.

I gasped as she yanked off her right foot.

"This is how I memorized all the bones in the human body!" she happily informed me. And then she began tossing the bones, one by one, into the toilet bowl. Yeah, *into* the bowl.

"WHAT ARE YOU DOING?" I screeched. *Again.* But the girl was just getting started. . . .

My eyeballs nearly hit the EJECT BUTTON as her bony fingers gripped the sides of her bony head and she popped it (it being *her friggin' head*) right off the rest of her!

Then, slowly, carefully, she set her freshly "liberated" cabeza down on the rim of the toilet seat and, even more slowly and carefully, turned it to face me.

"Don't worry," the head said with a cheery grin. "I can put myself together again!"

"Whatever you say, Humpty Dumpty!"

The hands of her now headless body groped blindly for the flusher lever.

"That's not gonna work!" I whisper-shrieked. "I mean, those bones aren't gonna go *down!*"

Fortunately, I was wrong. See, the bones in the bowl had turned all flexy, all Jell-O-y and gelatiny, and with a wild hiss and splash of water, they were sucked straight down the toilet hole, clicking and clacking and banging their way through the twisty network of pipes behind the wall.

"There are exactly two hundred and six in the human body," Esperanza's head explained. "They're made mostly of a protein called collagen and a mineral called calcium phosphate. And they can be surprisingly flexible when soaked. *Particularly* old calaca bones."

She was giving me an anatomy lesson I'd never forget. (And would probably have *nightmares* about later . . .)

With a snap, her humerus came free.

With a crack, her spine broke in two.

With a pop, her femur slipped out of her hip socket.

The girl worked with the efficiency of a machine: *Yank, toss, flush. Yank, toss, flush.* And before I knew it, the only part of her that was left was the grinning skeleton head on the toilet seat.

"I'm going to need your help with this last one," it said, still grinning at me.

"WHAT KINDA HELP?"

"A hand. Or, better yet—a *foot*."

"WHAT?"

"What I'm saying is you're gonna have to force my head down *the hole*."

¡Dios mío! I'd never heard anything so awful-sounding in my ENTIRE LIFE!

There was a tinny jingle of keys.

"*Yes, this door, Marty!*" I heard Mrs. Kirilenko shout. "*Open it! Open right now!*"

Marty was one of our school's janitors, and Esperanza must've read the thought—or, more likely, *the panic*—right off my face because she cried, "¡Dale! Hurry!"

With my heart trying to pound its way out of my chest (and probably on the verge of *succeeding*), I picked up her bony head—carefully, of course—and then dropped it, equally carefully, into the toilet. There was a satisfying *ker-plunk* as it went under, and I almost giggled.

Almost.

Then, gripping the flusher thingy, I gave it a nice firm *yank.*

Water hissed and swirled, but her head only hissed and swirled along with it. Translation: no flushy-flushy!

As the water rapidly refilled the bowl, Esperanza gurgled something at me (something that sounded *suspiciously* like, "NOT LIKE THAT, TONTO!"), so I tried again. And again. And again. But no matter how many times I tried or how hard I yanked down on the stupid lever, her stupid head just wouldn't go down the *stupid* hole! Sure, it was sorta soft and squishy like the rest of her bones, but it was still a *lotta* bone, no matter how soft and squishy!

And seeing as I didn't have any other options—like, *ninguna!*—I closed my eyes, sucked in a huge *oh God please help me* breath, and stuck my foot into the bowl!

Toilet water, cold and milky-colored and oh-so-*DISGUSTING*, instantly soaked my sneaker. I did not let out a manly high-pitched shriek. Okay, maybe I did. Then, squeezing my eyes even tighter, I began stomping on Esperanza's head, occasionally flushing, but mostly just grimacing and squirming as the pee-scented, puke-inducing nastiness splashed my knees and legs, licking coldly at the hem of my shorts.

My foot began to ache. A crack ran up the center of the porcelain bowl.

Water sloshed and splashed everywhere as I gave her cranium a final triple-stomp combination—stomp,

stomp-stttommmpp!—while simultaneously jerking down on the flusher, and finally—*finally!*—down swirled the water and down, down, down swirled Esperanza's big ol' skeleton head.

Breathing a Texas-size sigh of relief, I staggered away from the toilet, feeling kinda good actually . . . only to realize that—holy guacamole!—I'd lost one of my sneakers!

It must've been sucked right down the toilet hole along with Esperanza!

No, no, no, no—NO!

A key touched the lock.

A shiver of fear touched my heart.

On the other side of the door, I could still hear Mrs. Kirilenko barking orders, urging Marty to hurry up already, and: "Would you like *ME* to teach you how to unlock a door, *sir?*"

Not wasting a second, I snatched Esperanza's hoodie off the floor and practically jammed myself into it even though it was about three sizes too small and read I'M A MATERIAL GIRL! in huge pink letters across the back.

But no sooner had the lock clicked open and the doorknob started to turn than a familiar watery, liquidy, bubbly sound rose up behind me.

I turned, cautiously, and then peered, even *more* cautiously—and a little fearfully, too—into the bowl.

The toilet burped; it belched; it bubbled. The water gurgled. From behind the wall, the plumbing rumbled uneasily and an ominous hissing sound whispered through the air like the hiss of a hundred snakes.

The fudge funnels were singing to me again.

All of them.

I could hear their awful gurgly voices coming from everywhere. *Every. Single. Stall.*

I had time to think, *Not again,* and then "again" happened: A blast of whizz-scented nasty erupted from the center of the bowl, blasting me square in the chest.

I was flung off my feet on the explosion of water and never actually felt myself land. But when I'd finally blinked the water out of my eyes, I found myself staring up at the ceiling lights with my head spinning and the shocked, staring faces of Mrs. Kirilenko and Marty the janitor swimming in the corners of my vision.

I tried to sit up. Started to say, "I can explain," and . . . well, just gave up. No one could explain what had happened here.

No one should even *try.*

CHAPTER SIX

I should've been born with a warning label on my fore-head that read: CHARLIE HERNÁNDEZ, DESTROYER OF SCHOOL BATHROOMS—BEWARE! But fortunately for me, I wasn't. And fortunately for me, Principal García didn't even suspect me. In fact, he blamed the whole thing on the school's "very obviously faulty" plumbing and was even nice enough to find me a chancleta (in the lost-and-found box) to replace my "lost" shoe. Meanwhile, I just sat there, nodding enthusiastically and saying things like "Yep" and "I agree" and "That's too true" because it seemed like the best way not to get suspended for the rest of my natural-born life. And when Mr. García asked me what I was doing in the girls' bathroom, I told him that I'd had a taco-related emergency (spicy breakfast tacos had been on the school menu that morning), and he seemed to understand.

Anyway, when the final bell rang, I made my way out to

the stand of bleachers by the PE field to have a little heart-to-heart with Violet Rey. Violet was basically the coolest, smartest girl in all of Miami-Dade County—maybe even the entire *country*. Not only was she the captain of the debate team and cheerleading squad, but she was also the editor-in-chief of our school's newspaper, which didn't just put her out of my league. It basically put us in different *universes*. In third grade, she'd chased me around the art room with an opened paper clip. It might as well have been Cupid's arrow, though, because I'd tripped over a can of paintbrushes, taken the pointy end in the *bee*-hind, and had been seeing little cartoon hearts ever since.

"Let me guess the perfume," V said as I strolled up to her. "Dior de *Pee-pee*?" I could hear the laughter in her voice and see the sparkle of it in her eyes, and it was kind of annoying—but only kinda.

"*Ha. Ha.* You're *hilarious*," I groaned. "Please tell me it isn't true. Tell me you haven't heard about the bathroom."

"*Everyone's* heard about the bathroom, Charlie. Everyone in the entire school. Everyone in the entire *district*. In fact, there's already an article about it on our online rag."

"*YOU PUT IT IN THE SCHOOL PAPER?*" I shrieked; and then, getting funny looks from a couple of passing eighth graders, quickly shut up.

"*Had to*, Charlie . . . Our readers wanna know." Grinning,

Violet fixed me with those brilliant baby blues. I tried not to fall into them. It wasn't easy. "So what's the scoop, huh? What went down?"

"It wasn't what went *down*," I said. "It's what came *up*." (Which was about two hundred gallons of liquid *yuck*.)

Anyway, I told her the whole loco story, and by the time I was finished, her eyes had narrowed into concentrated little slits and her pretty pink lips were tight with thought.

She was now in full-on investigative journalist mode. And when she was in that mode, even Sherlock Holmes better watch out for those swinging blond pigtails....

Then Violet surprised me with: "She's cute, huh?"

I blinked. "*Huh?*"

"She is?"

"What? *No.* I said she had an *'interesting'* look.... That's a looong way from *cute*. But—why would that even matter?"

"Who said it did? Unless *you* think it does ..."

"Unless *I* think? You—you're the only one talking about it!"

"Yeah, but you're the only one *blushing*."

I probably was, too. Violet had a talent for making me feel like I was being grilled by some hard-edged police detective trying to badger a confession out of me. She usually got her confession, too....

"It's the heat!" I shot back. "It's this *SUN*! I think they took a buncha SPFs out of my favorite sunscreen and now I'm gonna have to change brands again."

Yeah, I was a sucky liar. Good thing Violet didn't seem to be paying me much attention. She was staring down at Esperanza's little card, the smooth, laminated paper gleaming in the blazing South Florida sun. "So this is all she gave you?"

"Uh-huh. And she wouldn't tell me any more about it either. Like she couldn't or something."

"That's . . . *interesting.*"

"We should probably hit up Whitepages.com or whatever. I'm guessing it's a person."

"You mean yellow."

"¿Qué?"

"Yellowpages.com. Pierre isn't a person. It's a place." V looked up at me. "And we gotta tell La Liga about this. . . . We need to see the queen."

"Uh, even though Esperanza *specifically* asked me *not* to tell La Liga?" I said.

"*Especially* because Esperanza asked you not to."

"What? You don't trust her or something?"

"I don't *know* her. But either way, she doesn't know Joanna like we do; she might *think* she can't trust La Liga, but we know she can. Plus, it's just something we have to do."

And, as usual, Violet was right.

CHAPTER SEVEN

The old Spanish monastery in North Miami Beach was about a twenty-minute bus ride from school.

On our very first visit here, I'd almost been chewed up and spat out by a psychotic, shape-shifting sorcerer called a nahual. (And yes, I do mean the *chewed-up-and-spat-out* part literally.) On our fifth or sixth visit, Violet and I had walked straight into a missing persons case that had almost turned *us* into missing persons as we went tumbling through the wild heart of Central and South America. Call me a pesimista, but something told me that this visit probably wasn't going to turn out much better. . . .

As we strolled through the high iron gates and underneath the green canopy of banyan leaves, I felt the sharp change in the air. That cool, almost sticky hum of ancient magia. It tingled up my arms and down my legs and made all the little hairs on my body instantly stand on end. The warm afternoon air sang with it, *sizzled* with it.

Now, on paper (or at least according to the "About Us" tab on their website), the monastery was an old church that had been built in the twelfth century in Sacramenia, Spain, and later brought over, stone by stone, and reconstructed here in North Miami. But in *actuality*, this whole place was what was known in the sombra world as a Provencia—an ancient, warded fortress used by La Liga and its allies since before the dawn of time. Well, maybe not *that* long ago . . . but you get the idea.

La Provencia itself put the *e* in enormous, spreading out over twenty-five sprawling acres of Spanish-style gardens, mango trees, and palm trees. It had enough alcoves, cloisters, walkways, and nooks to make you think you'd stumbled into some medieval maze, and enough rooms full of books, ancient scrolls, and otherworldly-looking artifacts to make you think you'd tripped into a world-class museum. There was even a family of lamiaks, mermaidlike creatures, living in the largest of the twelve stone fountains and a giant—aka a jentilak—who slept under the old bell tower.

Usually, though, most of the really important stuff went down in Queen Joanna's study, and today wasn't any different.

As we walked in through the magnificent fourteen-foot-tall iron-studded doors (which always opened for us even though no one ever seemed to open them), we saw a large group of sombras seated around the queen's desk. They'd been yapping at each other—and so loudly that we heard them *long* before we actually saw them—but they instantly shut up when they saw *us*.

"¡Niños!" the queen cried happily, her booming voice echoing through the grand chamber. "¡Sin pena! Come in, come in. . . . We were just finishing up."

For a moment none of the other sombras said anything. They basically just sat there, gawking at me like I was some newly discovered species of *green* flamingo or something. It was honestly pretty embarrassing.

Next thing, they all came leaping out of their chairs and nearly swept me away in a tidal wave of handshakes and hugs.

"Ay, Carlito, que placer!"

"A Morphling . . . I've lived to see yet another Morphling!"

"Charlie, es un honor! Es *mi* honor!"

A zip, no bigger than a bumblebee, flew over and shook my pinky finger with both of its tiny little hands and screeched, "*It's so wonderful to finally meet you in the flesh!*"

Two forest sprites—chaneques—bowed at me and patted me gently on the shoulders while a sisimite— which is basically a Mexican bigfoot—picked me up in its gigantic brown-furred hands (four-fingered, just like the legends say) and gave me a friendly full-body shake and an even friendlier full-faced grin before setting me back down again.

Then, all together, they filed quickly out of the room, chatting excitedly among themselves, and the great doors shut behind them (without anyone actually having shut them, of course).

"¡Niños! ¡Qué gusto de verlos! ¡Y qué sorpresa!" La bruja motioned us over, her jewel-studded crown glittering as it caught a shaft of fresh sunshine slanting in through the crystal ceiling. "¿Cómo están? You're both well, yes?" The Witch Queen of Toledo looked great for someone who had been born back in the days when people still thought that beavers were *fish*. Her eyes were bright and green, her hair was dark brown, and she wore enough pendants and necklaces and giant golden rings that she probably could've opened her own chain of ultra-high-end jewelry stores just with what she had on.

"I'm doing pretty good." Violet smiled.

"And you, Charlie?" asked the witch.

"Well, I, uh, had an *interesting* day."

"Yes, I read about it on your school's web paper."

"Did you, now?" I glared at V. "*That's so awesome.*"

"Pues, díganme más," Joanna urged, and so for the

second time today I told the story of the calaca girl, of Esperanza and her plea for help.

Slipping into her enormous throne, the Witch Queen listened silently while I spoke. Her glowing emerald eyes, which burned like those oddly colored torches we'd seen below La Rosa Cemetery, seemed to pull the words out of me.

But the more I talked, the more the light in her eyes appeared to darken and the frown on her face appeared to deepen. She looked worried. Which, naturally, made *me* worried.

At last the ageless Spanish bruja said, "This is all quite concerning." Her gaze was distant, far off, yet somehow fixed sharply on me. "Está bien extraño."

"Well, prepare to be even more concerned," Violet said. She opened her cheer bag, dug out a thick notebook covered with Hello Kitty stickers, and laid it in the middle of the queen's fancy-schmancy desk. Then she began paging through it and talking about some of the "cases" she was currently investigating for the school paper. She mentioned something about a missing person who lived a few miles from school and a pair of missing Chihuahuas, Chico and Chacha. She also brought out newspaper clippings about some tremors in the Little Havana neighborhood, which was one of the oldest and most well-known neighborhoods

in the entire city. The reports weren't super official or anything, but a handful of residents were claiming that they'd
felt something like earthquakes and claiming property
damage and stuff. I remembered hearing about it on TV.

Violet finished in typical Violet fashion with: "What if
it's all connected somehow?"

"How?" asked the Witch Queen.

"I—I'm not sure yet. But lookit: the missing person and
the dogs are both from Little Havana, and only a block or
two east of where we now have *three* different reports of
people having felt tremors. And guess what's right there, not
two blocks north of that? Pierre d'Exquis. I mean, you gotta
admit, the proximities are *at least* coincidental, no? And I
think everyone knows how I feel about coincidences...."

"She doesn't believe in them," I told Joanna. You know,
just so we were all on the same page.

La bruja was silent for a long time. When she spoke
again, her voice was about as bright and cheery as the eye
wall of a category-four hurricane. "I'm going to be comple-
tamente honest with both of you," she said. "I sense a looming calamity . . . a vague doom taking shape in the night. I
believed that when you cast La Mano Peluda back to the
Land of the Dead, its hold over this world would be broken. But it seems as though I was wrong. Its influence has
somehow been amplified; it festers now, unrestrained, in

all the forgotten corners of this realm. The sad truth is that if it hadn't been for your great victory in San Miguel, all would already be lost. For even now our alliances splinter like the bristles of an old broom." The witch frowned. Her eyes seemed to flutter behind heavy lashes. "I am troubled beyond the grasp of my own understanding. I wish I could describe to you precisely what I fear is coming, but alas, I cannot. And so I have made my judgment, niños: I must ask that you both stay out of this. All of it. That you make your own personal seguridad your *highest* priority."

"But we can help," Violet said. (Her personal safety—or even mine, for that matter—was *never* her highest priority.)

"You can," replied the queen. "And you have. But now I'm afraid the danger is too great. You are, after all, only children."

Ha. Like that would ever work on V. Still, I gave her a look like, *Joanna's right, you know,* and she just rolled her eyes at me.

Next moment, the door to the study cracked open, and in the crack, a duende appeared. The itty-bitty little castle elf stood about two feet tall and wore Spanish breeches, stony clogs, and a pointy straw hat that almost resembled a pyramid. A second later, another duende had hopped onto his skinny shoulders, then another hopped onto that one's skinny shoulders, and then yet another climbed up the back of that last guy until they stood in a stack that rose almost a whole six feet off the ground. Finally, the one at the top cried out, "¡Mi reina! ¡El concejo está listo! The council now awaits your presence."

When the queen gave a sharp, quick nod, the duendes quickly unstacked themselves, then sorta tug-of-warred the huge door shut with a soft bang.

Joanna sat as if lost in thought for several seconds. Then her glowing eyes flicked up and she said, "I'm glad you both came. Fue un placer verlos. But I'm afraid I must leave you now."

Violet reached for her notebook, but the long-ringed fingers of the witch pinned it to the desk.

"You won't be needing that," she told her. Then, fixing me with that piercing, regal gaze of hers, she said, "Charlie, la tarjeta, por favor," and I got a pretty good idea of what it must've felt like to have been one of her royal subjects back in sixteenth-century Spain.

So, naturally—like a loyal little subject—I obeyed, handing her the card Esperanza had given me. La bruja frowned at it and slipped it into V's notebook, and then slipped the notebook into the open, roaring mouth of a large bronze bull statue on the corner of her desk. In a blink, el toro seemed to go from inanimate to animate, wolfing down the notebook in a single giant swallow. I thought I heard a series of small locks clicking into place, but wasn't sure. Violet—surprise, surprise—didn't look too happy about the whole thing. She didn't look too happy *at all*. . . .

CHAPTER EIGHT

When we blinked again, we were back in South Miami, standing on a block of neat two-story houses with the slowly sinking sun setting in the distance. "I don't like this," Violet said, shouldering her cheer bag.

"Yeah, I hate when she does that too." Teleporting was mucho more fun in theory than it was in practice. Because in practice, it kinda felt like getting spin-kicked in *the brain*.

"I'm not talking about *brinco*," Violet said. "I mean everything that's *going on. . . .*"

Ah. Right.

"You saw how grabby Joanna got with my notebook? She wouldn't have traded it for the biggest cauldron in Diagon Alley."

"Was that supposed to be a witch joke?" I asked.

"Uh-huh. And *that* tells me we're onto something."

"*We?* You mean *you*."

"We, me—what's the difference?"

"The difference is that it won't be *my* neck on the pro-verbial guillotine when the proverbial revolution hits the proverbial fan."

"Oh, don't be such a proverbial Marie Antoinette." Violet bit her lower lip, thinking. I could practically hear the gears inside her brain grinding away on some idea that was probably going to get us—or at least *me*—into some serious trouble. She had an amazing talent for get-ting me into trouble.

"You already have a plan, don't you?" I said nervously.

V nodded. "I do."

(She always did.)

"And does this plan involve risking our personal well-being and ignoring the dire warnings of a six-hundred-year-old witch?"

"It does."

(It always did.)

Violet started up the sleepy, tree-lined street. "Meet me at the corner of Beacom and Eighth, say nine thirty sharp-ish. I'll explain then."

"*What?* Hey, wait—*no!* My mom isn't gonna let me out that late! Especially not after what happened in South America.... Did you forget *MEXICO?* I've been grounded.

For life! And I think it's pretty official, too. She even made me sign a semi-legal document!"

Violet grinned at me over her shoulder but kept walking.

"Hey, there's no way out of my house, anyway!" I shouted. "My mom's installed dead bolts ON our dead bolts. The house looks like it's been on *Extreme Makeovers, LOCKDOWN Edition!*"

"Try the window," V said as she disappeared around the corner. "Moms usually forget those."

CHAPTER NINE

"AY, UNA SERPIENTE!" screamed my mom el segundo I walked in through the door.

I shrieked, "SNAKE?! WHERE?" and nearly wiped out on one of her potted cactuses, trying to jump forward and backward at the same time.

Then I spotted the "snake."

Only it wasn't *quite* a snake. . . .

The half a foot of shiny black sleekness was much less reptile in nature and a whole lot more *electronic*: one of my dad's cell phone chargers curling out from underneath the entryway table, between its two wooden patas.

"Mom, *SERIOUSLY?*" I groaned, feeling my heart going all Canelo Álvarez on my ribs. "You know how much I hate snakes!"

"Ay, sweetie, I know. . . . I'm sorry! I wasn't trying to scare you. ¡Te lo juro!"

Lynda Eloise Hernández—aka my mom—was a pretty sneaky practical joker. She was always messing around, playing little tricks on me, and she was the exact same way with her students. She once faked a pop quiz, a midterm, and passed out a roomful of failing report cards—all in the *same* week. My mom taught Spanish and dance at my school but was currently on sabbatical (which is just a fancy word teachers use for vacation) on account of her only child being a shape-shifting superfreak who, oh yeah, just so happened to be target número uno for some of the evilest and most dangerous sombras in all of Latinx mythology. She was staying busy, though. She'd recently earned her purple belt in jujitsu, mastered the fine art of indoor booby-trapping, and had developed a weird soft spot for *Van Helsing* comics.

Her fiery reddish hair fell over my face as she wrapped me up in a hug. "You know how my nerves have been lately. . . . And then this morning I find a little piece of snakeskin behind *the fridge!*"

"You're not trying to be funny, right?"

"¡No, de verdad! A garden snake must've snuck in through the patio door. But don't worry . . . it has to be dead by now." She paused, giving me a suspicious look. "Or maybe your father's keeping a pet snake he doesn't want us to know about."

I'm not sure what kinda face I made, but apparently my mom found it pretty hilarious because she lol'd and planted a big ol' kiss on my forehead.

"By the way, your dad called a few minutes ago. . . . He said the conference is going great and that he'll be back early next week. Says he's never seen so many zoologists in one room. It reminds him of the Nigeria-Cameroon chimpanzee exhibit in Zoo Miami. Oh, and he said he's got a surprise for you."

"Better not be a pet snake . . . ," I grumbled. (Mi papá was *another* practical joker.)

My mom's hip pocket began buzzing and beeping. She dug out her phone and, swiping a finger across the screen, said, "Ay, I almost forgot! Your cousin Raúl gets here today. I think his plane landed half an hour ago."

"That's today?"

"Mm-hmm. I already registered him at our school y todo. He's going to be staying with us for a while. He's been having some . . . *issues* back home. But he's a good kid."

"Hold up. What do you mean *staying*? Like staying, *staying*?"

"Uh-huh. He'll sleep in your room. I put another bed in there this afternoon."

I gave her my best *you gotta be kidding me* look. "But why does he have to sleep in *my* room? He's a *stranger*!"

That wasn't me being all *drama, drama, drama,* either. Up until about a week ago, I didn't know I had a cousin. In fact, I didn't even know my mom had *a sister.* Supposedly they hadn't been on speaking terms in, like, forever. But according to my mom, getting turned into a muñeca (that's a doll, in case you're wondering) by one of the world's most terrifying brujas had given her a new perspective on life. Anyway, my cousin was born in Mexico (in the state of Sonora, I think), had spent a few years living in Texas, and was now apparently gonna be my new roommate. Yay me! (Major eye roll.)

My mom sighed. "He's not a *stranger,* sweetheart. . . . He's your *cousin.*"

"No, he's a stranger who *happens* to be my cousin," I corrected.

"No seas ridículo. And I don't see what's the big deal. Didn't you hound me for almost a year *straight,* telling me how badly you wanted a brother so you wouldn't have to sleep alone in your room because you didn't like how quiet it got or all the weird noises coming from the ceiling fan?"

"Yeah," I snapped, "when I was *eight.* And still afraid of the dark!"

I mean, *geez* . . . Did moms come with *photographic memories* of their kids' most embarrassing moments or what?

"Bueno, prepárate, because he's on his way."

Suddenly, the doorbell gave a sharp *DING-DONG!*

My mom grinned. "As a matter of fact, he's here!"

Standing at our doorstep, hefting a dark green military duffel the size of a large *asteroid*, was a kid of about my age. He was tall, almost as tall as my dad, and almost as broad-shouldered, too. His eyes were big and brown and his hair was all slick and spiky. A yellow bandanna was tied neatly around his squarish-shaped head, and he wore a tight black workout shirt (one of those stretchy performance fabric kinds) and loose black workout shorts of the same stretchy fabric. Ropes of muscles bulged underneath the shirt, and the legs sticking out of the shorts seemed to pretty much match what was going on upstairs. To top it all off, the guy was totally posing, sorta leaning up against the house and staring up at us from underneath long, thick eyelashes. He honestly looked like he belonged on *America's Next Top Model* or something. Like, a Latinx Justin Bieber.

"Primo!" he shouted, throwing his arms around me. And what a squeeze on this kid. Good thing he seemed to like me or he might've snapped me in *two*. . . .

"Hey, what's up, man?" I managed to choke out.

"Oh my gosh, look at you!" my mom said. "You've gotten so *big*! And so *handsome*!" She hugged and kissed the junior Mr. Olympia—I mean, *Raúl*. "How's my sister?"

"Está bien. Not too happy with me at the moment . . . but you know how it is." He paused, sniffing curiously at the air. Then his dark eyes sharpened on mine. "Is that—*albóndigas?*"

My mom laughed. "My gosh, you have a *great* nose! I haven't even started cooking those yet! You must be starving. . . . I'll start dinner a little earlier tonight." Giving me one of those *you better behave or else* typa looks, she shoved me toward the stairs. "Charlie, go show your primo his new room. . . . You two are going to have so much *fun* together!"

CHAPTER TEN

hich one's mine?" asked Raúl, tossing his Santa Claus–size duffel onto *my* bed. The mattress sagged, and the springs squealed in protest.

"The other one," I answered dryly. Then I watched him prowl casually around my room, looking at my books, at my desk, at my old-school mariachi guitar in the corner—plucking the C-chord with the perfectly manicured fingernail of his thumb.

"Cool guitarra," he whispered, his dark gaze flicking back to me. "You play?"

"When the mood strikes." I tried lifting his stupid sack of junk off my bed and nearly sprained *my spine.* Man, the thing must've weighed *five hundred pounds*!

"Let me help you with that, primo," he said, and picked it up, no problema, setting it easily down on the floor as if it weighed a couple of ounces less than *nothing.*

"Geez, you're pretty strong."

Beefy shoulders went up and down in a shrug. "I work out. Play a lot of sports. Oh, and that reminds me!" Next thing I knew, he began digging every kinda pelota you could think of out of that stupid duffel of his. Soccer balls and Ping-Pong balls. Footballs. A basketball. A whole buncha golf balls, and even a cricket ball. Initial diagnosis: The guy was *clearly* in need of a sports intervention. . . .

"Bro, how'd you stuff all that in there?" I said.

His lips split and two rows of perfectly white, perfectly straight chompers winked out at me. "Muscle, cuz . . . lots and lots of *muscle*."

Then he strolled into the bathroom with what looked like a large toiletry kit. I watched him unpack a bottle of gel, a bottle of hair spray, two bottles of cologne, some shaving gel, a can of aftershave, and one of those fancy electric razors you see advertised all over TV. He arranged it all neatly by the sink.

"Dude, you *shave?*"

His eyes found mine in the mirror. "Of course. Don't you?"

"I, uh—*yeah*, of course . . . ," I lied. "All the time. Sometimes *twice* on Sundays."

Raúl was grinning at me again. Lots of teeth. Lots of

dimples. "Man, we're so much alike, primo! That's the thing about blood." He dropped the empty kit into a drawer and turned to face me. His hands gripped my shoulders. He might as well have had a pair of pipe wrenches growing out of his sleeves. "We're gonna have *a blast, cuz!*"

CHAPTER ELEVEN

My mom served dinner at five thirty: sautéed albóndigas over arroz con frijoles, platanitos (fried bananas), yuca fries, and of course, her famous mango batidos. Raúl ate like he hadn't eaten in months, finishing off his thirds before I'd even asked for seconds. He chugged mango milkshake, vacuumed up rice and beans, and scarfed down the big, tomato-y meatballs like a wild animal. Dude could straight-up *chow*! No joke, he might've had a future in competitive eating....

Anyway, after dinner, we went back upstairs, and I showed Raúl my new PlayStation and a couple of the games my dad had bought me before he'd left for the conference. While we lazed out and button-mashed, we got to talking, and he told me all about everything that had gone down back home: how he'd gotten into a few fights with some older kids in his neighborhood—bandoleros, he called them—and how his mom had started to worry and decided to send him away for a while.

Raúl seemed like a cool guy. He was fun to talk to and crazy good at video games. Come to think of it, he might've had a future in that, too.

At around eight thirty, my mom told us both to go get ready for bed, and by nine o'clock we were already tucked in and Raúl was already snoring.

Which meant it was *go* time.

Silently, like a ghost, I slipped out from under my sheets, got dressed, snuck across my room to the window, and had just begun to unlatch the little metal hook (without even having made *a whisper* of noise so far) when suddenly a voice said, "Hey, you sneaking out?"

It was Raúl. The kid had the ears of a *jungle cat*!

For half a second, I straight-up froze. Like a burglar in a spotlight. Like Pooh caught with his hand in the honey jar! Then, realizing I'd better play this cool: "*What?* No, I'm not *sneaking out*. . . . You're dreaming. This is all a dream. Now go back to sleep!"

He gave me a funny look. "Looks to me like you're sneaking out," he said matter-of-factly.

"Now, what in *the world* would make you say a silly thing like that?"

"You mean besides your black gym shoes, black sweat-pants, and all-black hoodie?"

"For *your* information, I like to sleep prepared for any-thing *and* in tomorrow's school clothes. It makes getting dressed in the morning that much faster."

"You also prefer to sleep standing up by the window?" He eyed me with a knowing glint in those dark eyes, and I got the feeling that he worked the big muscle above his eye-brows just as much as he worked all the other ones below. This dude was nobody's fool.

In other words: *BUSTEDDDD!*

I sighed. "All right. *Okay.* You caught me. Happy? I'm sneaking out. I gotta meet up with a friend, okay? And my mom—well, she can be a little . . . *overprotective.*"

Talk about the understatement of the century. If there was an annual Olympics for overprotective parents, my mom would've taken home the gold *thirteen* years running.

I watched my cousin's eyes drift slowly up toward the ceiling, where the loaf of bread my mom had glued up there to ward off evil spirits was still molding away.

"It's an old superstition," I explained.

"I know," he said.

I sighed again. "Look, I gotta go. Please just promise that you won't rat me out. We're blood, remember?"

Raúl looked insulted. Like, *genuinely.* Or at least the

shadows slanting across his chiseled cheeks made it appear that way. "I would *never* rat out my own primo! ¿Estás frito o qué te pasa? How do you think my mother raised me, huh?" He frowned in the dark. "There is, however, one *teeny-tiny* issue."

My eyes narrowed on him. "Exactly how teeny? How tiny? And what exactly is the issue?"

"Well, I'm a bit of a sleepwalker. As a matter of fact, mi mamá says that I wander all over the house, into and through every single room, on any given night. She says I even have entire conversations with her when we run into each other in the hallway."

"Sounds like something you should get checked out," I said.

"But don't you get it? If your mom happens to catch me sleepwalking and we get to talking, I'm liable to say any- thing—cualquiera cosa—and in my semiconscious state, I might *unintentionally* give you away."

Unintentionally. Yeah, and my name was Clark Kent. I wasn't buying a word of that. Not even *a vowel*. But the hints he was dropping were bordering dangerously close to threats, which meant that I was going to have to pull up my shorts and play a little pelota. "Hmmm. That could be a problem. . . . And you wouldn't happen to have a solution to our little problema, would ya?"

"Actually, I do!" he said happily. "See, my sleepwalking is only a problem if I'm *asleep*. But if I were, let's say, out there with *you*, I'd be wide-awake, and your secret would be *oh so very* safe!"

"So, basically you wanna tag along?"

"Basically." Raúl grinned. Then he swept his sheets aside, and I saw that he was also wearing an all-black hoodie, black sweatpants, and black-on-black gym shoes! "Think you're the only one in the family who sleeps prepared?"

CHAPTER TWELVE

Violet was waiting for us on the corner of Calle Ocho and Beacom, straddling her bright red Mongoose eight-speed and looking all fly in a brown trench coat and matching brown boots. Miami's finest was messin' around on her phone, probably browsing the America's Most Wanted website (no joke— one of her legit favorite sites), and didn't spot us until we were only about half a block away—Raúl jogging along beside me, 'cause he'd flat-out *refused* to let me tow him on my bike. (He'd said he was looking forward to a little late-night jog—and also, that he didn't trust anything with two wheels.)

Anyway, when Violet finally *did* see us, she didn't look happy. Her left foot swept out the bike's kickstand while her right one tapped impatiently on the sidewalk.

"Charlie, may I have a word with you?" Then, pulling

me aside (well, more like *yanking* me aside), she hissed, "Who is *that*? And why did you decide to bring a stranger on a recon mission?!"

"Okay, first off, I didn't *decide* anything," I said. "*He* decided it when he caught me sneaking out. And second— he's not *a stranger*. . . . He's my cousin!" Yeah, yeah . . . I know. That had been my mom's comeback to *me*. But hey, she wasn't wrong.

"How much does he know?" asked Violet.

"Well, he's in seventh grade, so probably your basic pre-algebra and geometry, scientific classification, subject-verb agree—"

"I meant about *you*."

"Oh. Not much."

Her eyes flicked past me, narrowing cagily on Raúl. "I don't trust 'im."

"Whattaya mean, *you don't trust 'im*? You haven't even *met* him! Man, how do you live being so suspicious all the time?"

"Look, Charlie, I'm not a naturally distrusting person. I just like to operate under the assumption that everyone's lying and up to no good." She paused. "You vouch for him?"

"Yeah, I *vouch* for him. . . . Who are you, now, *the* God-mother? My cousin's cool."

"If he's so *cool*, why didn't you let him ride on the back of your bike?"

"Because he didn't *wanna* ride on the back of my bike. . . . He doesn't trust anything with two wheels. And, come to think of it, I don't exactly blame him. I mean, I can't even begin to count how many times I've fallen off that thing."

V ignored me. Then, loud enough so Raúl could hear: "So, are you going to introduce us?"

"Oh, right. Violet this is my cousin Raúl. Raúl, this is my friend Violet."

Bowing, Raúl took Violet's hand, planted a big ol' smoocharoo just above her knuckles, and flashed those perfect teeth. "Es un placer conocerla, señorita," he said in a low, velvety purr.

Dimples.

Muscles.

And manners.

Geez, this guy could be super annoying. . . .

"Wow," Violet said, surprised. "Your cousin's extremely . . . *polite.*"

I quickly slapped their hands apart. "A little *too* polite, if you ask me."

V wrestled back a smile as she glanced down at her phone. "All right, we don't have a lot of time. Pierre d'Exquis closes in exactly half an hour." She turned to Raúl. "So here's the 411: We're running a little investigation into that place.

For the, uh"—her eyes slid to me—"the school paper. We've heard rumors of some strange stuff going on in there and wanna see if there's any truth to them. So just act cool, *cool?*"

"Oh, I don't need to *act,*" replied Raúl in that purry and extremely *irritating* voice of his. "I'll just be myself in that case. By the way, you must be really busy, huh?"

V tilted her head. "Why do you say that?"

"Only because I'm assuming that apart from the newspaper club, you must also be one of the lead players in your school's drama club. Someone as inteligente and beautiful as you must surely be exploring the possibility of a fabulous career in showbiz, no?"

I sighed. Seriously? Out of all the roughly *seven billion* people on Earth, I had to be the one related to the Mexican *Casanova?*

Violet's cheeks turned a little pink. She gave a little shrug. "Oh, well, actually, I'm not. I mean, I *have* acted in a couple of plays. . . . But that was mostly in elementary school. Journalism is my passion. But thank you. That's . . . that's *very* nice of you to say."

I wasn't liking this guy all of a sudden. I wasn't liking him *at all.*

"Let's just get this over with already," I groaned.

CHAPTER THIRTEEN

ierre d'Exquis was a cozy little shop located on the south side of Calle Ocho, between a dance studio and a famous Cuban bakery ever so humbly named El Rey de los Pastelitos (or, the King of Pastries). The large front windows were lined with shelves, and the shelves were lined with all sorts of interesting-looking antiques: clocks and toys, dolls and stamps, statues, jewelry, and fancy-schmancy picture frames. We chained our bikes to a parking meter and went in. A small brass bell on the door said *ding!* and a tall lady in a smart black business suit said, "*Buenas.*"

Violet whispered, "I'll handle the sales force. You two pretend you're interested in the merch." And she shooed us away. "Browse ... *browse!*"

So while V made a beeline for the lady, Raúl and I made our way toward the nearest display table. A small plastic sign at its center read 35% OFF.

"These look pretty tasty," said Raúl, eyeing a flock of tiny ceramic chickens. He picked one up and—get this—started *sniffing* the thing.

I shook my head. "Dude . . . ?"

He shook his head back. *"Wha?"*

"What are you doing?"

His gaze flicked toward Violet, who was already in deep conversation with the saleslady. "She told us to go *browse*, no?"

"Yes, but what I mean is, why are you SNIFFING the chickens?!"

"Because they *smell* funny. . . . *Why else?*" He glanced around suspiciously. "This whole place does."

I picked up a pollito, took a whiff, but didn't smell anything even remotely giggle-worthy. "Just stop sniffing the porcelain poultry, will you?"

Just then, a voice boomed out of the back.

"Tilda!" it snapped. "Mr. C *clearly* said that he wanted these things outta here by midnight! An' I already told you, we need more CAGES!"

There was a rustle of plastic beads, and I looked around to see someone step through the colorful curtain to our left—a thick dude, half-hidden in shadow, with a tree-trunk-like neck and a shiny bald dome of a head.

"First all that *Golden Doom* business, and now I'm

practically running a ZOO out—" Seeing us, he broke off.

He gave Raúl a suspicious look, gave me a suspicious look, spotted Violet standing on the other side of the room and gave *her* a suspicious look, and then—equally suspiciously—said, "Oh, perdonen. . . . Didn't know we had customers."

Then, with what I guess was supposed to pass for a smile, Mr. Sospechoso melted back (and rather *suspiciously*, I should note) through the bead curtain.

"Well, *that* was suspicious," whispered Raúl. (See? It wasn't just me.)

Meanwhile, Violet had thanked the lady and started toward the door, motioning for us to follow.

Outside, we hopped on our bikes, rode about halfway down the block (Raúl jogged, of course), and when we were out of sight of the shop, V said, "That place isn't an antique shop. It's a front!"

"What are you talking about?" I asked. "What's a *front?*"

"A shady operation posing as a legit business. Basically, they wanna *appear* to sell antiques, but don't actually sell any."

"How do you know that?"

"Because I asked the saleslady for a Jaeger-LeCoultre Atmos clock; I told her we wanted an early 1920s rhodium-plated, gold-leaf-overlaid model."

"And what's that supposed to prove?"

"Well, there are no 1920s rhodium-plated, gold-leaf-overlaid Atmoses. There's only a 1910s rhodium-plated or a 1930s gold-leaf-overlaid, or a very early, very rare 1905 rhodium-overlaid. And anyone who specializes in clocks—particularly antique Swiss clocks like Pierre d'Exquis claims to—would have known that."

"And the lady didn't?"

"No. In fact, she claimed they had just sold their last one and would contact me as soon as she came across another."

"You know an awful lot about clocks," said Raúl, flashing those teeth and dimples again.

"I know an awful lot about *a lot* of antiques. My parents own a shop downtown." And—¡Dios mío!—now Violet was smiling back! "Maybe you should stop by sometime," she said. "See if you find anything you like."

"Oh, I think I will stop by . . . and I'm sure I'll find *many* beautiful things inside."

"Hey, *all right!*" I cut in. "What kinda conversation is that? Can we PLEASE go back to talking about clocks?" *Geesh!* "So what do we do now?"

Fighting down a giggle, V said, "It's simple. Investigative Journalism 101, really: When your lead turns out to be a front, you double-check the back."

"Uh . . . so that means we're gonna do *what* exactly?"

She gave me one of those looks girls give you to let you know you've just said something really dumb. "I just told you. We're gonna check *the back*. See what they're really up to."

"Oh, you meant that *literally* . . . like, the back of *the store*. Got it."

Yep. Master of reading between the lines, that's me!

CHAPTER FOURTEEN

We headed east along Eighth Street and then half a block south until we came to the mouth of the little alley that ran behind the mall. On our left were all the back doors and owner parking spaces; on our right, about twenty or so square acres of marshy woodland known in these parts as La Selva, or the Jungle. V and I stashed our bikes between the pair of big, stinky, rusted-out dumpsters at the corner, and then all three of us slipped into the trees, edging our way through saw grass and shadows until we were about twenty yards from the back of Pierre's. A large green cargo truck with a canvas top and huge mud tires was backed up maybe five yards from the small loading bay door. The suspicious-looking dude we'd seen inside the shop was helping two *other* suspicious-looking dudes (these with a little less neck and a lot more hair) load something like boxes into the rear of the truck. Thick black cloths were draped over the boxes, which made it impossible to tell what they were or what was inside. The whole thing practically screamed ILLEGAL ACTIVITY UNDERWAY—AVERT YOUR EYES!

"We have to get a closer look," Violet whispered. And so we crouched in the tall grass, swatting at mosquitoes and moths, waiting for the three dudes to finish.

When they finally did and had disappeared back into the store, we snuck up alongside the truck—on the opposite side—then quickly climbed into the back.

The canvas curtains were so thick that they blocked out every scrap of moonlight, but Violet already had her phone out, the harsh white cone of her flashlight app illuminating the boxes we'd watched them load in. There were about ten of them, stacked two high and five deep. But the weirdest part? They seemed to be making the strangest sounds: I could just make out faint panting and sniffing, and some small, soft scratching sounds.

"What do you think's in 'em?" asked Raúl, sounding very much the part of a soon-to-be victim in some scary movie.

"Let's find out," answered Violet, sounding like the very *first* victim. But when she lifted one of the covers, all we could do was gape.

"A . . . *golden retriever?*" whispered Raúl, frowning.

"And a Russian blue," said V, peeking underneath another.

So we peeked under maybe five or six more, and that was exactly what we kept finding: more dogs and cats. (Oh, and a hamster the size of a *turkey*.)

Raúl, his eyes all big and round and shiny, glanced up at me. "Can we keep one?" he whispered.

"*What? No.* Well—" I glanced at Violet. "Maybe?"

"They're not ours to keep," she said. "Check it out. . . . They're all wearing collars. They're all somebody's *pets*."

"But why would those guys have so many pets?" I rasped. I mean, I'm a huge animal lover and all. In fact, I'm *part* animal. But geez . . .

"I don't think they do," Violet said. "Look at the collars again. All different owners."

She was right. In the glow of her phone, I could see five different tags, and all five had different addresses and different phone numbers.

"So, what, then?" I said. "They're a *pet*napping ring posing as an antique shop? These people are *sick*!" Honestly, that was the only thing that made any sense to me. The question was: What could any of this possibly have to do with Esperanza's sister?

Next thing, Violet was opening one of the cages. A cat's. Its collar read *Kitty Purry* in swirling golden letters.

The blue-furred kitty blinked and its eyes sparkled, and it purred appreciatively as Violet brought it out of the cold shadows of the cage.

"Hey, what are you doing?" I whispered, and Violet said, "I *know* this address...."

I shook my head. "Whose is it?"

"Not sure, but I'm positive I've seen it before. Like, *one-hundo*." The cat purred again, louder this time. And now I watched Violet's lips pull down into a frown. "Where's Raúl?" she hissed.

"*Huh?*" I glanced left, right, left, spun *all the way* around, in fact—and realized my cousin had flat vanished on us. Like *poof!* "Where the heck did he go?"

Just then I heard a click. Somewhere close by, a door banged open. Then came the sound of voices. And then of footsteps—*approaching* footsteps!

"Someone's coming!" whispered Violet. "*Go, go!*"

We hurried out the rear of the truck, climbing backward down the tailgate, and had barely started to turn around when we ran into something—or rather, some*one*.

And, unfortunately, it wasn't my cousin....

"Hello, snoopers," a voice whispered by my ear.

I didn't need to turn around.

I recognized it.

And I recognized it because I'd just heard it.

Then Mr. Sospechoso—aka the suspicious weirdo from inside the shop—wrapped me up in his bulky arms, lifting me off my feet even as I kicked and twisted, trying to wiggle free.

Next to me, one of the other goons we'd seen helping him grabbed Violet. She struggled and screamed, and the cat leapt from her arms with a loud *meoooow!* to scamper underneath the truck.

"VIOLET!" I shouted. Then, yanking one arm free, I twisted around, already rearing back to pop this petnapping punk square on the nose—

Only what I saw when I finally got all the way around nearly made me swallow my *tongue!* (And a couple of teeth, too . . .)

What I'd *expected* to see—duh—was a human face. But what I *actually* saw was something else entirely. Up close, the best (and *kindest*) way to describe it was human-*ish* . . . except there was waaay more *ish* mixed in there than I was completely comfortable with. The skin on the sides of his face and under his chin was scaly, greenish, and bone-dry, like a crocodile's. His nose, which had just looked a little busted from across the shop, was, in fact, upturned, U-shaped, and rounded at the end, sort of like a shovel. A few long, crooked teeth (too big to be human, too sharp and serrated to be fake) stuck down over his lower lip, and

I could hear this totally creepy, rattlesnake-like hiss rising from deep inside his throat. But the freakiest thing about him? No doubt about it, *his eyes!* They were greenish, yellowish, and black, with dark vertical slits for pupils. *Those are the eyes of a reptile,* I thought numbly. *The eyes of a PREDATOR!*

Resisting the temptation to go all Little Red Riding Hood and shout, "GRANNY, WHAT FREAKY EYES YOU HAVE!" I swung my head around and saw that his buddy (the one who'd grabbed Violet) had the same weird skin and the same reptilian eyes!

Call me thick, call me slow—call me whatever you wanna call me!—but it was slowly beginning to dawn on me that these guys weren't *exactly* human . . .

CHAPTER FIFTEEN

P anic rose like a hot-air balloon in my throat. But not just because we were outmuscled, outarmed, and *completely* outsized. But because I didn't have the *slightest* clue what the heck these things even were! When I was growing up, my abuelita had taught me hundreds, if not *thousands*, of myths from all over the Spanish- and Portuguese-speaking world. She'd taught me them in order to protect me, knowing that one day I'd probably run into a few. And it had worked, too. Her stories had saved my life more times than I'd ever admit. (*Especially* to my mom, because she freaks out about stuff like that . . .) But now, as I took a panicky nosedive into the ocean of my hippocampus, searching through murky memories for stories of croc people, of walking, talking alligator monsters, I came back up with a big fat nada burger. *Nothing!* Which of course begged the question: Had my grandma never heard of these things? Had she forgotten about them? Or—and maybe most concerning of all—had she not told me about them *on purpose?*

"What are we gonna do with 'em?" asked one of the goons—er, *croc things.*

"Exactly what Mr. C would want us to . . . ," answered the croc thing currently squeezing me like his favorite stuffed teddy. "Make 'em *disappear.*"

"Well, let's hurry up and start the magic show," hissed croc number three, "because this one's scratchin' my wrists all up!"

"*Charlie!*" Violet shrieked, still kicking and struggling. But it was useless. These things were RIDICULOUSLY strong!

A wave of fear crashed over me, followed by a tsunami of anger, and I screamed, "LET. ME. GO!"

And—surprise, surprise—Mr. Sospechoso actually did!

Just opened his arms and fumbled back a step, gawking at me like I was some five-headed, fire-breathing burro.

Then he started gawking at himself, at the dozens and dozens of long brown somethings—*thorns,* maybe?—sticking out of his arms and chest. (I'm not even half-kidding when I say that the dude looked like he'd just belly flopped into a ball pit of thorny cactuses.)

The croc monster's slitted eyes now rose slowly to

mine. A cold, reptilian anger burned in their dark, greenish depths. "You pricked me!" he hissed.

"*What?* No, I didn't!" I shot back.

"Yes, you did!"

"Did not!"

"Did too!"

"Did—"

"Charlie, your back!" Violet yelled, a sudden hopefulness filling her voice.

I twisted, turned, trying to get a look at what she was pointing at—

And saw—well, *pointy* things . . .

A forest of them. A forest of bristly, spiky, needlelike quills—yeah, *quills!*—stabbing out of my back. Stabbing right through the soft cottony fabric of my T-shirt! They were long and greasy-looking, tipped with these cool backward-projecting barbs, sorta like the ones on the ends of fishing hooks. And no joke, it looked like I was wearing *a cape* of them!

Holy porcupine quills, Batman! I'd gone full-on Erethizon dorsatum*!*

And thanks to my dad's nonstop talk about all things animalia, I knew a thing or two about porcupines.

For instance, I knew porcupines were herbivores. I knew they were the third-largest type of rodents on the planet. I knew they had terrible vision but a great sense of smell. *And* I knew that the average porcupine came equipped with right around thirty THOUSAND quills. In other words . . .

"I got *plenty* more where those came from, boys!" I shouted, shaking my booty to make my quilly cape rattle. It made a nice chunky-clunky sound. "So, let her go or prepare to find out *just* how many!"

"What the heck are you, kid?" shrieked one of the crocs.

So I told him: "The name's Charlie Hernández, and I'm just your friendly neighborhood Morphling." Yeah, I know—that was Spidey's famous line. But c'mon now, it wasn't every day you got a chance to give it a whirl.

"You tell 'em, Charlie!" Violet cheered.

But Mr. Sospechoso only frowned. "The *who?*"

"The Morphling?" I repeated. "You know, El Cambiador? Never heard of me?"

"The heck's a morp*lang* . . . ?" he hissed.

"It's Morph*ling*, thank you very much. And I'll take that as a *no.*" Suddenly I spun to face croc number three. The one holding Violet. "Let her go, or I'm quilling *you* next!"

Now, did I *seriously* think that threat had a snowball's chance in Havana at working? Duh. Of course not. I mean, just how dumb would someone—or, in their case, some*thing*—have to be to fall for that?

Fortunately, croc number three was just about that dumb. He panicked and, with a little shriek, let Violet go, and she came scrambling over next to me.

"Ay, whatcha do that for?" Mr. Sospechoso snapped at his buddy.

"'Cause the kid said he was gonna *quill* me!"

The overgrown, overmuscled, alpha croc shot him a glare that could've sliced guava. "The freak's some kind of preteen *porcupine*. . . . You ever heard of a porcupine that *SHOOTS* its quills?"

"*Yes?*"

"NO! You haven't! 'Cause they CAN'T!"

Now croc number three's leathery face wrinkled like a grape taking a sun-dried detour over into Raisinville. Wrinkled in anger.

"You tricked me," he growled, his dull yellowish eyes narrowing angrily on me. "And I don't much like being *tricked. . . .*"

He stepped forward then—they all did, in fact—and as my back bumped up against the side of the cargo truck, I suddenly realized one very unfortunate fact: We were *done-zo. Trapped!*

There was nowhere to run.

Nowhere *at all . . .*

CHAPTER SIXTEEN

My life was just about getting ready to flash before my eyes the way lives tend to do right before you get viciously mauled by a gang of meatheaded, killer croc monsters, when a roar—I'm talking a *RAWWWARRRR!*—erupted from behind us. Deep inside La Selva.

Only it wasn't like any roar I'd ever heard. Not in Miami, anyway. No, this was the ferocious, bloodcurdling, skin-crawling, heart-*melting* cry of something very wild, and very, very angry. And, quite possibly, very *hungry*.

The crocs froze.

We froze.

Everyone just *froze*.

"Wh-what was that . . . ?" stammered a goon. "What even roars like that?"

"I believe that would be genus *Panthera*," I informed him. (Aka, a big cat.)

And that's when V made her move. Like a flash, her hand disappeared into the pocket of her trench coat, and—ta-da!—reappeared with a bright red can of pepper spray.

She readied said can.

She aimed said can.

Then she fired said can.

What came next was—well, *muy caliente*. . . .

A spicy hot cloud of capsaicin exploded from the tiny plastic nozzle, blasting croc número uno directly in his nictitating blinkers.

He howled, whirling away from her, temporarily blind and temporarily unable to make his feet do what he wanted them to do. That is, of course, unless he was trying to dance some ridiculously uncool, doubly left-footed version of La Macarena. . . . (It was pretty much all I could do not to bust out laughing and singing the chorus line—the croc looked that silly!)

Violet, meanwhile, being her usual generous self, treated the other two croc freaks to a whiff and an eyeful as well, then quickly tossed the empty can, sprang forward, and—"Hi-ya!"—karate-kicked one right where the sun don't shine.

"Oof!" The goon arched back, not sure whether to grab his aching heinie or his burning eyes.

"Time to go!" Violet said, stooping to retrieve the cat (Kitty Purry), and there was no need to check my watch on that one.

We dashed wildly into the trees, doing our best Barry West impersonations (that's the Flash's real name, for any of you non–DC Comics buffs)—jumping over logs and puddles, ducking under branches—and kept running until I almost couldn't breathe anymore and all my quills had fallen off.

"WHY ARE YOU STOPPING?" shouted Violet.

"Because we have to go back!"

"We can't go back!"

"But what about *Raúl?!*"

"We don't even know where he went!"

"We can't leave a man behind! That's the promise we make to each other!"

"This isn't *Saving Private Ryan*, Charlie!"

"I know, but he's my cousin!"

"What about those *crocodile* things?!" she shouted. "I mean, what kinda sombras are those, anyway?"

"I—I don't know...," I admitted. And the concern that swirled in Violet's eyes was only about *half* as much as was currently swirling in my belly.

"*You don't know?* I thought you were a walking *Merriam-Webster* of myths!"

"I am, okay? I—I just . . . I don't remember my abuelita telling me any stories of half-human, half-croc people."

V thought about that for a second. "It's a clue, then."

"*What?* How can me not knowing something be *a clue?*"

"Because sometimes the absence of a clue is a clue."

My eyes narrowed on her. But before my mouth could open to say, *¿De qué estás hablando, chica?* I heard the rustle of leaves . . . the thump of pounding feet . . . and next thing I knew, the wall of leaves to our left exploded like a leafy green piñata, and someone plowed straight into me, knocking me off my feet!

Panicking, I quickly scrambled up, preparing to unleash my inner Bruce Lee when I saw—

"Raúl!" shouted V.

"Primo!" shouted me.

"Cuz!" Raúl grinned, flashing that trademark teeth-and-dimples combo.

"Oh, put that away!" I snapped. "This isn't a Crest commercial!"

As he pushed to his feet, Violet said, "Where'd you go?"

And Raúl said, "To search the front of the truck. See if I could find anything interesting."

"Did you?"

"I found these." He held out a couple of pet collars, one pink, one blue. One read *Missy*, the other *Fu*.

"Nice!" Violet snatched them out of his hand, stuffing them into her pocket; and right as she did, Raúl noticed the cat cradled comfily in her other arm.

"Hey," he said, glaring at me. "How come she gets to keep one?"

"Because this isn't a pet," said Violet. "It's a *clue.*"

CHAPTER SEVENTEEN

Well, in all fairness, it does *appear* to be more pet than clue," I pointed out as we continued into the trees.

La Selva was basically your typical marshy South Florida woodland, which is to say it was very woody and very marshy and swarming with all sorts of insects and frogs and probably more than a few crocodiles, too. We made our way through the mushy tangle slowly, carefully, trying not to lose our way (which was pretty hard), and trying not to get eaten alive by mosquitoes (which was pretty much impossible).

Eventually, though, we left the trees behind and about a mile or so north hit civilization—a sleepy residential neighborhood maybe fifteen minutes from Coconut Grove and only a mile or two from home.

"I'll have my dad get our bikes in the morning," Violet said as we started east along a block of old-fashioned streetlamps, walking in hazy light one moment and in pitch-darkness the next. "They should be good for tonight."

Raúl shrugged. "I say good riddance."

"Oh, that's right. A little birdie told me that you don't trust anything with two wheels."

"That little birdie told you right. I don't. And it's worked out pretty good so far. No broken bones."

"I'm a little different," said V. "For me, it's the things with two *legs* that I find hard to trust."

Raúl grinned. "Ah, so you're suspicious of people?"

"Sometimes. Like right now."

I turned to Violet. "What are you talking about?"

"Methinks we have a tail. And not the kind you're familiar with either." She made a tiny movement with her eyes. "We're being followed."

"Followed? By who?"

And without missing a beat, Raúl said, "Young guy. Kinda bony. Maybe six feet tall, wearing a big hoodie, cachucha, and hugging the houses so close you'd think he was trying to make friends."

Violet looked pretty impressed. So I said—or rather *lied,* "Yeah, uh, I spotted him too . . . a *whiiiile* ago. Didn't wanna say anything until I was absolutely sure, though."

Kitty Purry meowed at me. I think she knew I was

lying. I gave her the stink eye, then started to turn to get my first *actual* look at our tail, but Raúl stopped me.

"Don't let 'im know we know," he whispered. "It'll make him more careful next time."

Buttoning the top two buttons of her trench coat, Violet nodded up ahead. "As soon as we turn the corner, we start running. I know the neighborhood pretty well. We'll lose him in a couple of blocks."

CHAPTER EIGHTEEN

No big surprise, Violet's plan worked. After zigzagging our way between houses and through yards, over a tall wooden fence and around doghouses and little kids' swing sets, we'd left whoever was tailing us in the dust (and dark) and probably wandering around in confused circles, too. Heck, *I* hardly even knew where we'd ended up, and I lived around here.

Within a couple of minutes, though, Violet's pretty pink house came into view at the end of the cul-de-sac. I walked her up the little path to her front door, trying to think of something cool to say that might impress her or make her laugh, couldn't think of anything, panicked, stumbled over a few words, somehow made her laugh anyway, then told her I'd be dreaming of her.

Yeah. Those words actually came out of my mouth.

Naturally, I quickly autocorrected that to: "I meant

texting! I'll be *texting* of you!" Which, of course, made zero sense. And that's because it was a lie. But now it was a lie that I had run with, so I ran with it: "In other words, I'm gonna text you in a little bit to make sure you get . . . *upstairs* . . . safe and stuff."

Violet laughed again, told me she'd be waiting for it, and whispered, "Good night, Charlie Hernández," smiling at me now, giving me that half-sly, half-shy look that always made my insides twist up like the world's twistiest churro. Then she shut the door, slowly, wholly, while I stood there on her front porch, feeling like a complete *goof* and already sort of dreaming about her. I mean, she was, after all, my dream girl. . . .

"You're pretty smooth with the ladies, huh, cuz?" said Raúl, smirking, as I joined him on the sidewalk.

"Oh, *shut up*," I groaned.

The moon was only a bright silver sliver in the sky by the time we got home, and the good news was that all the lights on the second floor, and down in the living room, were still off, which meant my mom probably hadn't discovered the two empty beds.

We were halfway to the wicker trellis that ran up to my bedroom window when a huge—I'm talking MASSIVE—shadow detached itself from a nearby tree,

CHARLIE HERNÁNDEZ & the GOLDEN DOOMS

standing nearly as *tall* as that tree, and began waving at me.

My breath caught. My blood froze. Every single thought in my brain *instantly* cut off. That is, every single thought besides the one screaming *RUN!*

+ 85 +

CHAPTER NINETEEN

Fortunately, I didn't run, though. I mean, it would've made me look like a total Patrick Star (y'know, the brainless starfish from *SpongeBob*?), because the waving tree-size shadow was just Juan—Juan the basajaun!

I turned to Raúl. "Hey, you go ahead. I'll be right up. Gotta make a quick phone call."

He showed me his teeth. "Who you gonna call?"

"Ghostbusters," I teased.

"You mean Violet, right?"

"Uh, yeah . . ." Sounded like as good an excuse as any.

"You *seriously* gonna call to see if she made it upstairs?"

"Uh, *yeah* . . . And what's so bad about that? Stairs can be—*tricky*."

He was still grinning at me. "So can love, primo . . . And I smell it all over you."

"What you're smelling is *sweat*," I said. "Also, mind your own business."

Once Raúl was inside, I slipped off into the shadows to holla at my boy Juan. Basajauns were probably some of the most beloved creatures in all of Basque mythology. Their stories were as old as civilization—and that's probably because basajauns were believed to have helped start the very *first*. Juan was one of the greatest warriors their warrior tribes had ever produced. He'd once routed a clan of marauding vampire dogs (aka Dips) with only a rag, a butter knife, and half an avocado. (Don't ask.) He was also Queen Joanna's personal bodyguard and my unofficial guardian angel, having saved my life more times than I could count on my fingers. (Probably even my toes, too.) Juan was taller than most houses, smarter than most geniuses, and hairier than—well, just about anything with hair. He had this thick Spanish accent (which was totally awesome and which I'd pretty much gotten used to), and he just so happened to be one of the kindest, gentlest sombras you could ever hope to meet.

"Juan, hey, what's up, dude?"

"Buenas noches, Charlie." He smiled broadly at me (which is really the only way you can smile with a mouth as broad as his), and the assortment of crude tools hanging in the tangles of his yellowish beard clinked together like the chimes of a wind chime. I saw my own smiling reflection in the square silver head of a hammer. "¿Y quién es ese?" he asked.

"Oh, that's my cousin. Raúl. He's from Mexico."

"He smells . . . *interesante.*"

"Yeah, it's his cologne. Guy basically drowns himself in the stuff."

"How much does he know?"

"Some. Not too much."

"Does he know you are a Morphling?"

"Nah, not yet. Don't wanna freak the kid out too bad. He only just got here."

The twelve-foot-tall hairy hominoid whose ancestors had taught early Spanish settlers the secrets of blacksmithing, farming, and milling nodded like he understood.

"So, would you like to tell me where you went tonight?" he asked pleasantly enough. "Perhaps an evening stroll through el barrio with your primo? Because I *know* there's no way you would have so blatantly and so *recklessly* disobeyed Queen Joanna's wishes only hours after speaking with her."

I didn't say anything. I didn't want to lie to him.

Sighing, Juan shook his head at me, looking very much the part of a disapproving parent. The world's hugest, hairiest, most *ginormous* parent, that is. "Ay, Carlito, Carlito . . . You see, mi niño, you are like the great beech tree with wild-growing branches that must be pruned if you are to one day grow into your full glory."

"Uh—*come again?*"

"You are like a cold lump of iron ore that requires hammer and anvil and fire and the skill of a blacksmith's hands to form into the *perfect* horseshoe."

"*Huh?*"

"You, Carlito, are like the inland field that must be rut and cut with irrigation canals so that a generous harvest may, in autumn time, spring *bountifully* forth."

"Yeah, I'm having a little trouble with your metaphors . . . ," I admitted.

"Then allow me to be more literal: You are young, Charlie. And in one's youth, it is quite wise to heed the counsel of the old and wise. And Joanna is one of the oldest and wisest. She knows more about the evils of this world than most. And she is trying to protect you. But as they say in my mother country, 'Puedes llevar al caballo al agua, pero no puedes hacerlo beber.'"

I knew that saying. My abuelita used to say it all the time. It basically translated to: You can lead a horse to water, but you can't make it drink.

Juan's leathery lips crinkled into a small frown. "In the end, you will do what you will. For that is your greatest strength—*and* perhaps your greatest weakness."

"What's that supposed to mean?"

"Which Morphling before you has heeded wise counsel? Have they not all readily thrown themselves into the fire for both honor and glory? The stories of cowards are not told. But their stories you *have* heard. . . . The animal spirits are woven into your very blood, Carlito—your *hot* blood—and you will go wherever their wild calls lead you. I, as part beast myself, understand this. Perhaps Joanna yet does not. You will not be the first Morphling to hack your own path through the jungles of this life, mi'jito; but I fear that if you are not careful, that path will be regrettably short."

He dropped a massive, padded hand on my head (basically swallowing *up* my head) as he said, "Charlie, understand: you are still el gran premio—the grand *prize*! And perhaps now more than ever. If La Mano Peluda was able to hurt you—or God forbid, *worse*—that would single-handedly win them this war overnight, for nearly all the sombra clans across this world would cower in fear. You are the light that shines upon what little hope we have. You *are* the Morphling, and for ten thousand years my kin have been loyal to your predecessors. So my heart—mi corazón—is always with you. I will not lie to you. And so I freely tell you that the queen has instructed me to shadow you, to not let you out of my sight, and to report back to her as to your comings and goings. I will not tell her about where you were tonight, because tonight I saw nothing, and so there is nothing to tell. Pero otra vez, I *implore* you, be *smart*, Carlito—and be *careful.*"

"But, Juan, they're *up to* something . . . ," I said.

"*Who* is?"

"Whoever owns Pierre d'Exquis. It's an antique shop in Little Havana. We ran into some really weird sombras there. These weird *crocodile* people I've never even heard stories about . . ."

"Crocodile people?"

"Yeah. Big guys with scaly skin and croc eyes."

The basajaun only stared at me for a moment before saying, "I've also never heard of such sombras. You are certain this is what you saw?"

"Do octopuses have three hearts?"

He blinked. "No sé. Do they?"

"Well, *yeah* . . ."

"Ya veo," he said slowly. But I could tell from the way his eyes had sorta crossed that now *he* was the one having trouble getting *me*. Guess that made us even.

Juan wiggled his shoulders like he'd just have to take my word for it, then reached a great, apelike hand into the strands of his scraggly beard and brought out a smooth gray stone. "Para ti," he said, holding it out like a telephone.

"What . . . *is it?*"

"Someone would like to speak with you."

"Say what?" Yeah, it seemed to me like Juan might've spent one too many nights alone in the woods. . . .

"It is a linka," he explained. "One of the ways we sombras communicate across *vast* distances. Notice the witch runes."

I had noticed them. Carved into the smooth face of the stone, they looked like a cross between a tic-tac-toe grid and ancient Maya script.

"Do I just, like, say, 'Hello?' or something?"

"You don't have to say anything," replied the basajaun. "All you have to do is *touch.*"

So that's what I did. I reached out and touched the stone. But about half a second *after* I'd touched it, I sorta wished I hadn't.

CHAPTER TWENTY

The runes on the stone began to glow. Shafts of brilliant purplish light blazed out, illuminating the yard and my house and making me wish I had my pair of anti-glare snowboarding goggles handy. I felt a sudden dizziness, a sudden shakiness, a strange wooziness, and then an odd giddiness. An instant later, the ground seemed to tilt, and it was as if an enormous force seized me and yanked me forward while my insides shrank and shriveled and the world around me blurred to blackness.

When I blinked again, I realized I wasn't in Miami anymore. Or at least no part of Miami that I recognized.

I was standing in the middle of a dark, wild . . . *forest* maybe? A sliver of yellow moon peeked through the dense canopy, and all around me trees like skyscrapers burst toward the night sky, their trunks wrapped with colorful mosses, their branches wound with flowering vines. The air was thick with humidity and even thicker with foresty smells—bark and earth and rain and leaves.

With my pulse beating in my ears like bongo drums, I turned in a slow circle while my eyes rapidly scanned the black-green darkness.

I could feel the swish of the high grass against my ankles and hear the flutter of wings and the hooting of owls—

And then a voice.

A *familiar* voice.

It spoke up from among the trees.

I whirled—

And my heart instantly jumped in my chest!

It was El Cadejo!

The divine protector who takes the form of a ginormous white dog emerged from the darkness of the forest like he was emerging from another dimension. His deep azure eyes blazed like cold fire, and his snow-white coat glistened brilliantly, almost blindingly, as he strode toward me.

"*Cadejo*," I breathed. "Wh-where are you? I mean, where are *we*?"

Estamos in the wilds of Galicia, he answered, speaking directly into my mind (as he always did). *In the land of witches.*

"You mean we're in *Spain*?"

Sí, España. Though you are not here physically. Rather, in espirito.

And as he touched the tip of his nose to mine in greeting, I whispered, "And what are you doing here? I mean, there . . . wherever."

I am tracking a thief, he said. His gaze sharpened, and now he looked past me to where the trees were thickest and the ground first dropped, then sloped sharply upward like a rolling black wave. *Just thirty miles north of here, in the foothills of the Macizo Leonés, lie what is known as Los Castillos de Brujas, the Witch Castles. They are among the oldest enclaves of brujas in the entire world, and the home of the first witch ever born, Silva Villalobos. Less than fifteen miles east spread the vast Witch Markets of Galicia, the most important trading hub in all the sombra world and, until now, the safest. But there has been a robbery at the market. Various items of importancia mágica fueron robados.*

"Like what? What was stolen?"

That matters little. What matters much is why they were stolen and who stole them. That is why I am here. The ancient guardians of these woods, the curupira of Western Amazoa, have suffered a great embarrassment, for it is they who protect the market. I am now assisting them in hunting down this thief—or perhaps thieves; we are not yet sure, for we have yet to find any tracks in el bosque. He shook his shaggy head. Pine needles and glittery stuff rained from his thick mane. *But that is not why I wanted to speak with you, Charlie. See, I fear that the robbery might merely have been una distracción—a distraction. And if La Mano Peluda is, in fact, behind this, as I suspect they are, then I have no doubt the true and deadly point of their scheming will, in the end, be thrust in your direction. I sense you are in great danger, Carlito. Dark forces are still very much at work in this world. Rumors of war have already begun to spread in the south. As we speak, Juesto Juez is trying to rally our allies from Ahuachapan to Ushuaia, but even the very jungles struggle against us now that Madremonte has turned. We are stretched thin, mi niño, and the hourglass of time is running out beneath our feet. But I wanted you to hear this warning from me so that you will be on your highest guard. Remember, La Mano Peluda will stop at* nothing *to return to this world. And it will stop at nothing to get* you.

Suddenly, from deep in the woods, there came a shout: "¡Cadejo, encontramos algo!" And a moment later a figure melted from the shadows of a giant pine.

A figure I *instantly* recognized!

Well, from the legends, anyway . . .

For a sec, I went all fanboy thinking, *A curupira—a real-life CURUPIRA!* Thing was, I remembered listening to my abuelita tell me their stories like it was yesterday! Though their tales had first been told by the Tupi people of Brazil. They believed the curupira to be the guardians of all wild things. Mischievous and teasing, yet kindhearted and giving, they were said to protect the jungles and forests from the greed of humankind, preying on poachers and hunters who kill for pleasure. The legends claimed that the curupira set traps among the trees and that they knew all the secrets of the forests. Particularly the healing properties of herbs, which they'd mastered over the millennia.

This curupira, however, was young. Maybe a little younger than me. She stood about four feet tall and wore something like a dark leather tube top and a dark leather skirt fringed with grasses and dry leaves. Her fiery reddish-orange hair was wild, almost as wild as the woods around her, and her golden-brown skin was crisscrossed with stripes of blue and yellow war paint. A spear that could've doubled as a pole-vault pole was gripped tightly in her right hand, and her too-large eyes narrowed as she scanned me from head to toe.

She said, "That face is familiar."

Dude, a curupira recognizes me! I thought, and nearly lol'd.

"Ha. Yeah. *Hi* . . ." I could feel a hot little blush creeping up my cheeks. "I'm Charlie Hernández. You might know me as the fifth and final Morphling?"

The mythical forest guardian shook her head. Her hair

seemed to crackle and hiss, like her entire scalp was on fire. And maybe it was. . . .

"Not your face," she said. "*That* face." She jabbed her spear at my T-shirt. My "Havana" song T-shirt.

"Oh . . . *gotcha.*" My cheeks burned some more. "That's, uh, Camila Cabello. The singer-songwriter?"

The curupira wagged her head up and down like she remembered now. Then, twirling her spear in a blur, she turned back to El Cadejo, saying, "Encontramos huellas."

"You found tracks?" I asked.

She nodded. Then, to El Cadejo again: "They lead into el río, but no one could have escaped by it. That river is caiman territory, and constantly patrolled."

El Cadejo's wise eyes otra vez fixed on mine and his "voice" was rich and deep as he said, *Charlie, I must go now. But remember what I have told you. And keep close to your friends, for there is safety in friendship.*

When I blinked again, I was back in my yard, standing exactly where I'd been standing when my fingers had first touched the stone.

But both the stone and the basajaun had vanished.

CHAPTER TWENTY-ONE

The next morning, the earsplitting crow of some *annoying* rooster woke me up first at 4:30 a.m. Then at 5:00 a.m. Then at 5:30. Then again at 6:01. And then yet *again* at 6:22, and by the time 7:45 rolled around and Raúl and me had to get up and get ready for school, we felt about as fresh as last week's guacamole.

I could barely keep my ojos open through my first two periods, and in third period, when someone called my name, I shouted, "$E = MC^2$!"

Ms. Alonso, my history teacher, frowned. "Charlie, we are currently investigating the socioeconomic effects of the Industrial Revolution, not Einstein's theory of relativity."

A few people giggled.

Someone yelled, "D'oh!" in their best Homer Simpson impersonation.

Ms. Alonso flicked a finger toward the door. "In any case, the principal wants to see you," she said.

I looked and saw Alvin Campbell standing there, waving at me with a big silly grin on his face. Alvin was one of my best friends in the entire world and made up exactly one-half of Los Jimaguas (aka the Twins), which included my other best friend, Sam Rodriguez. The three of us played video games together, had started our own Latin-rock band together, and usually ended up on the wrong side of the bell curve in math together. (Well, most of the really low scores were Sam's handiwork, but Al and I weren't exactly a couple of Pythagoreans, either.)

A couple of months ago, Alvin signed up to be the seventh-grade hall monitor, and Ponce's security chief, Mrs. Simon, had made the biggest mistake of her life by giving him a badge and a matching orange sash. Now Al thought he was the Wild Bill Hickok of Ponce Middle.

He raised a yellow notice slip over his mop of curly orange hair like it was a mini wanted poster or something. A wanted poster with *my* picture on it. "Sorry, but I gotta bring you in, pard."

I gulped. A meeting with the principal could mean only one thing: They must've discovered my sneaker in the plumbing! Or worse, Esperanza's *HEAD*!

I was about to be brought up on destruction of pri-

vate property charges. Maybe even falsely accused of
MURDER!

Once I'd gotten all my stuff together and we were all
alone in the hall, I rasped, "What does Principal García
want with me?"

"Nothing," Alvin said, and relief—sweet relief!—came
crashing over me like a glorious waterfall.

"Nothing?"

"Nope. Someone else wants you."

"Who?" I asked as we came around the corner.

But Alvin didn't answer; just stopped in front of room
1105—aka our school's media center and home of the
Daily Galaxy, aka our school's newspaper. Then, adjusting
his hall monitor's sash (which he did proudly *and* often—
very often), he went all deep-cover spy mode, glancing
suspiciously right, then suspiciously left, then suspiciously
right again before hissing, "I'll play lookout!" and shoving
me quickly inside.

Just two steps into the newspaper club's editorial room
and already I could feel the fluttery wings of panic tickling
my stomach. See, when your body is as prone to suddenly
and spontaneously manifesting any range of ridiculous animal traits (I'm talking anything from the tiny little horns of
a Jackson's chameleon to the long, hairy, pointy ears of an
Iberian lynx), the newspaper jocks aren't exactly the kind of

peeps you wanna hang with. They all had camera phones and notepads and weren't afraid to use them. But today it was familiar faces all around. In the center of the room, Violet stood over the large square-shaped desk, studying a mess of papers, while at the table behind her, Sam, the other half of Los Jimaguas, was messing with what looked like the PA system and bobbing his head up and down to Bad Bunny or whatever he had playing on his phone.

"HEY, CHARLIE! 'SUP, HERMANO?" he said—more like SCREAMED—when he saw me.

Violet flung an eraser at him, then gave him the classic *Shut up and take off the headphones!* gesture.

"Let me guess," I said to her. "You're playing principal for the day?"

V grinned at me. My heart did not go *ba-boom*. (Okay, it always did that when she grinned at me. But so what?) "Had to get you out of class somehow," she said.

"And you figured forgery was your best bet?"

The grin got bigger. "It was definitely top three."

Before I could ask what the other two were, the door to the media center swung open again and in came Alvin.

Only not on his own two legs. More like, on *Raúl's* two legs. 'Cause Raúl was carrying him, both hands jammed underneath Al's armpits, sorta like you would a baby with a dirty diaper. . . .

Alvin wasn't struggling or anything, but he did look *mighty* concerned. "Sorry, guys," he said, sounding embarrassed. "Couldn't stop him." Then, to Raúl: "Dude, you're, like, *super*strong. You pump iron, huh?"

"Hey, primo, put him down. . . . That's Alvin. He's a buddy of mine."

"Watch the door!" Violet hissed at Al, and he snapped her a quick little military-style salute before zipping back outside.

Raúl turned to me. His spiky black hair gleamed like onyx in the strip lights. "Oye, I heard you talking out in the hall. What's up?"

I started to answer, but then a thought smacked me in the face. "Wait. Aren't you in third-period biology?"

"Yeah, so?"

"Isn't that Mr. Binner's class?"

"Yeah, so?"

"Well, isn't that on the *other side* of the building?"

"Yeah, so?"

I opened my mouth to scream, *You just said you HEARD me!* but decided to let it go. Honestly, I wasn't in the mood. . . .

Raúl leaned across the table toward Violet, flashing those annoying dimples again. "¿Hola, señorita, y cómo está usted hoy?"

"De lo más bien," V said, smiling back. "Gracias."

Man, her Spanish was getting worrisomely good. And in this case, it was more worrisome than good.

I elbowed Raúl in the ribs. (It hurt. *Me.*) "Hey, stop smiling at her like that."

"Like what, cuz?"

"Like *that.*"

"I'm not smiling at her in any special way. This is how I smile. *See?* Now I'm smiling at you."

Bah, those perfect teeth and dimples! Seriously. Why did girls care about stuff like that anyway? Far as I was concerned, teeth were overrated. And *dimples?* Don't even get me started on dimples. I mean, what could you even do with those? Store a *penny* in them?

"Put those chompers away," I told him. "I left my sunglasses at home."

"Guys, focus," Violet said. She slid a sheet of paper across the desk toward us. "Check that out."

I quickly snatched it up before Raúl could. *Ha!* "It's . . . *blank.*"

"Sharp eye. And that just so happens to be about all the info I was able to dig up on Mr. C. You know, the name those goons at Pierre d'Exquis mentioned? Turns out he's the owner of that Shop o' Fakes, but I couldn't find an address, a picture, nothing on the guy. But here's where things get interesting. . . . So, you remember Kitty Purry?"

"I don't know a Kitty Purry," I said.

"You don't remember the cat we rescued last night? The Russian blue?"

"Oh, that Kitty Purry. Go on. . . ."

"I love cats," Raúl said, showing us his dimples again. "The bigger the better."

V gave him a strange look. "*Right*. So, anyway, I tried calling the number on her tag, you know, poking around a little—and guess what? No answer. Tried calling a buncha times this morning, too, but all I got was a machine, and the machine was full. Which naturally made me even more curious."

"Naturally," I said. Because what *didn't* make her curious?

"So I ran the address on her collar, and it turns out that Kitty Purry is *Mrs. Sifle's cat!* That's why I knew the address! I helped her ship some things home from a PTA meeting last year."

I shook my head. "I don't know a Mrs. Sifle."

"You don't know Mrs. Sifle? The school's longest-tenured lunch lady? The one who's been helping you open your milk since *second* grade?"

"Oh, that Mrs. Sifle. Wait. So, for real? That's her cat?"

"Uh-huh. And it gets more interesting. . . . Mrs. Sifle

hasn't shown up at school for the last *two days*! Hasn't called in sick or anything."

"Hol' up. So who's gonna help Charlie open his milk now?" Sam asked, looking genuinely concerned.

Violet ignored him, went on. "I checked with the lady who runs the school office, and she hasn't been able to reach her either. She's worried. So in homeroom I tried calling Mrs. Sifle's closest neighbor—found his number in the directory—and get this." She slid over a newspaper with a big missing persons ad in it. "His daughter put that in the *Herald* exactly thirty-six hours ago. He's been missing for three days, according to his family."

"That's Mrs. Sifle's neighbor?" I said.

"Yep. But there's more. His daughter claims it's the oddest thing—I got her on the phone this morning, after breakfast—anyway, she says that all his stuff is still at his house—his car, all his clothes, everything—but he's vanished without a text. She claims that the last time she spoke with him was Wednesday evening, around seven o'clock, and she heard something like a strange whistling sound in the background, far-away sounding, and then the line went dead. Oh, and she mentioned that he'd been complaining about being dehydrated for about a week now and had even made a doctor's appointment. An appointment he never showed up for."

"I don't blame him," Sam said. "I wouldn't have shown up either. I always get super nervous in those sterile little waiting rooms."

Violet looked like she was seriously regretting having invited Sam to our little powwow. "And get this," she said. "Mr. Miller—Mrs. Sifle's neighbor—he's the lunch aide over in GWC, our rival school!"

Man, that *was* kinda weird. "So, two neighbors, two missing people. You know, maybe they ran away together. A couple of cafeteria aides fall in love and swear to leave cafeteria duties behind forever. That'd make a cool book, actually."

V quirked a brow at me. "You been reading your parents' romance novels again, huh?"

"What? *Nooo* . . . Okay, so I might've *glanced* at a chapter or two. They leave those things lying around *everywhere*. And just so you know, they're actually pretty good."

Raúl, meanwhile, was staring down at the newspaper, rubbing his chin and sorta purring deep in his throat. Finally he looked up at us. "Sounds to me like someone's kidnapping lunch ladies—er, *people*."

"That was my initial hunch too," said Violet. "But then I ran a quick search for anyone else recently reported missing in the area, and I found another person who claimed their aunt and uncle had gone missing. It's only been a day, but they posted on social media about it. They're florists. But look where they live. . . ." She slid the newspaper aside and brought a big blowup of South Miami from inside her book bag. At the top left-hand corner, a large red circle had been drawn around a house. "That's them there. Only eight blocks from Mrs. Sifle's *and* Mr. Miller's. All their houses are up in Little Havana, not too far from La Rosa Cemetery. Oh, and I almost forgot! Remember the pair of pet collars Raúl found inside the truck at Pierre's? Missy and Fu? Well, they belong to them! To the florists!"

Whoa. Okay. Now things were getting interesting. Weird. *Really* weird. But also really, really interesting . . . Shaking my head, I studied the blowup. I mean, that was just *a lot* of kidnapped pets and *a lot* of missing people living kinda nearby to each other. Sure, the people hadn't been missing for long, and who knew if they were actually missing at all (I still liked my theory about the two lovey-dovey cafeteria attendants), but it was still strange.

The only question was, how did all this tie in with what was going on at Pierre's? Or with Esperanza's sister? Or even with those earthquakes people had been reporting in the area? (And what was up with that whole ominous-sounding Golden Dooms thing we'd overheard Mr. Sospechoso blabbing about?) Honestly, I didn't have the slightest clue. And I didn't have a plan for helping us get a clue either. So I turned to the one person I knew already had a plan. Because she always had a plan. And they were always pretty good, too, which was why I never really bothered coming up with one.

"So, what are you thinking?" I asked our resident Sherlock, and watched her lips curve up into the type of smile I knew meant trouble.

"I'm thinking this calls for some *serious* snoopage," she said mischievously.

I sighed. *Ya tú sabes . . .*

CHAPTER TWENTY-TWO

Violet's plan was pretty simple. Head back over to Little Havana, snoop around the houses of a few of the missing people, try to talk to someone, and see if anything turned up. Her plan was so simple, in fact, that it was basically foolproof. Except . . . there was a *snag*. We'd overlooked one critical—maybe even *fundamental*—element: a mother's intuition.

See, moms just *know* when their kids are up to something they shouldn't be up to. And the sharpness of my mom's intuition made Excalibur's legendary blade look like a butter knife.

"Oh, no, I don't think so," she said when we came to her with the whole "sleepover" cover. "You and your friends are up to something, and I don't like it."

"Mom, we're not up to anything! What could we *possibly* be up to?"

"¡Charlie, no quiero oírlo más! I don't wanna hear it! Just wake up extra early tomorrow and bike over to Alvin's. And if you wake up early enough, it'll be just like you slept there!"

My mom was a tough cookie. And tough cookies don't crumble. Not on their own, anyway. So I dug right into my bag o' tricks, all my tried-and-true staples:

"But, Mom, Sam and Alvin are counting on us being there!"

And "Mom, this isn't *fair!*"

And "But everyone *else's* mom said yes!"

Oh, and let's not forget the classic "Mom, I'm gonna be *an adult* pretty soon. You can't just keep me locked up forever!"

Yeah, that one never even had a chance. The truth was, my mom would *gladly* keep me locked up well into my eighties and wouldn't think twice about it. She probably wouldn't even think *once*. To her, age really was just a number. . . .

Anyway, I was all out of guilt-trip-inducing material and the clock was ticking. Which meant I needed to call in reinforcements. Translation: I called Violet.

After I'd explained the situation to her, she told me that the mission was still a *go*, and to, and I quote, "Sit back and wait for the cavalry."

So that's what Raúl and I did. We sat back and waited for the prancing pony soldiers, watching the little digital Power Rangers alarm clock on my nightstand.

Then, at 6:02, the phone rang.

At 6:03, my mom answered.

6:05, my mom said, "Oh."

6:06, she said, "Oh, *wow*."

6:07, she said, "Well, I had no idea. . . . No. He doesn't tell me things like that."

At 6:09, she hung up.

And at 6:10 she shouted, "Charlie, get down here!"

Raúl and I traded *uh-oh* looks.

That didn't sound so good.

CHAPTER TWENTY-THREE

Down in the living room, Mommy Dearest was waiting for us in that classic *you've-just-been-busted-sucka* mama pose, hands on hips, eyes narrowed in righteous and all-knowing indignation.

"Charlie, ¿por qué no me dijiste?" she snapped. "Why didn't you tell me?" And I, of course, nearly swallowed my tongue.

I mean, what had Violet told her? *The truth?* You can *NEVER* tell my mom the truth. It doesn't work on her!

"Mom, look—" I started to babble, sounding a lot like my dad when he got caught sneaking Kit Kat bars into his lunch bag, but she cut me off, shouting:

"How could you not tell me you and Violet were going on a date?!"

"*A DATE?*" I screeched.

"Honey, you don't have to be *embarrassed*! And you don't have to make up lies about sleepovers and pajama parties. . . . You and Violet make the CUTEST couple! Besides, everyone knows you're in love with her."

"*Mom!*" I shouted. Honestly, I could've died of embarrassment. I really could've. But maybe even *worse*, I would've bet *ANYTHING* that Violet was probably laughing her brilliant little head off right about now, just imagining how all this was playing out.

Man, sometimes I really hate smart people. . . .

"Oh, and it's a *double date*, tía," said Raúl, with that sly dimply charm of his.

My mom blinked. "You too?"

"Sí, I met a very nice girl who's on the soccer team. She does an *amazing* wheel kick! Violet introduced us."

You would've thought he'd told my mom that he had discovered the cure for zits or something. "Ay, my two little hombrecitos! Growing up so fast!" She dabbed the corners of her eyes like she might burst into tears any second now. "It's just a lot, you know?"

"Uh, right . . . Anyway, we better get going," I said. "Don't wanna be late for our big *double date*."

"GOING?" my mom shrieked. "You can't go on a date with Violet looking like *un zaparrastroso!*" Her hand shot out, quick as a cobra, snatching mine. I tried to pull away, but it was useless. All moms come equipped with that secret mommy strength. And mine wasn't any different. "C'mon," she said, "it's time for a mommy makeover!"

CHAPTER TWENTY-FOUR

"W"ell, don't you shine up real nice," Violet said as she came pedaling up my driveway to where Raúl and I were waiting for her. "Who's the lucky girl? Does she go to our school?"

"*Ha. Ha*," I said dryly, really playing up my annoyance, even though it was virtually impossible for Violet to annoy me. "Well, if it isn't the neighborhood *comedian*. Do you have any idea what my mom put me through in there? I had try on *fifty* different guayaberas. That's, like, three MIL-LION total buttons! My thumbs might never recover!"

It hadn't stopped there, either. In the bathroom, she'd spotted Raúl's assortment of beauty products and had plastered my hair with gel and doused me in enough of his stinkin' cologne (Aqua de Gato, I think it was called) to drown a manatee. And all that for a *fake* date. I could only imagine what prom was gonna be like. . . .

Grinning, Violet looked me up and down. "Your hair— it's . . ."

My heart sort of skipped a beat. "Yeah?"

". . . *interesting.*" Then she said, "And you smell . . ."

"Yeah?"

". . . *musky.*"

"Thanks?"

Then, frowning a bit: "And I gotta say, your fashion sense is *a little*—"

"Please, just stop."

A large red egg yolk of sun was melting into the horizon by the time we set out for Little Havana, Violet and I riding out in front on our red and yellow eight-speeds, Raúl jogging behind and sometimes between us, laughing, making jokes, and generally just showing off.

Man, handsome cousins can be some of the most *annoying* kinds of cousins. . . . I'm pretty sure that's, like, a universal truth or something.

At any rate, Alvin and Sam weren't joining us on this one. Not physically, at least. We wanted part of the team sitting safely in the comfort of their own cribs in case things got dicey and we needed to send out an emergency SOS text. And, naturally, Alvin had quickly volunteered them both for that "risky" job.

In hindsight, though, it might not have been such a

terrible idea, because less than three minutes into our ride, I began to have this sneaking suspicion that we were being followed. Seven minutes in, my suspicion was no longer sneaking. And ten minutes in, it was no longer a suspicion.

"We got another tail," I whispered, trying not to look back again. Our personal paparazzi was straddling a low, old-school, rust bucket of a bicicleta. And when I say old-school, I'm talking a total blast from the past, the kind of bike you'd probably only find on some vintage bicycle collector's eBay store.

"Pretty sure it's the same tail as last time," Violet said, using the reverse camera function on her cell phone to scope him out. (This apparently wasn't news to her.)

"Definitely the same guy," agreed Raúl. "Same crusty sneakers—high-tops."

V snapped a picture. "Looks like a 1905 Schwinn. That's a *seriously* cool vintage. . . ."

"Maybe we should let him catch up," I suggested. "We can all go for some guarapo and have a nice little chat, if you know what I mean."

Raúl, jogging next to me now, cracked his knuckles and grinned. "I like the sound of that."

But then, as if sensing danger—or maybe just suddenly needing to *pee*—the rider veered off, disappearing behind a row of Spanish tile roofs.

"You want me to chase 'im down?" Raúl asked, staring after him.

"No point," Violet said. "If he's involved in this thing, we'll see him again."

CHAPTER TWENTY-FIVE

We reached the house in Little Havana—the two missing florists' house—at a little after seven thirty and found a car parked in the driveway and most of the indoor lights off.

Violet tried ringing the bell, knocking on the back door, banging on all the bedroom windows, even pounding on the flimsy garage door, but no one answered.

The big bay window overlooking the front yard gave us a pretty good look at what was happening inside, and that was nada. The only sign of life was a large red-feathered rooster strutting and pecking around the side yard. I'm not gonna lie. I thought about asking Raúl to catch it, thinking it might've been the same useless chicken that had "serenaded" us out of some sweet REMs, like, *fifty times* this morning, but I couldn't see a chicken making it this far across Miami roadways (which are, of course, *zooming* with Miami-style drivers) without having quickly become *roadkill*.

On the side of the house, near the AC unit, we found some kind of huge feather. It was the oddest shade of black-green, which meant it wasn't the rooster's, and my only guess was that someone around here was keeping a crested argus as a pet. (In case you're wondering, a crested argus is a wild pheasant, which basically has the longest and *widest* feathers of any bird.)

"Looks like it's on to our lunch lady's," said Violet.

House #2 (Mrs. Sifle's pad) was a lot like house #1 except that there were a few more cars in the driveway and a lot less flowers planted around the yard and in window boxes. We tried the whole knocking, ringing, banging, pounding, shouting routine again (just in case), and again got the same result. A stack of big cardboard boxes was piled by the front door. They each had a red LIQUID sticker on the side and had apparently been shipped from the Coca-Cola Company's official headquarters. There must've been close to a dozen boxes.

"Apparently Mrs. Sifle takes the 'obey your thirst' slogan a little too seriously," I said.

Around back, we spotted a second red-feathered rooster pecking and clucking around the yard, and I couldn't help wondering if these things were the latest breed of invasive species threatening to destabilize the delicate balance of South Florida's diverse ecosystem. Personally, I had no clue; but my dad was always worrying about stuff like that.

"I don't like this," Violet said, toeing the edge of an unopened newspaper. "It looks like there're people in there, but nobody actually *is*. It doesn't make any sense."

Ten feet away, Raúl—who was now down on all fours—sniffed the tailpipe of a little frost-gray station wagon. "This car hasn't been started in days," he said, glancing up at me.

"You can tell like that?" I asked, surprised.

"Yep. You'd be amazed how much you can learn by sniffing something's rear."

House #3 (Mr. Miller's) was where things got . . . well, even *weirder*. There were more cars in the driveway, more lights on inside, but all the blinds were drawn, and the whole place smelled oddly of an old musty sack. The weirdest part, though? We ran into yet *another* red-feathered rooster! This one was strutting around the neat little yard, squawking and beating its bloodred wings. Now, one red-feathered rooster was odd. Two was a coincidence. But *three*? Three had me un poquito nervioso. . . .

"This can't be right," I said as V disappeared around the side of the house. "Every single house is totally abandoned, and every single one has a rooster pecking around the yard. I don't think I've ever even *seen* a chicken that shade of red before. And now we've seen *three*."

"It's true," Raúl agreed. "I grew up on a farm and never seen a rooster that color. I thought maybe it was a South Florida thing."

But the roosters were far from the only surprise. An instant later, a strange whistling sound filled the air. No, not just a sound, I realized. A tune: *Do, re, mi, fa, so, la, ti.* Only it was the single most *awful* rendition I'd ever heard! The notes seemed to scratch at the air—to *tear* at it. They crawled over my skin and dug into my ears and seemed to worm their way deep into my heart, sending a cold tingle of fear down my spine.

Not five seconds after it had started, the whistling was already twice as loud as it had been to begin with. Then, just as it reached a deafening pitch, it cut off.

"*The heck was that?*" I hissed, turning to my cousin.

Raúl was shaking his head, his dark eyes trying to scan in every direction at once.

"A demented *ice cream truck?*" That was my one and only guess. I mean, what else?

"That's what I was thinking, cuz."

"Guys, what was that?" Violet rasped, poking her head around a clump of red bougainvillea.

"No idea," we both answered, and then she began frantically waving us over. So we hurried over and found her standing by the side door. The *open* side door.

"I just nudged it and it opened," she said. Her voice was an innocent little kid's.

I said, "You mean you *picked* the lock, *then* nudged it, *and then* it opened, right?"

"I'm not saying the thought didn't cross my mind, *Charlie* . . . but no. Honest. It was open."

"Maybe we should have a look inside," suggested Raúl.

And when V said, "I agree," my eyes popped so far out of my face that they probably looked like they were attached to selfie sticks.

"Are you two being *serious* right now?! You want to *sneak* into some STRANGER'S house? That's—that's called BREAKING AND ENTERING! It's a *CRIME*. And in all fifty states!"

"Only if we get caught," Raúl said with a smirk.

"And we didn't actually *break* anything," Violet pitched in. "The door was already open. So that would only make it half a crime, if you think about it."

"Yeah, well, you're the one who's gonna explain that half to the SWAT TEAM when they handcuff us and throw us in the back of a squad car!"

Violet didn't say anything. Only grinned at me. She knew I was gonna give in to her. I always did. I'm blandito like that.

CHAPTER TWENTY-SIX

The aluminum door creaked open (its rusty hinges practically screeching WARNING! DELINCUENTE ALERT!) as the three of us stepped inside along with a gust of fallen leaves. And the moment we did, all I could think was *Yuck.*

The door had let us into a small, plain-looking kitchen, and that kitchen was a total *mess.* A half-eaten bologna sandwich sat moldering on the countertop. Clouds of fruit flies were swarming around a plateful of sliced guava paste. There were empty water bottles, empty milk cartons, half-empty soda cans, and a couple of plastic pitchers—empty, of course—piled almost to the ceiling by the sink. Call me capitán Obvious, but something told me that whoever lived here must've had a *mighty* thirst.

"Check these out," whispered Raúl.

Crouching, I could just make out faint, S-shaped tracks

on the tiles. Long zigs and zags. *Snake tracks.* In fact, I even spotted what looked like a bit of shed snakeskin in the corner by the sink!

"Looks like somebody's got a pet python," I said with a shiver. "Watch your toes."

I had just walked over to get a closer look at the bit of skin—to see if it actually *was* python skin—when a sound caught my ear. A low, frightened whining. A sound a baby might make. Standing very still, I listened very hard . . . and the sound grew louder and louder until I was pretty sure it was coming from the other side of the wall. In the living room.

"You both hear that, right?" I whispered.

Violet's head wagged up and down.

"Whatdya think that is?" asked Raúl. And exactly five seconds later, as we tiptoed cautiously out of the kitchen and even *more* cautiously through the swinging door and into the big living room area, we saw *what*: Trapped inside a small steel cage, pawing and gnawing anxiously at the bars, was a fuzzy, brown-furred puppy. Isabel, according to the tag.

"It's the same kind," Violet said, squatting beside the cage.

I shook my head. "The same kind of *what*?"

"Same kinda cages that were in the cargo truck behind Pierre's."

"It's true," Raúl agreed. "Same style."

It was then—right as my eyes drifted a little way past the cage—that I noticed something else: more tracks on the tiles. Only . . . these weren't snake tracks.

No, these were big and muddy and looked more like footprints—or, more specifically, *boot* prints. Dark and moist-looking nearby, but growing lighter and fainter as they tracked past the puppy and past a pair of love seats, disappearing into the big closet along the wall.

"V, check those out," I whispered, pointing.

Violet's eyes narrowed as she leaned over to examine the prints. "They're *huge* . . . ," she rasped. "Size twenty-twos at least. Working boots, it looks like from the shape of the heel." Her eyes, suddenly full of concern, rose to mine. "And . . . they're *fresh*."

All three of us looked anxiously around at each other.

And anxiously down at the prints again.

And then anxiously back up at the closed closet doors.

I had time to ask "*How* fresh exactly . . . ?" Then the doors exploded open—I'm talking into little *bits* and *pieces*!—as three Dwayne Johnson–size dudes came bursting out!

Two leather-jacket-wearing goons—the croc things we'd run into behind Pierre's—and something else. Something even *uglier*, if you can believe it.

My first thought when I saw it was *¡Santo cielo! That thing doesn't have a head! It's all legs and torso!*

But as my eyes ran up . . . and up, and up, and up, they finally found a head. And a face, too. Well, not exactly "a face" per se. . . . It was missing eyes and ears and a nose, sorta like its body was saying, *Hey, I got you to ten feet tall. What else do ya want from me?* The thing did have a mouth, though. A particularly *flexible*-looking mouth, too . . . all soft and mushy, apparently muscleless.

The monster looked like a hybrid between the world's ugliest sock puppet and the world's ugliest Venus flytrap. (Totally weird combo, I know. But that's just what it looked like.)

Hands like meat hooks hung down around its ankles. Eyes the size of headlights blinked up at us from its knees. Yeah, *its knees*. Strapped across its narrow chest was a bow of brown birchwood and a single birchwood arrow.

In all my fear and shock, and with the way my pulse was pounding painfully in my temples, I almost didn't recognize the thing; but recognize it I did, and mostly because it was basically *un*mistakable: that thing was a Munuanë! Those infamous jungle ogres from Colombia and Venezuela!

My abuelita had told me pretty much all their stories, and none were, shall we say, particularly *flattering*. . . . They mostly involved this monster and others like it slinging arrows at anyone who happened to wander near their parts of the jungle or raiding villages for baked goods. (Apparently this particular species of ogres had a bit of a sweet tooth; which was kinda funny, considering they didn't seem to have any *teeth*.)

"Lookie, lookie, if it isn't porcupine boy . . . ," said one of the croc things—Mr. Sospechoso, I was pretty sure. Except . . . he looked almost completely *human* now! Not as many scales. No croc eyes. The grin he flashed us was still just as ugly, though. "And he's even got himself a new hairstyle!"

"And a new smell," said the other one. "*Phew!* What'd ya do, *bathe* in the stuff?"

"It was my mom!" I shouted. "She just wanted me to try something new!"

"Well, in that case," said croc número uno, "try some of *this*." Then, turning to the mush-faced Tower of Ugly: "¡Cómetelos vivos!"

And since he'd basically just told the Munuanë to, and I quote, "Eat them alive!" we did our finest imitation of the Olympic-gold-medal-winning sprinter Mr. Usain and *bolted* for our lives!

We flew down a hallway and scrambled through the first door we found. (Because, really, any door will do when you're running for your life.) It happened to be a den. Small, no windows. ¡No bueno!

Thinking fast, V shut the door and locked it, and just as she did, I realized, with a surge of panic, that we'd forgotten one *itty-bitty* little thing—

"WHERE'S RAÚL?" I shrieked. Yep, in our mad scramble, we'd totally forgotten my cousin!

"He's probably trying to split up!" shouted Violet. Then: "Help me!" And together we toppled a huge, heavy wooden dresser by the door, creating a makeshift blockade.

"I wanna see 'em get through *that!*" I said. Looking back on it, though, I probably should've just kept my big mouth shut, because I got *exactly* what I asked for.

There was a great splintering crash as the Munuanë came barreling through the door. Except it didn't simply *barrel* through it. It *EXPLODED* through the door and through the dresser and came hissing and snarling into the bedroom. Guess jungle ogres don't knock. . . .

As we fumbled backward, I realized my phone was still in my hand. (I'd brought it out to shine some light on the piece of snakeskin by the sink.)

I didn't think. Just flung it at the monster's smooth, featureless face. Yeah, not my smartest move ever. But then again, when facing certain death, smarts are usually the first thing to shrivel up and die.

Anyway, my phone bounced off nothing in particular

and clattered noisily to the floor as one of the Munuanë's giant apelike feet came down on top of it, crushing it like someone squashing a pesky cockroach.

Munuanë—*one*.

Charlie's flying cell phone attack—*zero*.

Fortunately, now it was Violet's turn. And she was usually much more heavily armed than me.

Her right hand slipped into her purse and came out with a sleek black Taser (her *dad's* Taser, it looked like). Then she lunged forward, touched the business end to the side of the Munuanë's leg, and hit the deep-fry button.

Nothing happened. Actually, something *did* happen. The Taser lit up. The two metal prongs at its end spat an arc of blueish sparks. But other than that, the sock-puppet-faced monstruo was completely unfazed.

V's hand slipped into her purse again, and this time came out with a mega-Slurpee-size can of pepper spray. Her eyes narrowed, her arm aimed, and her pretty little thumb with its pretty little manicured fingernail did the deed, unloading roughly half the can's misty, liquidy, burn-your-friggin'-*face-off* contents into the ogre's hissing punim.

The cloud of weaponized capsaicin wrapped around the monster's egg-shaped head like a peppery crown.

But—just like with the Taser and my cell phone

attack—*nothing* happened! The Munuanë didn't gasp, didn't cough, didn't even *flinch*!

Violet, on the other hand, frowned. "Not exactly what I was hoping for . . . ," she said. Honestly, it wasn't exactly what I'd been hoping for either.

But that's when I remembered something: Munuanës had a weak spot! It was super consistent throughout all their legends!

Only it wasn't their *faces*—it was their *knees*!

"V, its knees!" I shouted. "Give its knees the bizness!"

I didn't need to tell her twice. She let him have it—a big spicy blast right in the kneecap—er, knee *eyeball*.

And this time the result was much more to our liking.

The faceless freakazoid let out a single piercing shriek. (Which, by the way, sort of reminded me of the shriek Sam's mom gave every time she saw one of his report cards.) Then the skin around its knee rippled and its pepper-sprayed eyeball retreated deep into the knee joint, burrowing like a wounded worm.

A lot of good it did us, though, because right at the same moment one of el monstruo's twig-thin (but obviously pretty freakin' *powerful*) arms swung up in a wide arc, connecting with Violet's wrist and knocking the can of pepper spray out of her hand.

The Munuanë hissed at us. It growled. Its toothless

maw opened wide, revealing a purplish-reddish tongue that was so yucky and crusty it made me wanna find a scrubber and go all Mr. Clean on the thing. Its other knee eyeball glared angrily up at us—glared like, *Ahora it's MY turn!*

In a blindingly fast move that would've made even Robin Hood blush, the ogre unslung its bow, nocked its deadly arrow, and drew, taking aim at Violet.

Time stood still.

My breath stopped.

My heart stopped.

Everything around me just *stopped.*

Except, of course, for me, myself, and I.

Without even thinking, I lunged, throwing myself in front of Violet just as the ogre released his arrow.

I really wasn't interested in seeing the arrow that I would soon be *feeling,* so I sorta turned away, in midair, figuring it would hurt less this way. Stupid, sure. But that was exactly the sort of stupid stuff that felt supersmart at moments like these.

Anyway, I knew from the legends that the Munuanë never missed.

Not once.

Not ever.

And on this occasion the result was no different.

The arrow sang through the space between us like a heat-seeking missile, flying straight for its target.

Fortunately, I was in the way.

Unfortunately, it found a new target.

Me.

CHAPTER TWENTY-SEVEN

There was a dull *thud!* as the arrow buried itself in the middle of my back. It hit me with the force of a Mack truck, and the impact flung me clear across the room, where I banged my head hard enough against the wall for a whole flock of yellow Tweety birds to suddenly appear, chirping and flapping, flying dizzy circles around my ringing cabeza.

Weird thing was, the arrow itself wasn't causing me much pain. None, really.

Or—more likely—it was causing me SOOO MUCH pain that my overloaded nervous system simply decided not to bother sharing it with the rest of me.

Violet rushed over, shouting, "Oh my gosh, Charlie!" Then, as her wide, frightened eyes ran down my back to where the arrow was: "Oh my gosh, Charlie!"

"IS IT BAD?" I shrieked.

V made a face. "Actually, it's kinda . . . *good*."

Scrambling to my feet, I tried to reach a hand around back there, but realized I couldn't. It felt . . . *weird*. As if some sorta big, dome-shaped, sentient bookbag had latched itself onto my back.

And that's when it all clicked together!

A shell.

I'd morphed a freakin' TURTLE shell!

Beneath my searching fingertips, I could feel its unique smoothness, its oily hardness—the tough hexagonal texture of each large individual piece—or scute—that made up the outermost layer.

Dude, I'd gone full-on Teenage Mutant Ninja Turtle!

And suddenly that epic theme song of theirs was blasting through my head: *THEY'RE HEROES IN A HALF SHELL AND THEY'RE GREEEEEEEN!*

I checked my arms.

Not green.

Just nicely tan.

Oh, well, nobody's perfect. . . .

But that's why I hadn't felt the arrow, I realized. That's why I wasn't *dead*!

The Munuanë, meanwhile, had just been standing there, kinda gawking at me via one kneeball (see what I did there?). It didn't have much in the way of what you might call "an expression." Which was no big surprise, seeing as the thing hardly had any facial features. But you could tell it was surprised.

Yanking la flecha out of my *sick* new shell, I began waving it around in front of the ogrezilla's faceless face so it could get a good look at it.

"This belong to you?!" I shouted. Then, remembering its eyes were actually down at its knees and adjusting accordingly, "Is that all you got, you overgrown *PUNK?*"

The Munuanë—who apparently spoke at least *some* English and who apparently didn't appreciate being called a punk—flapped its floppy lips at me.

Then it shouldered its bow, dropped into an angry crouch, and let out a hiss so loud it shook the world—or at least it shook *my* world—as globs of mucusy spit flew from its maw, splattering my arms and face. *Yummy!*

V looked at me like, *Bad move, kid.* And I looked back at the Munuanë and was all like: "I WAS ONLY ASKING!"

But it was obviously way too late for I'm-sowwys. (Note to self: Do *NOT* go flexin' on ten-foot-tall killer sombras with serious temper issues. On the bright side, I don't think that was going to be a tough one to remember. . . .)

The ogre came forward, clawed fingers spread like a fan of deadly daggers. V and I stumbled backward, too scared to scream, too terrified to run.

We butted painfully up against the wall and then just sort of threw our arms around each other in what was probably going to be our last terrified act on this side of things.

Well, it was weird while it lasted, I thought. And by "it" I meant *my life. . . .*

Suddenly, out in the hall, something roared. A blur of silver shot in through the wrecked doorway, slamming into the Munuanë like a runaway Metro Rail.

Then ogre and blur went crashing into the far wall, and also *through* it, and into the next room.

The silvery blur came out on top, pinning the Munuanë beneath massive furry paws.

And as its furry head flew back, letting out a mighty jungle-cat-like roar, I realized (with something between relief and a high-pitched shriek) that it was more creature than blur and more jaguar (or, more specifically, *were*jaguar) than any creature I'd ever seen.

Cords of muscles rippled beneath its midnight-colored fur. Gold-rimmed eyes peered out of a face that couldn't seem to make up its mind between kitty-cat or human, and its fang-choked mouth hissed and snarled, roaring down at the Munuanë, who kicked and struggled fiercely underneath it.

One of the ogre's clawed hands slashed across the

werejaguar's upper arm. Blood gleamed in its thick fur, but it didn't back down.

Next moment, the Munuanë seized the werecat around its spotted neck and slammed it first into the wall—*bang!*—then into the floor—*crack!*—and then flung it, furry head first, through the bedroom window—*crash!*—and out into the backyard.

Which was obviously no bueno—not for us and not for the cat.

"C'MON!" Violet shouted, snatching my hand.

We rushed out of the little room and back into the messy kitchen, stumbling over water bottles and each other, and had just started for the side door when a massive, mammoth, mountainous, absolutely MONSTROUS figure filled the doorframe, blocking our way.

And *that's* when I knew it was all over. . . .

CHAPTER TWENTY-EIGHT

t wasn't another ogre. That was the good news. The bad? Whatever this thing was, it was even *BIGGER!*

From that point, everything happened in ultra-slow-mo.

V and I began to retreat—if you could call tripping and fumbling over each other retreating—as a ginormous shadow fell over us, and eyes like burning torches glared down at us from an incredible height.

My Panic-o-Meter spiked. My legs tangled. I fell flat on my butt but managed to scramble back up just as the Munuanë, all snapping saggy mouth, appeared at the other end of the kitchen.

In its huge apeish hands was its bow, the arrow already notched and ready, its deadly point already leveled on us. (Guess we were just lucky like that.)

A millisecond later, something like a hairy tree trunk

swept through the air, shoving Violet and me first aside, then behind, and then out the side door and out of the house as the shadowy figure put itself between us and the Munuanë. And right at that moment, right as a pool of bleary light from the ceiling fan lit up the figure's face, I heard myself cry, "¡Leche frita!" Because the figure with the burning eyes was *Juan!*

Juan the basajaun!

The Munuanë changed its mind. Well, more like *its target.* It swung the bow smoothly toward Juan, drew, and, just as smoothly, released.

The arrow sliced through the air, too fast to track. But at the last moment, Juan's massive fist batted it away like it was nothing more than an annoying fly, and it went spinning and twisting away, embedding itself in the wall.

Then, with a mighty roar that shook the floor (and the whole wide WORLD beneath it), the basajaun charged.

He tackled the Munuanë around its skinny waist and drove it through the kitchen wall, through the living room wall, and the fireplace, and a bedroom, and a closet, and another closet, and finally into the big bedroom.

I wondered if there were insurance policies that covered "acts of sombras." My guess was probably not.

"LET'S GO!" Violet shouted, and we hurried to the front yard, looking desperately for my cousin.

A half second later, I spotted him—and with a HUGE surge of relief, too—coming around the other side of the house.

"¡Ahí!" I pointed. "There he is!"

Raúl's right arm appeared to be dangling at his side, and there was a gash in it and fresh blood on his sleeve.

I ran toward him. "¿Dude, estás bien?"

"Just a scratch," he said. "I'm good."

Behind us, another mighty roar shook the house, nearly bringing *down* the house. (And not in the fun mega-concert kinda way.)

"We gotta help Juan!" I shouted, starting toward the front door. "It's three against one!"

"Yeah, only I feel bad for *the three*," said Raúl.

There was a huge crash as the wall on the garage side blew apart, and the Munuanë and the two crocs came stumbling and bumbling out. Another earthshaking roar, and this time several windows exploded outward in a shower of sparkling glass.

The ogre and the two goons apparently didn't want to stick around to find out what was making Juan so cranky, 'cause they immediately hightailed it outta there, scurrying off into the night like a trio of cowards with their tails tucked tightly between their legs. (Though, for the record, only the Munuanë actually *had* a tail.)

"Hey, they're taking the puppy!" shouted Raúl, looking like he wanted to chase after them. But there wasn't much we could do about it now.

A moment later Juan emerged from the darkness of the little house. His thick fur rippled in the breeze as he strode quickly toward us, seeming to melt in and out of the shadows of lampposts. "¿Están heridos?" he asked sharply.

"We're okay," Violet said. "But he's bleeding."

Raúl shook his head. "I'm fine. I tol' you it's just a scratch."

The leathery skin around the basajaun's mouth tightened, and his wise eyes flashed as he looked sternly around at us from his absurd height.

"This was *incredibly* reckless of you three—*tontísimo!* That Munuanë is a well-known *mercenary,* un matador for hire! It would have gladly boiled your bones jess to make itself a fresh bowl of sopita!" Digging a wrench out of his bushy blondish beard, he began wringing it between his hands like a wet rag. The metal squealed and bent, and I got the feeling he was doing that to the wrench so that he wouldn't do it to *us.* Overall, I thought that was a very solid idea. . . . "Joanna will hear of this!" the basajaun growled, twisting the wrench into a pretzel. "¡Se los juro!"

"Juan, no, c'mon!" Violet and I started to beg, but the hairy hominid wouldn't hear it.

He roared, "And then I'm going to tell *TU MAMÁ!*" looking straight at *me* now. And if looks could kill, his would've blown vital parts of me into *Biscayne Bay.*

"Juan, dude, not *my mom!*" I shouted. "I mean, she'll *KILL* me!"

"I hope she does! It will save *me* the trouble!"

Violet put both hands on the woolly Schwarzenegger's huge biceps, trying to calm the man—er, *beast.*

"Juan, listen," she said, "we're *all over* them. . . . We're close to tearing this whole case wide open!"

"You're close to getting *YOURSELVES* torn wide open!" he snapped. "Like a flock of helpless sheep without a shepherd!"

"But, Juan, *it's true!*" I said. "We can already pretty much prove that Mr. C's goons are involved with the people who've been going missing around here. At least a few of them. And at the very *least* they're kidnapping their pets."

Now, how any of that tied into whatever had happened with or was currently happening *to* Esperanza's sister was still YTBD (yet to be determined). But at the very least we were slowly starting to peel back the layers of the orange— or was the expression "onion"?

Juan, meanwhile, was still shaking his head like he didn't want to hear it, but asked, "Who is Mr. C?"

"He owns Pierre d'Exquis," explained Violet. "The

antique shop. It's a front. We know he's up to something—something bad enough to make a calaca leave the cemetery to try to help her sister."

The wise forest lord whose ancestors had invented both the horseshoe and the dress shoe said nothing for several seconds. His jaw worked like a meat grinder. The corners of his mouth were drawn back in a snarl, and his eyes grew dark and sorta distant. "I am already investigating that place," he growled finally, "because of what Charlie told me the last time we spoke. BUT if there is anything to find, *I* will find it. *Not* the three of you."

Then he went quiet again, the muscles along his shoulders tensing and untensing, and it seemed to me like he was trying to decide how much of this he was going to tell Queen Joanna.

I gave him a few secs, then decided to shoot my shot. "Hey, uh, maybe on second thought there's no need to tell the queen about what happened here, you know? It's not like any of us are *hurt* or anything. . . . And we probably don't wanna worry her for no reason. She's already got enough to worry about."

Juan gave me a look that was a little too much beast from *Beauty and the Beast* and not enough of that friendly blue monster from *Monsters Inc.* "There is no use trying to manipulate me, Carlito, for I have already made up my mind *not* to tell Joanna about today. . . . You speak truly when you say she has much on her mind as it is. *But if I ever catch any of you three within ten blocks of that store or ANYWHERE ELSE near those monstruos*—te lo juro—you are going to have a lot more than just a bruja to worry about. . . . Do I make myself *absolutamente* clear?"

The tone of his voice could've boiled platanitos. Still, I grinned up at the lovable giant and said, "Does a manatee love to swim in warm, shallow water?"

(Hint: They sure do!)

CHAPTER TWENTY-NINE

A few minutes later, as we were making our way back home along Calle Ocho, something hit me. Something that probably should've hit me, like, *twenty minutes* ago. And something that had me suddenly EXTREMELY concerned. . . .

I whirled on Raúl and—in my most accusing tone—shouted, "Hey, *wait up*! I just realized that you didn't freak out—like, *at all*—when you saw those croc things *or* when you saw the Munuanë, or even the entire time Juan *the basajaun* was talking to us! What the heck gives, bro?" I mean, *sure*, the kid was cool. Supercool. Arctic, even. But THAT cool? Nah . . . Nobody was *that* cool.

Violet sighed. "*Of course* he didn't freak out, Charlie. Why would he?"

Confundido, I shook my head. "What's that supposed to mean?"

"Charlie, *he's* the werejaguar!"

"You mean the one that jumped the *OGRE*? Did you crack your coco or something?"

"C'mon, Charlie. Look at the gash on his arm. His *right* arm. The same arm and the *exact same* place where that Munuanë thing slashed the werejaguar. *And* look at his hair and eye color. Pretty much identical to the werejaguar's hair and eye color ... Not to mention the fact that it keeps popping up *every single time* we lose track of Raúl. Remember the roar behind Pierre's after he disappeared?" V gave me a deadpan look. "Is it really even that much of a stretch? He's *your* cousin, for crying out loud!"

"And what's *that* supposed to mean?" To some people, those would've been fightin' words. I turned back to Raúl. "Dude, tell her she's gone loca! Tell 'er, dude!"

But Raúl didn't tell her anything. Didn't say *a word*, in fact.

"You're not gonna ... *deny it?*"

"I *would* ... ," he said slowly, carefully, "but I really don't wanna lie to my own primo. It's not my style."

You know in cartoons when they get whacked in the stomach by a giant wooden mallet and their eyes pop way out of their faces? Yeah. Well, that's how my eyes felt right about now. "So you're *ACTUALLY* a werejaguar—a nahual?"

"Hey, you ain't exactly the one to be pointin' fingers. . . ." He grinned at me. "Know what I mean, Mr. Fifth and Final?"

"You know about me being a Morphling?!"

"How could I *not* know? It's like having Shakira in your family tree! You're famous, cuz!" But suddenly his expression changed, growing dark. "There's something else you gotta know, too. . . . I—well, my mom didn't send me over because I was getting into fights and stuff. Actually, it wasn't my mom who sent me over at all. It was the tlatoani."

"*The tlatoani?*"

"They are the governing body of all Jaguar Warriors— or ocēlōtl—in Mexico. They are closest thing our kind has to a royal family. They lead our tribes, our *Shadows*, as we call them. And it was them who sent me to protect you."

"What?!"

"I just completed my cuāuhocēlōtl training in Mexico City. Our facilities are carved into the sides of the Black Mountains, hidden deep beneath the great catacombs below what you might know as the Teotihuacán ruins. That's where we send our most promising young cubs to learn the ways of the jaguar and become our most elite warriors. And when the tlatoani remembered that I was your cousin, they figured who better to send to watch over you than your own blood?"

Okay. I mean, that *did* sort of make sense and all. But . . . "But then why didn't you just *tell* me?"

"Because I couldn't! I swore secrecy to the tlatoani! But my oath was only to last for as long as I remained undiscovered. And since, well, she pretty much *discovered* me, I figure I'm now free to talk."

My head was spinning. Raúl was grinning. The moonlight flashing off his too-white teeth wasn't helping my head any.

He said, "There's *sooo* much going on right now, primo. . . . Our Shadows are preparing for all-out guerra—for *war*! My tío says he hasn't seen anything like it in almost *fifty years*! We know that La Mano Peluda is scheming in the darkness, but we don't know what to do to stop them. Queen Joanna and La Liga have their own ideas, but the elders do not trust las brujas. Not since they betrayed our clans during Las Guerras Negras. So the tlatoani has been trying to come up with some other way to fight against La Mano Peluda. And I guess that *I* was it." Gingerly, he pulled up the sleeve of his right arm to show off some neat little design, three horizontal, jade-colored marks, stacked one on top of the other on his shoulder. Something like a tattoo, but cooler-looking. "I received Las Líneas upon completion of my training. They are proof that I have been initiated into the ranks of the most elite warriors and am now ocēlōtl."

The marks seemed to glow in the moonlight. I stared at them, speechless.

Violet, flashing me one of her extra grin-y *I told ya so* grins, said, "Looks like you're not the only animal in your family."

And yeah, I guess she had a point. . . .

CHAPTER THIRTY

Jaguar Warrior or not, the whole twenty or so blocks back to Violet's house Raúl wouldn't stop wincing and glancing down at the gash on his arm. But whenever V or I would ask him about it, he'd say that he was fine, that it didn't hurt, though he wouldn't quit touching it, and it hadn't exactly stopped bleeding. "*At least* come inside and wash it out with soap and water," Violet urged him.

"Dude, her parents are gonna have a first aid kit in the house," I said. "Let's just get you patched up."

Raúl sighed. "Could both of you please *chill* . . . ? Remember, I am an ocēlōtl. I am a Jaguar Warrior. *And* I'm a man. I don't need to be babied."

I rolled my eyes at him. "Dude, machismo is so 2007."

"I don't know what you're talking about, cuz. All I know is that I'm a macho. And real machos don't cry about little scratches. We don't cry at all, in fact. We don't feel pain, either."

"Bro, seriously?" I was pretty sure he'd basically given me a textbook example of machismo. "Raúl, you look like you're hurting, man. The *least* you can do is be honest about it."

"It can't possibly look that way," he said, "because I'm not hurting."

"But look at *your face.* . . ."

"I can't. Without the use of some kind of reflective surface, that would simply be *impossible.* Even for an ocēlōtl. There's nothing to see, anyway. This is just my normal, usual face."

"So your *'normal, usual'* face is a pain-stricken grimace?"

"Yes. And see? I smile sometimes too." He tossed in a side of teeth with his grimace.

"Look, all I'm saying is that it's okay to show your feelings. Your *true* feelings . . . If something hurts or you need help, it's okay to say so. You don't always have to pretend to be so tough or whatever. I mean, even MJ cried. Championships two, three, and five."

Raúl shook his head. "Who's MJ?"

"*Michael Jordan* . . . ? Greatest basketball player of *all time?*"

He shrugged. "Never heard of him." Then: "And I bet I could take him one-on-one."

When we reached Violet's, I walked her slowly up the little stone path that led to her house and then up the four or five steps that led to her front door.

Leaning up against a porch column, V sighed and smiled at me and, tucking a long bang behind one ear, said, "Whatta day, huh?"

I smiled back. Tried to, anyway. Whenever Violet smiled at me, my motor skills usually took a siesta over to No Trabajasville. "You can say that again. . . . You okay?"

"I should be the one asking *you* that," she said. Then, after a moment: "That was . . . *really* cool what you did back in the house, Charlie. You saved my life."

"Oh, yeah. Well, it was nothing. . . . Don't mention it."

"Oh. Okay. I won't ever bring it up again, then."

"Wait. *What? No.* I was just saying that. I thought that was something people said. I *definitely* want you to bring it up. . . . And *often*, as a matter of fact."

V was smiling at me again. "I'm just messing with you, Charlie." But slowly, slowly her smile faded and the glow in her eyes dimmed, and her words shook a little when she spoke. "Seriously, though, you could've gotten yourself *killed*."

I shrugged. "Would've been worth it."

Violet blinked. "Excuse me?"

"Hmmm?"

"You just said, 'Would've been worth it.'"

I had just said that, hadn't I? And out loud, too. "Uh, yeah, I guess—I *did*."

V looked steadily at me. "Are you saying you would've been okay sacrificing your life to save . . . *mine?*"

"Well, *yeah*," I admitted, and that was the honest truth. "I mean, you're like my best friend, V. I couldn't let some stinkin' *ogre* hurt you."

Violet didn't say anything; for what felt like a long time, she just stood there, staring back at me with the wind blowing between us and the big bluish moon reflecting in her big blue eyes. Then a sweet little smile began to tug at the corners of her pretty pink lips. "Even though the context is *a bit* strange, I'm pretty sure that's the sweetest thing anyone has ever said to me."

Her fingertips grazed my arm, and my breath caught. We were standing so close now that I could smell her perfume: she smelled of sugar and spice and everything nice.

My heart began to race. Violet's eyes searched mine like she was trying to read my thoughts or something. Too bad for her I don't think I had any at the moment. There was probably an OUT OF ORDER sign hanging from my frontal lobe.

Honestly, I felt more nervous standing in front of Violet right then than I had facing down that killer Munuanë.

The world grew hazy around us. The air felt charged somehow, like it was alive with some kind of electric magnetism. Something pulling us closer and closer even though neither one of us had moved. Sweat prickled my skin, and I knew it had nothing to do with the suffocating 105-degree heat *or* the 99 percent humidity, which was about your typical South Florida weather forecast. I wondered if Violet could hear my pounding heart. I thought I could hear hers.

"So, uh, you okay?" I asked, hardly knowing what to ask.

V's smile grew wider. Her eyes shone brighter. "You already asked me that, Charlie."

"Oh, right. Well, it's just—I wanna make *sure*, you know?"

Her eyes never left mine. "I know . . ."

Next moment, she was leaning toward me, slowly, quietly, like she was about to whisper the great secret of the world; only an instant before she could, the front door swung open and a little girl who looked like a shrink-rayed Violet (and that's because she kinda *was* a shrink-rayed Violet—it was Maggie, Violet's kid sister) blinked up at me. Kitty Purry meowed in her arms. A chubby little finger pointed in my general direction.

"Is that the bird boy?" she asked Violet.

And *WHOOOSH!* She might as well have flung a bucket of *freezing ice water* at my face!

"The *WHAT?*" I shrieked.

Violet quickly steered her back inside. "And off to bed you go. . . ." Then, shutting the door again: "Sorry about that."

"Wait. So you told her about me?!" I hissed.

"Of course not!"

"You can't tell things like that to little kids! They'll tell the *WHOLE WORLD!*"

"Dude, chill. I just told you I didn't. The little ankle biter reads my journal. . . ."

"Hold up. You . . . *write* about me in your journal?" For some reason a big goofy grin had hijacked my face, and it was all I could do not to bust out some of my spiciest salsa moves.

Smiling her patented sweet/sly/shy smile, Violet said, "I write about *a lotta* things in my journal, Charlie. . . . But yeah, you happen to be one of them."

I was just beginning to feel that strange electric pull again when an annoyed voice from inside the house shouted, "VIOLET, WHAT DID YOU DO TO YOUR LITTLE SISTER?"

Violet blinked. "I gotta go," she said (even though it really didn't look like she wanted to). And as she started inside, and our eyes caught, and the bright full moon reflected in hers, she whispered, "Good night, Charlie Hernández. . . ."

Still sort of dazed, I said, "Good night, Charlie Hernández—er, I mean, Violet. . . ."

Yep, the King of Smooth. That's me!

Anyway, the real King of Smooth was waiting for me by the sidewalk, grinning like a wolf—scratch that, *a jaguar.* "Man, ella te gusta, huh, cuz?"

"Yeah, so? I like a lot of people. I even like *you*, if you can believe it."

His dimples deepened. "Only something tells me you like her *un poquito* más than the rest of us. . . . ¿Sabes lo que digo?"

CHAPTER THIRTY-ONE

I t was almost nine by the time we finally made it back to my house, and by that point I was *completely* exhausted. All I wanted was my pillow, my blanket, a cozy pair of pj's, and a nice soft mattress to pass out on. But, apparently, the night had other plans. . . .

We'd barely made it across my backyard when a voice whispered my name from the shadows.

I turned, looking toward the swing set by the shed—

And saw the slim form of a calaca melt out of the night.

It was Esperanza. She was wearing dark leather huaraches and a beautiful Mexican crochet dress, kinda like the ones my mom sometimes wore.

"A *muerto*," growled Raúl, moving between us. "Stay back, primo. . . . I'll handle it."

Esperanza—who'd *obviously* heard that—retreated a step. But her gaze never left mine.

Putting a hand on Raúl's shoulder, I whispered, "It's cool, dude. . . . That's Esperanza. She's the one who gave us the antique shop lead."

"Oh." Raúl sounded a tad embarrassed. He gave her a quick little wave. Then, after looking between us a couple of times (and I guess noticing that Esperanza still hadn't taken her eyes off me), he whispered, "Dude, I think that calaca's got the hots for you!"

"*What?* What do you mean, 'the hots'?" I hissed.

"I mean, she's totally crushing on you, man!"

For some reason those words really cranked the dial on my Panic-o-Meter. "H-HOW CAN YOU TELL?!" I whisper-screeched.

Raúl made a face like, *Brah, you serious?* "Animal instincts, cuz . . ."

I glanced back at Esperanza, giving her a big, *never-mind-our-secretive-little-whisper-fest* sorta smile and couldn't help noticing that she was *still* staring at me. And *just* me! As if Raúl didn't even *exist.* Someone gulped. (It was probably me.)

"Guess I better run along now . . . ," Raúl whispered with a mischievous glint in his eyes.

"What? *No!* Don't leave me alone with her!" I rasped, grinning casually at Esperanza again while simultaneously trying to hook a finger into my cousin's pocket so he couldn't run away on me.

And, of course, the double-crossing half kitty-cat was all grins. "Scared, primo?"

"Now I am! Now that you brought up all that *JUNK!*"

He showed me some teeth. "I'll be upstairs. Growl if you need me."

"Bro! Stop playing!"

But he'd already yanked himself free of my finger hook and was starting toward the house. "Imma give you two un . . . *momentico*," he said loud enough for Esperanza to hear. "I gotta go, anyway. Gotta . . . lick my wounds and whatnot. *Meow*. Er, I mean, *chao*."

Turning slowly back to Esperanza—and by the way, feeling SUPER awkward now (gracias, Raúl!)—I said, "So . . . I guess it's safe to assume you know where I live, huh?"

"It's safe to assume I know *a lot* about you." She smiled. And if she hadn't been so innocent and sweet-looking, a comment like that might've really freaked me out.

After a second Esperanza said, "You smell . . . *musky*."

I frowned (on the inside mostly). "You can smell that, eh?"

"I'd have to be *dead* not to smell that. . . . Well, dead *and* nose-deaf."

She came closer, and for the first time I noticed that the designs on her face had a shiny, glittery quality to them and that they were way more intricate and colorful than

I'd first thought. There were swirls inside of swirls inside of perfectly formed dots and miniature rose heads of reds and greens and golds. In the gloom and the slowly falling moonlight, the designs seemed to leap off her snow-white bone.

"Man, that's *awesome* . . . ," I said, sorta lost in the designs, my eyes tracing them like they were some rare work of art. A Picasso or something. "Like, how did you do all that on yourself?"

"I didn't," she whispered. "They're called Decoritas. They are the adornments of the dead. You receive them on the birthday of your death. Calacas believe that death is a celebration, and these are the scars of your new life." She looked away, as if suddenly self-conscious. Then her eyes fell and her face blurred and began to change as the glamour covered bone with muscle and sparkles with skin, and all of a sudden all the perfect imperfections of her real face—her *true* face—were replaced by all the imperfect perfection of her fake face: a living, human mask, which was no longer hers and no longer suited her. She looked more self-conscious than ever hiding behind that lie.

"You don't have to do that," I whispered. "You look so . . . *cool*."

Esperanza made a face like she'd bitten into the bitterest fruit. "Don't say that."

"Don't say what?"

"Don't lie to me. I know I don't look 'cool.'"

"What are you talking about?"

"Death isn't something nice, Charlie. . . . It isn't awesome or cool or even *pretty*. It's ugly. Death is *hideous*. And death is all anyone can see when they look at me."

A calaca who wasn't so hot on death. Guess I'd heard it all now.

"That's not true," I said, shaking my head. "I mean, I was just looking at you right now and I think you—well, I think you're *beautiful*."

¡Dios mío! Did I seriously just say that out loud?!

Esperanza blinked. My words hadn't just shocked me apparently; nope, they'd also given *her* such a shock that her glamour began to flicker, like a channel with bad reception, before vanishing altogether.

"You think I'm . . . *beautiful?*" she breathed. A sudden hopefulness had filled her face, her voice.

My mouth opened, but no words came out. I honestly didn't know what to say. I didn't want her to get the wrong idea or whatever. Problem was, when I get nervous, the most embarrassing stuff just seems to spew right out of my mouth. Man, this was ALL my cousin's fault!

Whatever. Damage-control time.

Except . . . I had no idea *how* to control the damage!

Just say something, idiot!

So idiot spoke. I said, "Well, *yeah* . . . But I was just sort of speaking for *most guys*, you know? *Other* guys. What *I* think *they'd* think . . . Though, not necessarily what *I* think, even though I'm not saying that I *don't* think it. Whatta you think?"

A small smile blossomed on Esperanza's ruby-red lips, but she stayed silent.

Say something ELSE, idiot!

So idiot spoke again. (And this time he decided to change the subject.) "Oh, by the way," I said, "we checked out that, uh, store from the business card you gave me. . . ."

Esperanza hesitated. Like my sudden change in topic had caught her off guard. Or had maybe disappointed her somehow. "You did?"

"Yeah. Seems like they're running some kind of pet/people kidnapping ring. Sounds super weird, I know. But at least a few of the pets we found there belonged to people who've recently gone missing. Still not sure what any of it has to do with your sister, though."

Esperanza said nothing. But I could tell something was bothering her. And I didn't think it was just plain ol' worry, either.

"What else do you know?" I asked, looking straight at her. "What aren't you telling me?"

She averted her eyes again. Her whole body shivered. "Nothing."

"*Nothing* or nothing you wanna talk about?"

"It's not that I don't want to. It's that I *can't.*"

"Why not?"

"You won't understand."

"Then help me understand."

For a few seconds Esperanza looked just miserable, staring down at her feet and twisting the heel of her chancleta into the soft ground. Her voice was strained. "The reason I can't say more is that I cannot be *involved.* I can't risk *any* of this being traced back to me. No puedo. You don't understand calaca política. But, please, whatever you do, find something on those criminals. I'm begging you! You have to stop them! For my sister's sake!"

"But stop *WHO?* We don't even know who *owns* that store. We just ran into a couple of their *goons.*" Frustrated, I let out a loud sigh. "Look, I gotta be honest with you. If you really want my help with this and you *really* want me to help your sister, you're gonna have to tell me *everything* you know. Todo. That's the only way this is gonna work."

All the color seemed to have gone out of Esperanza's face. And there hadn't been much to go. "It's so much worse than you think," she whispered, still not meeting my eyes.

"Try me. What *exactly* is wrong with your sister?"

"It's not *what*," Esperanza sighed. "It's *who*. It's the monster she's with."

"Hold up. Are we talking a *literal* monster here or more metaphoric?"

"Yes."

"To which one?"

"*Both*."

CHAPTER THIRTY-TWO

H e's the owner of the antique shop I sent you to," Esperanza explained. "Pierre d'Exquis."

"The monster is *Mr. C?*"

"That's not his name. Well, not *all* of it . . . His first name is Saúl, but he goes by the name Mr. Caiman. He is *extremadamente* dangerous, Charlie. Un matador! A killer! And he's keeping my sister from me. . . ."

"What do you mean, *keeping her from you?*"

"He won't let me see her. The last time I spoke to her was in his shop, but she's not there anymore, and I have no idea where he's keeping her." Her expression was grave, but for a moment, there was a brightness in her voice: "I remember when we first met, Charlie . . . when you sprouted feathers. It reminded me *so much* of my sister! I took it as a great omen! See, she loved feathers. Their colors. Their wonderful textures. She even dreamed of flying! But now she's *trapped*. Like a caged bird."

"I—I don't get it. . . ."

"My sister's been *kidnapped*, Charlie!"

So there it was. Finally. The truth of what had happened to her sister and the reason she'd asked me for help. Apparently, the creeps over at Pierre d'Exquis *were*, in fact, some kinda kidnapping ring. And, apparently, they didn't just specialize in the four-legged and furry.

"So . . . they *kidnapped her*?" I asked uneasily (not that I hadn't sort of expected it; but to hear her actually say it was still pretty scary).

"Sí. This all happened some time ago . . . many months now." Her voice had turned small—so small. "Ese *monstruo*, Mr. Caiman—he saw her swimming at the Venetian Pool. You know, the one in Coral Gables?"

"Yeah, I know it."

"My sister would sometimes slip out from among the graves late at night to go for a swim. She loved the feel of the water against her cold bones. It was there that they first met, that my sister recklessly befriended an upworlder and that he kidnapped her. And now . . . now she won't *leave* him."

"Leave *who*? Mr. Caiman? Her *KIDNAPPER*?"

"That's right. She won't leave his side! Not for a moment. Not even to see her own bone and marrow!"

"You're talking Stockholm syndrome?"

"No, I'm talking about *amor*, Charlie! I'm talking about a *love potion!*"

My eyes bugged out, cartoon-style. "*Whoa, whoa, whoa.* A *LOVE* POTION?!"

"Yes! He must've given it to her while he was keeping her prisoner. It's a specialty of his. He's a known potions master. My sister would *never* have fallen for a monstruo like him! Not on her own. And now she . . ."

"She *what?*"

"She—well, she wants to *MARRY* him!"

"Holy guacamole. You mean *holy matrimony?*"

"Till death do them part."

Geez, man . . . This story had more plot twists than a telenovela!

"He's a villain, Charlie! A vile, vicious, *venomous* villain!" Esperanza's cold fingers wrapped tightly around my arm. They felt like frozen papitas against my skin. "And now that he's planted the idea of marriage in my sister's head, there isn't a shovel in this world capable of digging it out! She's always been so hardheaded. ¡Toda su vida!" If possible, her voice became even grimmer, dragging her expression down with it. "Y la va a *matar*, Charlie. . . ."

"¿LA VA A QUÉ?"

"He's going to *kill* her!"

"*KILL HER?!* You just said he was going to *MARRY* her! Besides, how do you kill someone who's already *DEAD?!*"

Esperanza's gaze darkened. She said, "Oh, there are ways. . . . And you must understand: Caiman is a *shaman.* He trained under a sorcerer of the most *ancient* order. And every shaman of that order has, for one thousand years, sacrificed their first wife to their gods of the jungle. It's their oldest and most *sacred* ritual!"

Okay. Now I felt like I was *trapped* in a telenovela.

"It gets worse," she whispered.

"Worse than bridal sacrifice?!" *This*, I had to hear.

"Yes. You see, my sister is a Puesha!"

"A *whatsha?*"

"A Puesha! Since the beginning of time, our kind has found it necessary to keep accurate records. Places to store the names of the dead, such as the Book of the Dead, and maps of our vast underground labyrinths. However, our most *important* records were never written on parchment. The ancients believed that such things had to be recorded on the longest-lasting material possible. So, from the beginning, we've kept our most sacred records on *ourselves*—on calacas. Those on whom this great honor is bestowed are called Pueshas. No two Pueshas keep the same record. And my sister keeps perhaps the most sacred and secret record of all: *the map of the Golden Dooms.*"

There it was again, I thought as my heart began using my rib cage as a punching bag. That ominous-sounding phrase: *the Golden Dooms.*

I was shaking my head without even realizing it. "The map of the Golden Dooms?" I repeated slowly. "Wha-what are Golden Dooms?"

Esperanza gave her head a firm shake. "I can speak no more of it. But understand that if La Sociedad de Calacas hears of my sister's plan to wed an upworlder, thus betraying one of the tenets of her Pueshahood, they will immediately hunt her down and kill her to retrieve the map; for they will never allow such secrets to float among the living." Her voice was low now, panicked and scared. And her pale hands trembled. "Don't you see?" she whispered. "If I let them marry in secret, my sister is dead; Caiman will sacrifice her to his jungle gods. But if I go to the Sociedad de Calacas, or even to La Liga, all will be revealed and my sister will be tried for treason and executed anyway."

"The ultimate catch-22," I whispered.

"¡Exactamente! And that is why I *need* your help, Charlie. . . . I need *proof*! Proof that he potioned my sister, and because that proof will be almost impossible to come by, I need proof of his other crimes, of which I assure you there are *many*. Any crime will do. I simply need some evidence that can be used to lock him up, to take that monster out of my sister's life before he marries her and *ends* it."

¡Santo cielo! Drama, drama, drama. It was like a bad episode of *The Hills!* "But—but why didn't you tell me all this before?" I said.

"Because I was protecting my sister. *And* I was protecting myself. I had to make *absolutamente* sure I could trust you. Perdóname. But now I believe I can." Then, gazing intently up at my face and taking my hands in hers, Esperanza whispered, "My sister needs you, Charlie Hernández. . . . And *I* need you."

CHAPTER THIRTY-THREE

Cock-a-doodle-doo-doooo-de-do-do-do-o-o-o-o!

The shrill crowing of some good-for-nothing rooster jerked me out of a deep, sweet sleep Saturday morning. It was the same stupid-sounding crow as yesterday, which meant it was probably the *same* stupid rooster. Someone was *definitely* gonna have to make a bowl of chicken noodle soup out of that thing. . . .

Rolling over, I glanced up at my alarm clock and groaned. It was 6:30 a.m., and I'd never felt so exhausted in my entire life. My bones ached, my temples were throbbing, and my mouth couldn't have felt any drier if I'd spent the entire night munching on handfuls of sand.

The tall glass of cold water I poured myself from the tap didn't help much, so I downed a second and then half a carton of orange juice just to wash the dryness away. Geez. I honestly couldn't remember the last time I'd been *this* thirsty.

Apparently late-night sleuthing really takes a toll on you. I had a newfound respect for Violet's chosen line of work—er, line of *hobby*.

Through the window over the sink, I could see our neighbor, Mr. Hiriart, chasing a fat red rooster out from between our houses with a broom. *Good!* I thought. But, *man*, those things really were everywhere. . . .

Sam showed up a few minutes after breakfast. He said he was here to "escort" Raùl and me somewhere, but he wouldn't say where and wouldn't say why.

The "why" was easy: probably because Violet hadn't been able to get ahold of me on account of my phone having recently met its untimely demise at the hands—or rather, beneath *the foot* of a rampaging killer ogre.

The "where" turned out to be the beautiful Bayfront Park, just a few blocks east of Little Havana.

Out on the thick, rolling lawns that curved all the way along the western side of Biscayne Bay, Violet had set up what appeared to be some kind of mobile military command center, complete with an impressive array of gizmos, gadgets, and a couple of radio-looking doohickeys. I spotted something like a small satellite dish next to a picnic basket and something like a seismograph next to her book bag and a soccer ball.

"Charlie!"

I turned toward the sound of my name to see Alvin jogging toward us from across the park. He was holding some kind of weird contraption in his hands—something between a stake light and a Slinky.

"Al, what is all this stuff?" I asked him.

"Dude, you haven't even seen the *half* of it! Me and Sam have been helping the cheer squad set these sensor-hick-a-ma-bobs up all over town. Violet told them it was some kind of science fair project or something. But I've been hanging out with cheerleaders all morning, dude . . . CHEERLEADERS!"

"I can tell," I said. "You're *peppier* than usual."

Over by the seawall, Violet was chillaxing under the shade of a tall coconut tree, studying something—a map, it looked like. Raúl and I went over to ask her what the whole Rambo-style picnic was about, and she told us that she'd bought the equipment off eBay, from a retired geophysicist. Then she said, "You know all those reports of quakes around Little Havana? Well, I think they're really happening. And look at the locations of some of the eyewitness reports." She held out the map, which was a bird's-eye view of South Miami with points plotted in bright green marker. "They're a bit spread out, but look at the ones near the top. Those quakes were all reported on the *same blocks* as all four of our confirmed missing people."

"So you think it's all connected, then?" I asked.

"It's been my working hypothesis, yeah. And I think it's really our best lead at the moment. We can't go anywhere near Pierre's at the moment because Juan will probably twist us into churros if he catches us. Plus, after our little run-in at the Miller house, this Mr. C or whatever is probably gonna start being *extra* careful."

"Mr. C is actually Mr. *Caiman*, by the way," I said.

Violet blinked. "How do you know that?"

So I told her how, told her all about my late-night rendezvous with Esperanza. Raúl—who'd already gotten the scoop—nodded along, occasionally purring, regularly mentioning how cute he thought Esperanza was and how he was pretty sure she had the hots for me.

V gave me a few funny looks, and I, in turn, gave Raúl a few friendly elbows to the ribs to make him shut up about all that.

Not surprisingly, Violet didn't seem to know what to make of Esperanza's story. She thought the whole thing was kinda weird and didn't like the fact that Esperanza hadn't been up front with us. But she found the love potion/bridal sacrifice stuff pretty interesting. She also thought the whole "Golden Dooms" thing (whatever it was) might be playing a big role in all this, seeing as we'd also heard one of Caiman's goons mention it in his shop.

"So you have any theories about how the earthquakes tie into the missing people?" Raúl asked, cracking a coconut against a rock and slurping some fresh juice.

Violet said, "You mean besides the earth randomly opening up and *gobbling* them? Not yet."

Anyway, with all the fancy earthquake-reading equipment in place, it was now just a big waiting game. So we waited. And while we waited, we talked. And after we'd talked, we decided to play a little soccer. First, it was me and Raúl versus Violet, Sam, and Alvin, and we won. Then it was Raúl and Violet versus me, Sam, and Alvin, and *they* won. And then it was Raúl versus me, Violet, Sam, and Alvin, and he *still* won. What can I say? My cousin was apparently a magician with a ball at his feet.

After that embarrassment—I mean, *the last game*—we sat down for a bite. V had brought lunch from one of my favorite local spots, Versailles. We had medianoche sandwiches, which are these glorious melty, gooey, and oh-so-yummy sandwiches made with pork, ham, and Swiss cheese, all pressed in a roll of sweet Cuban bread. And we washed that down with mango and strawberry batidos from El Palacio de los Jugos.

After, we just sort of hung out for a while, joking and laughing and staring out over the bay, dark blue and rippling, looking as big as any ocean. Relaxing here by

Biscayne, breathing in the full, rich salty smell of the Atlantic, brought back so many old memories of my abuelita. When I was little, me and her would hang out at places like this all the time, picnicking on guava and cream-cheese-filled pastelitos and jugo de mamey (that's mamey juice) while she told me stories of all the cool villages and tiny rural towns she'd visited in order to collect her cherished myths (or should I just finally start calling them *truths* now?).

Two of our favorite spots were Jungle Island—that awesome wildlife-themed adventure park right near South Beach—and Zoo Miami, down by the Everglades. My abuela loved animals (no big surprise there), and she loved spending time around them and watching them (also no big surprise). Funny part was, Raúl and I got to talking about her, and it turned out that she'd spent a lot of time down in Mexico with him and his mom. Apparently, she'd taught him a bunch of the same folklore and legends she'd taught me, but she'd also taught him a lot of outdoorsy stuff too, like how to make a lean-to (which is basically a makeshift shelter), how to start a fire with rocks, how to build traps and snares, and even how to leave trail marks in the wild so that you don't lose your way. According to him, my abuelita was super into nature, and one of the things they loved to do together was to hike up the Cerro de la Campana, which was this humongous hill overlooking the beautiful Mexican city of Hermosillo.

Sitting there listening to him, I felt like I was getting a sneak peek into a whole different side of my grandma, and that was awesome. Only the more we talked about her, the more I realized just how much I missed her, which kinda sucked; but I also realized just how much I loved her—how much we *both* loved her—so it wasn't all sad.

Anyway, I figured we'd probably be hanging out here all night, waiting. But as it turned out, I was wrong. Just as the sun began to set over the horizon of concrete high-rises, one of the radio-looking thingies began beeping and beeping and something else began screeching and shrieking, and we all quickly gathered around.

"Whatta we got?" I asked V, peering over her shoulder, reading everything on the small square screens but understanding none of it.

"Well, the equipment isn't exactly state-of-the-art, and I'm not exactly a pro, but from these readings, it's pretty clear. . . . All the tremors appear to be tracing back to a *single* location. Maybe along fault lines or something."

"And what's the location?"

Violet stayed quiet, her expression turning grim.

"V, where are the tremors coming from?" I pressed.

Finally, she answered. Though when she did, I almost wished she hadn't. . . . "They're all coming from La Rosa," she said in a tight voice. "They're coming from the old cemetery up on Bonita."

CHAPTER THIRTY-FOUR

L a Rosa cemetery in South Dade was a relic from the 1800s, built way back before Miami was even recognized as a city. It was probably the oldest cemetery in all of Florida—if not the country. But the old graveyard wasn't just ancient or abandoned-looking or spine-tinglingly *creepy*. It also happened to be home to the largest pasillo in North America. Pasillos are basically passageways between the Land of the Living and the Land of the Dead, and right below La Rosa, La Sociedad de Calacas had set up what was rumored to be their largest regional headquarters in the entire Western Hemisphere. La Sociedad—or the Society—was the global organization of undead skeletons, who spent their sleepless nights ferrying the souls of the recently departed across the chasm between worlds. And this old boneyard was the very place where Violet and I had run into our very first calaca,

Gregory de Esqueleto. A pretty cool dude, actually—aside from that one time when he'd almost bashed our heads in with his pala (that's a shovel). But since he was no longer around—he'd been sent to the Land of the Dead by that evil shape-shifting bruja infamously known as La Cuca—my hope was that we could find another equally friendly (though maybe slightly less *violent*) calaca to help us out.

La Rosa's massive iron gate, which was bent in places, twisted in others, swung noisily in the breeze, groaning on its huge rusty hinges.

"I don't like this," Alvin rasped as we parked our bikes by the low concrete wall that ran around the cemetery proper. "I never even *been* to a cemetery before!"

"It was really only a matter of time," said Raúl, smirking at him.

The wind rustled through the trees and whined between the old tombstones and mausoleums as we walked on, deeper and deeper, into the cold heart of La Rosa. The five of us seemed like the only warm bodies within a million-mile radius.

"Doesn't look like anyone's home," I whispered, listening to the creepy, creaky, eerie sounds of the boneyard.

"Totally with you," Alvin quickly agreed. "We should probably go. Come back tomorrow when it's still light out."

A soft crunch of pebbles had me whipping around. I held my breath, my eyes scanning the shadows.

Then, an instant later, I caught a blur of movement— there and gone—between two headstones, maybe fifteen yards back the way we'd come.

And it didn't seem like I was the only one. Beside me, Raúl froze. He must've seen it too.

"*What was that?*" Violet rasped, making it three of us now.

Alvin and Sam shook their heads but didn't make a sound. *Ni pío.*

"Looked like a ghost," whispered Raúl.

"Dude, you don't say *GHOST* in a graveyard!" Alvin hissed.

"Yeah, don't say that," I agreed.

"What am I supposed to say, then?"

"*Shhhhh!*" Violet scolded them. "I think I hear something. . . ."

"Whatdya hear, huh?" Sam asked anxiously. "C'mon, what was it? Whatdya hear?"

"No idea, because you four won't *SHUT UP!*"

The ground was cold and squishy beneath our feet. A thin bluish-gray mist rose from it in curls, coiling around our lower legs like restless, dewy snakes. A cloud passed over the moon. The dark cemetery grew even darker.

I'd just opened my mouth to whisper something when a voice as hard and rough as the blade of some rusty old shovel—and about as cold, too—said, "El cementerio is *closed.*"

CHAPTER THIRTY-FIVE

We all screamed, "AAAAAAHHHHHHHH!" and whirled around, holding on to each other. And when we saw the tall man with the huge dirt-streaked hands and the pale dirt-streaked face and noticed the giant shovel-ax clutched between those huge hands and the hardness of that pale face, "AAAAAAAAHHHHHHHH!" was what we all screamed next, and "AAAAAHHHHHHHHHH!" was what we screamed again right after.

Funnily enough, the gravedigger looked almost as terrified as we did. "¿Qué fue?" he whispered, looking wearily around. "You see something scary?"

"*Just you. . . ,*" squeaked Alvin.

"Oh. Bueno, that's real good, 'cause I get un poquito jittery on nights like these. . . . *Bad things* tend to happen on nights like *these.*" Saying it with all the tremble and spook of someone telling a campfire ghost story. Al and Sam gulped.

Violet, on the other hand, got right to business. "We need your help," she told him.

"¿*Mi* ayuda . . . ?" The creepster looked around at us like we'd just asked him to solve for *x*. "What would you need *my* help for? I'm just a simple gravedigger. See?" He held up his shovel-ax like it was some huge, rusty photo ID or something.

"Dude, we know you're a calaca," I said.

"*Calaca?*" His pale lips frowned. "No sé lo que es eso. Never heard that before. Like I said, all I do is dig holes and put people in them. So why don't all of you run along now before I decide to dig five *more* holes, if you smell what I'm stepping in. . . ."

"Loud and clear!" shouted Alvin. "I mean, strong and stenchy!" Then, nudging me from behind: "Dude, let's make like leaky faucets and run!"

I ignored him. "We've been down there, hermano," I told the calaca, pointing at a grave. "We've *seen* it."

"Bah, I don't got time for this!" he snapped. "I'm working. And *you're* trespassing!"

"Figured this might be an issue," said Violet. Then she turned, signaling to Sam, and said, "*Light 'im up.*"

At her command, Sam's shaky fingers slipped into his backpack and came out with what looked like some kind of portable headlight. His thumb flipped a switch.

Instantly a flood of bright white light shone out, washing over the gravedigger in a glittery wave, and as he shrank back, raising both hands to shield his face, the skin and muscles and veins that had a moment ago covered his hands, face, and neck suddenly vanished, leaving nothing but an esqueleto of gleaming, undead *bones*. A walking, talking, shovel-wielding skeleton-man.

A calaca!

"Witchlight isn't the only kind of light that can penetrate a glamour," V explained. "From my research, it seems that xenon also does the trick. Which explains why most calaca sightings happen near highways and at night."

"*That's gotta be the sickest thing I've seen in my entire life,*" Sam murmured.

Violet smirked at our bony new friend. "So, gonna stick with the 'I'm just a simple gravedigger' spiel, or can we start talkin' turkey?"

CHAPTER THIRTY-SIX

The calaca, lowering his bony, ancient hands and peering steadily back at us out of his bony, ancient face, looked none too pleased. When he spoke again, his voice sounded parched—you might even call it *bone*-dry (ba-dum-bump-ching!). "So, you've caught me. . . . *Congratulaciones.* You're a lively bunch, I'll give you that. And not short on inteligencia, either. Especially *you*," he said to Violet. "But, you see, now that you've seen me for what I truly am and quite obviously know this place for what *it* truly is, regrettably, it looks like I'm gonna be digging those five graves, after all."

He stepped toward us, raising his shovel in a not-so-friendly gesture, but Violet stopped him dead (pun totally intended) in his tracks.

"Sure, go ahead," she said a little too nonchalantly for my taste. "That is, if you wanna be known as the calaca who tried to kill the fifth and final Morphling . . ."

The skeleton's face paled. Which was pretty impressive considering it had already been bone-white to begin with. "*What did you jess say?*"

"I said, *he's* the Morphling. And this place is covered with the wings-and-horns symbol, so we know you're allies. We're investigating a case. We think we're onto something, but we need *your* help."

Raising an eyebrow—er, a brow *bone*, the gravedigger leaned toward me, the hollows of his eyes looking me suspiciously up and down.

"Pruébalo," he said finally, shouldering the shovel.

I shrugged. "Prove *what?*"

"Prove that you're the Morphling. ¿Qué más?"

"Then you'll help us?" asked Violet.

The calaca looked like he wanted to roll his eyes at her. If he'd had any, that is. "Yeah . . . then I'll *help you.*"

Now every eye (and *eyehole*) turned to me.

I said, "Uh, okay . . . So, how can I prove it?"

"Go ahead and manifest something for us, chico. How about a nice pair of horns?"

"Horns? Fine. I can do horns." I mean, horns *were* the first thing I'd ever manifested. Way back before I'd even known I was a Morphling. And I'd done it without even trying, too. *This'll be no sweat,* I thought to myself.

Only, as it turned out, it *was* a sweat. Because *this* time, even though I *was* trying—and trying hard, too—nothing happened. Nothing at all. I felt no tingle, no itch, no stirring animal forces of any kind. Or, as the wise Jedi Master Yoda might say, "Manifest horns I currently cannot." Talk about epically embarrassing.

"Uh, yeah, so, I'm sorry to say that it doesn't look like horns are in the cards today. . . . Probably haven't been drinking enough milk. You know, for the calcium and stuff? But I'll do something else. Anything else. What do you wanna see?"

"How 'bout a couple wings, then?" said the gravedigger.

So I tried to manifest a pair of those instead, but— surprise, surprise—nada. Nothing was happening!

Violet sighed. Raúl began shaking his head.

"Hey, you guys think it's *sooo* easy," I said. "YOU manifest a pair of wings!"

My cousin's hands flew up like, *I didn't say anything.*

"Hey, I'm curious," said the calaca. "Are all Morphlings this bad at morphing or just *you*?"

I turned to glare at the bonehead. "Look, I'm sorta new at all this, okay? But it's true. I'm a Morphling. You're just gonna have to trust us on that."

"I don't think so, chico. I know las leyendas: A Morphling can manifest *anything.* And if *you* can't manifest *nothin'*, then you ain't no Morphling."

"Hey, MANIFESTING something doesn't *make* me a Morphling!" I snapped, feeling a hot rush of anger bubble up in my belly. "I AM a Morphling. And I don't gotta prove it to you or anyone else in this daisy farm! You got that, *Bony?*" Now, was I being a little touchy? Sure. But he'd started it.

"Charlie, look!" Violet gasped, pointing behind me. So I turned, twisted—and what did I see? A fluffy snow-white rabbit's tail!

It was sort of puffing out the top of my shorts, above the waistband.

"Aha!" I shouted triumphantly. "*SEE?!* What I tell ya, huh? What I tell ya?"

Raúl whispered, "Cuz, *a rabbit's* tail . . . ?" He sounded pretty embarrassed for me. But he couldn't possibly have felt *half* as embarrassed as I felt for myself. Still, like my mom always said: trabaja lo que tienes. So that's exactly what I did. I worked it.

"Yeah, *and?*" I said. "Rabbit tails are *the bomb!* They look great and they're super fluffy. Everybody loves them. I mean, they even make awesome good luck charms."

"Those are *rabbit feet,* dude," Sam whispered in my ear.

"Well, *whatever,* guys! I mean, c'mon! Gimme a break here. Rabbit tails are nice too. Look how neat that looks. Anyone wanna pet it?"

Ryan Calejo

There didn't seem to be any takers.

"Don't all jump on me at once!" I shouted.

And, of course, because I'd called them all out:

"Oh, yeah . . ."

"*Wow.*"

"Yeah, very soft . . . very nice."

"It's great, Charlie. It's really great."

The undead undacova gravedigger, meanwhile, was giving us all a sorta disgusted look. "Qué desgracia," he murmured to himself. "I'm sure La Mano Peluda's fingers are all atremble because of this chavalo."

I glared at him again.

He raised his bony hands. "All right, all right. A deal's a deal. ¿Cómo te puedo ayudar?"

"What do you know about the quakes?" asked Violet, getting right to it.

"What *quakes?*"

"The ones coming from here. We've tracked at least a dozen different mini quakes happening within a twenty-five-block radius, and they all seemed to be leading back here. In spectacularly straight lines, too."

"Those quakes got nothing to do with us," said the gravedigger, shaking his head. "What I mean is, they are not of supernatural origin. We have already investigated the occurrences."

"You sure? Because earthquakes aren't exactly typical for South Florida."

The calaca shrugged. "That is all I know."

Violet turned back to me. "What do you think?"

"I don't know," I said. "Maybe it's nothing. Maybe the quakes and the missing people aren't connected."

"The muerto doesn't seem like he's lying," whispered Raúl. "I can usually sniff out a lie . . . *literally*."

V thought for a sec, biting her lower lip. "We're missing something," she said at last. "I can *feel* it. . . . As Cap McCaw would say, 'We're missing the hair in the chicken salad.'" Her eyes locked on mine. "We're gonna have to regroup. Maybe even start from scratch." Then, turning back to the gravedigger: "Well, gracias por todo."

The esqueleto tipped the brim of his wide straw hat in reply. "Un placer, señorita. Nos vemos . . . in about eighty or so years."

Alvin was already yanking me back toward the entrance when Violet turned back to say, "Oh, one more thing."

"¿Sí?"

"What do you know about the map of the Golden Dooms?"

If right at that moment a giant flying elephant would have taken a giant flying *poop* all over the skeleton's bony head, I don't think he would have looked any more stunned.

The calaca froze. His jaw dropped. *Literally.* It detached from his skull and clattered to the ground between his bony feet. The black sockets of his eyes stared back at us like we'd all suddenly turned into bright pink flamingos and had begun flamenco dancing in pairs among the graves. Picking his jaw up from the misty grass and snapping it back into place, he whispered, "*What did you just say?*"

"The map of the Golden Dooms," Violet repeated. "What do you know about it?"

The gravedigger's gaze darkened, narrowing on V's face. His voice was pitched low, deep, and very hollow-sounding. "The question is, what do *you* know about it?"

"Not much. That's why we're asking."

"Who mentioned this to you?"

"Just . . . rumors and stuff," I lied.

The skeleton hesitated, thinking. "Rumors, huh?" The hollow eyes stared unblinkingly, and his too-big shirt flapped and rippled in the cool wind. At last he said, "I think there's something you all should see. . . ."

The calaca led the way deeper into the maze of tombs, and eventually we came to a familiar sight: the grave marked by the giant statue of an angel. The last time we had been here, some months ago, Violet and I had followed another calaca beneath that very statue and into the underworld—or at least the *in-between* world. But on this occasion, our calaca tour guide did not approach the angel. Instead, he stood before it, staring back at us.

"What's wrong?" he asked.

I nodded at the ground under his bony feet. "Aren't you standing on the way in?"

"Actually," said the undead, "that is the *guest* entrance."

"So where's the main entrance?" Violet asked.

A small grin touched the calaca's mouth. "*You're* standing on it."

Then he drove his shovel into the weedy, mushy earth, and the huge square-shaped grave we were all standing on suddenly opened up—opened like a huge, hungry mouth!

I had time to think, *¡AY, CARAMBA!* and the next moment, all five of us went plunging into darkness.

CHAPTER THIRTY-SEVEN

For the record: I've never been swallowed alive by a grave before. And it wasn't one of the more pleasant experiences of my life. My initial (and most *honest*) assessment of the situation was: "AAAAAAAHH-HHHHHHHHHHHHHHH!" And from what I was hearing, everyone else pretty much seemed to agree.

Down, down, down, we plunged, kicking and screaming and smacking into each other as we picked up speed. Just when I started to feel a lot like Alice tumbling down that never-ending rabbit hole, the tunnel or whatever abruptly leveled off, and we were sent flying through wide-open air to land, breathless and a little bruised, in a heap smack in the middle of some dusty underground cave. Green-flamed torches burned along the walls, and in their dancing glow a humongous door in the shape of an enormous marigold flower loomed up before us.

A moment later the calaca dude came flying out of the same hole in the wall. His bony feet hit the ground with a loud *crunch!* and he crooked a creaky finger at us. "Vamos, niños...."

"Where are you taking us?" Sam asked warily.

But the calaca didn't answer. He simply approached the massive door, which swung silently inward, as if thrust by an equally massive, though much less *visible* hand. And the instant we'd followed him through, my eyes nearly flew out of my *face!*

The space beyond was *huuuge.* So huge, in fact, that it could've easily housed *two* Miami International Airports and still had room for LAX, LaGuardia, and probably Dolphin Mall (and the Dolphins stadium) too. A massive square-shaped hall spread out before us like an endless sea, and yet nearly every square inch of that sea, every nook, every corner, every cranny, was packed from wall to wall with calacas. The throng of esqueletos bustled busily about, marching up and down the zigzagging staircases, along the connecting catwalks, under archways and through doorways, and into large, square-shaped holes in the ground. All of them laughing and shouting and calling to one another in loud, happy voices while the click and clack of old bones played in the background like the inner workings of some ancient machine.

"Welcome to the Dancing Tombs," our undead tour guide announced with a grand sweep of his shovel. "The undisputed hub of the World In-Between."

Then he started into the throng of the undead, and we followed, huddled closely together. All of us were sorta trying to blend in, but—surprise, surprise—failing miserably on account of the fact that we happened to have eyes and skin and hair and, oh yeah, *inner organs.*

We were about a quarter of the way into the great hall when there came a series of loud, clunking sounds and the stamping of quick little feet, and I looked around to see a bunch of mukis hurrying toward us. Large silver anvils were strapped to their tiny little backs, and together the gang of cave-dwelling dwarfs was hefting an elaborate wooden coffin nearly as long as a school bus.

"*Dude*, I gotta get a vid of that!" whispered Alvin, whipping out his phone. "My Insta followers are gonna *LOVE* this!"

"Al, you don't *have* any followers on Instagram," I reminded him. (I don't think *I* was even following the kid.)

"You mean *not yet!*" But just as he summoned his inner Steven Spielberg, carefully raising the phone like he was about to film some epic piece of cinematic history, the muki bringing up the rear of the coffin-towing crew reached out and touched a stubby, dirt-streaked finger to Alvin's phone.

The instant he did—¡Dios mío!—the entire thing turned from cheap gray aluminum to gold—*solid gold!*

The muki snapped, "¡Nada de fotografías!"

But Alvin—along with the rest of us—only gaped. Finally Al cried, "I'M RICH!"

The crowds thinned a bit as we took an open stairwell down to a lower level, and the air seemed to grow cooler, drier. Down here was a maze of rocky red tunnels, and as we came around a corner, I heard this huge, earthshaking, ear-popping roar and glanced back to see an absolutely GINORMOUS comelengua—a real-life tongue-eater!

The thing was easily over eight feet tall, with a pinched, batlike face and a wingspan that would've made a wandering albatross turn verde with envy. Dozens of calaca soldiers brandishing bony spears had surrounded the thing, poking and jabbing at it, trying to corral it back into what looked like a giant birdcage made of elephant bones. But the tongue-eating monster was having none of it. It squawked and shrieked, flinging the soldiers against the wall so that the skeletons went all Humpty Dumpty, clattering to pieces.

"What's going on?!" I shouted at the gravedigger.

But he only shrugged like, *Oh, a rampaging killer monster? No biggie.* "Some things don't like to stay dead. Can you blame them?"

Guess not, I thought.

"It seems to be a growing sentiment nowadays," added el esqueleto as we rounded another bend.

"What do you mean by that?" asked Violet.

The calaca's pace slowed, and his voice pitched low, taking on a nervous edge. "Deathly rumors are being whispered among the tombs. . . . Reports of the dead marching. Whispers of La Mano Peluda's forces massing on the other side, organizing. *Preparing*." Hollow eyes slid sideways to me. "I heard the story of what happened in San Miguel, young Morphling. I know you sent that evil back to La Tierra de los Muertos. But apparently it is quite *eager* to return."

CHAPTER THIRTY-EIGHT

Finally we came to a kind of boarding area—maybe twenty rickety old mine carts sitting on tracks that ran off into the dark. The calaca climbed into the first one in the line, motioning for us to follow. So we followed, cramming in like sardines, even though I really wasn't all that stoked about the idea, seeing as how "wonderfully" my last two experiences on these things had gone.

"Is this thing even safe?" Alvin asked.

"Extremely," replied the gravedigger. "Not a single calaca has died on one yet. Then again, we're *already* dead!" He began laughing, a high, terrifying cackle, and the cart began rolling, a slow, shuddering lurch.

"Let me off this thing!" Sam cried, reaching for the door.

But it was too late.

Icy-cold air washed over us as we shot into the

pitch-dark mouth of a tunnel. My hair flew back from my face, and I saw the cart's headlamp snap to life, illuminating a world of hanging teethlike stalactites and reaching handlike stalagmites. Bits of stone and dust drizzled down on us as we began to plunge.

"*Whoa, whoa, whoa*—slow this thing down!" shouted Raúl, gripping the walls of the cart. But the calaca only grinned, his face deathly pale in the yellow glow of the headlamp.

We picked up speed, wheels screeching. Glittery minerally walls zipped past. The cart rattled and jumped and bounced so violently that the stupid thing started to come apart!

"I don't like this!" Sam shouted as lugs and bolts went twirling off into the dark. We dropped into a series of sudden dips, plunging deeper and deeper into the icy belly of the earth.

The clanking, clacking, clattering sounds of the cart on the tracks grew louder and louder, and the next moment, with a lurch that jammed my stomach halfway up my esophagus, we came to a sudden, jarring, and oh so wonderful stop. Then the cart's side door swung squeakily open, and we all tumbled out, a little green, a little dizzy, and a lotta grateful to still be alive.

"This way," ordered the calaca.

Maybe fifteen yards down a narrow tunnel we reached what looked like a dead end: two undead soldiers, their spears crossed, identical *don't mess with me looks* on their bone-white faces, flanking an intricate stone monument—a Maya stela—which had been carved into the wall.

I recognized the carving because I'd seen dozens just like it inside my mom's travel books. Carvings like that had been discovered inside countless Maya ruins and Maya temples and all over the lowlands and valleys across Central and South America for countless generations.

This particular stela, like so many, depicted a king. And this particular king was sitting, sorta lying back on a massive golden throne, looking supercool, with a double-headed jaguar scepter in his hand and a headdress of animal faces and teeth on his head.

Like the image in the stela, the soldiers also wore headdresses—these of green quetzal and nearly as spectacular, adorned with gold and jade and rows of smaller feathers in blues, yellows, teals, and reds.

Surprisingly, the skeleton soldiers did not move as we approached, but what was even *more* surprising, the stela *did.* . . .

There was a loud crunching, grinding sound, a tremble in the walls and the ground, and a noisy rattle of chains—

And for a second it looked like the carved figure—the

Maya king himself—was rising out of his stony throne!

But then I realized what was *actually* happening: As we watched, jagged cracks appeared in the wall. The cracks began to spread, zigging and zagging like the course of some wild river, until finally, with a series of loud clicks and clacks and hisses, the wall slid all the way open, revealing a long, shimmering passage beyond.

"Por aquí," said the calaca.

CHAPTER THIRTY-NINE

The first thing I noticed about the tunnel: It had cost someone a pretty penny to build. Or more like a pretty *fortune*. Every inch of the ceilings was covered in golden tiles, and every inch of the floors had been paved with golden bricks. And the polish on both was so meticulous that I could see our reflections, clear as day—Raúl's wide eyes, Violet's slack jaw, Alvin's trembling lower lip, and mine and Sam's bug-eyed stares—as we followed the gravedigger down it.

"*Dude . . . ,*" Sam whispered.

"*Yeah . . . ,*" Violet agreed.

"Gold is the only substance on this Earth that can conduct the magia," the calaca said in a voice of hushed reverence. "You see this place? There are others just like it branching out from underneath La Rosa. Some stretch for many miles. And that's most likely what you detected:

vibrations in the earth channeling into these underground tunnels and being conducted by them to make it appear as if the quakes were originating from or converging here."

Ahead of us, the walls and ceiling shimmered like light playing over water. I could sense magic all around us now. That familiar hum and sizzle. And with each step we took, the stronger it became.

But the most incredible sight of all awaited us at the tunnel's end. In the middle of the glittering golden space was what appeared to be a . . . a *skeleton*.

A calaca.

Except, it was like no calaca I had *ever* seen.

First off, it was ENORMOUS, easily fourteen or fifteen feet long, floating in the light like someone would in a pool or one of those standing suspension tanks you see a lot in science fiction movies. Its hands were huge and gnarled. Tiny arcs of reddish something—*electricity*, maybe?— danced along its bony arms and along its bony spine and down its long, bony legs. The freakiest part, though? As we approached slowly, its hollow gaze seemed to follow us just as slowly.

Even from twenty or so feet away, I could feel the magic pulsing through and around and out of that thing like a low-voltage current. And it pulsed through and around and out of us in much the same way. It felt like old magic, old and forgotten, magic long since buried away in this ancient place between worlds. And the calaca itself looked just as old and just as forgotten. A slumbering, skeletal giant.

And yet . . . I could somehow *sense* its life force. Its *consciousness*. The unseen force of it curled around my arms and legs, slithering its way into my skin—searching, seeking, like it desperately wanted to know who the heck we were and why the heck we'd come. Whatever that thing was, it was *far* from dead. Though it was hard to say that it was much closer to being *alive*, either.

Alvin's trembling fingers reached slowly toward it—

But the gravedigger instantly caught his hand. "¡NO TOQUES!" he hissed. "For the magical force field that is its eternal tomb will destroy any flesh that so much as touches it!"

Al gulped.

"Wha-what the freak is that thing?" I murmured.

"That, young Morphling, is one of the twelve *Golden Dooms*."

CHAPTER FORTY

Violet asked, "*That's* a Golden Doom?"

"Sí," replied the skeleton coolly. "That is how they are known, numbered among the oldest of our kind, from the time of the Great Shaking. These are the pillars of the ancient wall."

I shook my head. "What wall?"

"The supernatural veil that has been drawn between our worlds. Between the Land of the Living and that of the dead. The barrier that keeps us separate. That keeps us safe."

"You're talking about the chasm?"

"I am. And these are its bearers."

"I—I don't understand."

"See, long ago, in the beginning, there existed a divide between our worlds, a gulf of immense time and space. This kept the two 'dimensions'—as you might call them—separate. But as the worlds grew older, that space grew smaller, and soon the two worlds were nearly touching, separated only by a narrow gap, no wider than a river.

It was around this time that the first unfound pasillo was discovered by a wandering spirit who had been cursed to forever wander the dark and lonely places of the dead. With this discovery, that secret place was no longer secret, and other unfound pasillos were searched for and likewise discovered; and soon the dead began to pour across. But the living and the dead were not meant to coexist. And so there was war and death, and soon we calacas were overrun as the old dead and the newly deceased came back across the worlds, seeking a second chance at life. It was at this apocalyptic juncture that La Sociedad de Calacas convened to discuss what should—or even *could*—be done.

But the solution was not a simple one. And so we called upon all the most powerful sombras of this world: brujas de Galicia, brujos y basajauns, nahuals, curupira, and all manner of hadas. These came together to solve the great riddle of the age, and at last a solution was found: a magical veil, one to be drawn across the chasm between worlds, thus sealing off the pasillos—or at least the vast majority of them. A barrier that would stand for all time, unchanging throughout the eons, so that the safety of this world would be forever guaranteed. That is the story of these Ancient

Ones. It was they who proposed the solution, offering themselves up as eternal watchmen. The most powerful magia has been bound to their very marrow, and they are constantly recycling its power and channeling it together to form the great veil. Together the Dooms hold back the flood of the dead, and that map you spoke of—the map of the Golden Dooms—is *their* map. A map to the secret locations of the twelve."

For several seconds no one moved.

No one even breathed.

Finally Violet said, "Can we have a moment?" And when the calaca tipped the brim of his straw hat, we all huddled together.

"What's up?" I asked.

V's voice was hushed. "It's La Mano Peluda!" she said firmly.

I shook my head. "*What is?*"

"They're the ones after the map! It's *them*! Which means they're *also* the ones that had Mr. Caiman kidnap Esperanza's sister. He must be working with them!"

"What makes you so sure?" asked Raúl.

"Don't you remember what the calaca just told us? La Mano Peluda's forces are massing on the other side. They're organizing—*preparing!*"

"Preparing for what?" whispered Alvin.

And when Violet answered, "*An invasion,*" the sound of his gulp echoed all the way back down the tunnel.

She said, "They need the map in order to learn the secret burial sites of the twelve Golden Dooms—so that they can *destroy* the Dooms and then unleash their armies!"

It made sense. A lot of sense, actually. And maybe that even explained why Mr. Caiman was planning on "sacrificing" Esperanza's sister. Getting rid of the only witness type thing.

Yeah, the puzzle pieces were starting to click into place, and I was starting to get *pretty* worried.

"Okay. So, what are we waiting for?" said Raúl, anxiously rubbing his chest. "Let's tell that muerto and get the heck outta here already. Am I the only one craving some fresh oxígeno?"

He wasn't. I was craving a bit of fresh air myself. So we told the gravedigger our theory. But Mr. Old and Bony didn't really seem too concerned. In fact, even *that* was an overstatement.

"Impossible," he said with an easy (and borderline *terrifying*) grin. "For the location of the twelve is the most closely guarded of *secretos,* and the map to their golden tombs is not easily stolen."

"But what if it *was* stolen?" said Violet. "Then La Mano Peluda would only need someone on this side to destroy the Dooms, bringing down the veil, and they could unleash their invasion from the other."

This didn't faze him either. The calaca was still grinning, almost as if he found our concern kinda cute. "Señorita, if that map *was* ever stolen, I have a sneaking suspicion that *I* would be the *very* first to know."

"How come?" asked Raúl. And for the first time during our conversation, the calaca removed his raggedy straw hat, revealing the domed white hump of his fleshless cranium. And there, chiseled into the hard plates of fused bone, like a sketch or a painting or some futuristic glittery tattoo, was a map. A map on which I could just make out about a dozen big, elaborate, X-ish-shaped calaca heads.

"Because," the gravedigger said with a grand bow, "*I am the Puesha assigned to keep its secret!*"

CHAPTER FORTY-ONE

My nombre es coronel Diego de la Sociedad," said the skeleton-man. "I am el comandante of the third legion de los muertos, and it is my *own bones* that keep the secret of the Golden Dooms."

Violet and I exchanged total *uh-oh* looks. Not twenty-four hours ago Esperanza had told me that it was her sister who was the Puesha in charge of keeping the secret of the Golden Dooms. Now here was Diego the gravedigger telling us basically the opposite—that *he*, in fact, was that Puesha. Clearly—*very* clearly—something was rotten in Denmark.

The bony colonel continued. "Además, what you skin people do not understand is that this is only *one* of twelve Dooms, and in order to bring down the veil, all twelve must be destroyed—and destroyed *simultaneously*. That is how

the magic was designed—that is the genius of the Dooms."
His jawbone stretched into a grotesque grin. I thought I
heard Alvin whimper. "No, an attack on the Dooms does
not concern me. No living thing can penetrate their magical force field and survive. However, what *does* concern me
is how so many of my kind's deepest secrets are finding
their way up to the surface world. And *that* is why I have
brought all of you here. Why I have let you behold what no
mortal eyes have ever beheld. So that I may demonstrate
my trust in you and, in so doing, perhaps earn yours in
return."

"Why do you want our trust?" I asked.

"Because I must discover the traitor within our ranks.
The secrets that are being whispered into the ears of the
living are being whispered by undead lips. And I must
know exactly *whose* lips. For this traidor must be brought
before El Skeletario, the high court of the undead, and they
must be sentenced to the most *severe* punishment our kind
can deliver: the Second Death." His hollow gaze silently
searched our faces. "Now, tell me . . . how did you hear of
the map of the Golden Dooms? Which among us betrays
their own bone and marrow?"

"Sorry," Violet said. "Even if we knew, we couldn't tell
you. We can't blow our sources. It's Journalism 101."

Replacing his straw hat, Diego whispered, "Perdón?"

"She's an investigative journalist," I explained. "They take an oath. Like doctors!"

His bony face went rigid, and the empty sockets of his eyes were like a pair of bottomless black holes. "Please, tell me that is what passes for a *joke* on the surface."

V glanced at me like it was my choice. So I said, "A sombra told me about the map. But I didn't get a name. Didn't even see them. They spoke to me in a . . . *bathroom*. From another stall." Eh, at least that wasn't *all* a lie.

The Puesha's stare didn't budge, geez, like he was trying to break me with it. Y'know, the way detectives use those bright lamps in interrogation rooms. "You expect me to believe that?" he said finally.

"It's . . . *the truth*." I gulped.

There was a long silence, and when the skeleton-man spoke again, his voice would've made an ice cube shiver.

"Did you know that we calacas are considered intermediarios? That is to say, we belong to neither world. We are the workers of La Catrina—her very hands, if you will. So in a manner of speaking, all five of you are currently standing six thousand feet below ground, staring into the very eyes of *death*." Hollow sockets, darker than night, stared back at us. Seemed to stare *through* us. "Now, I have never been a subtle man, not even in life, so I shall plainly lay your choices before you: Either begin talking or begin *dying*. . . ."

"TALK!" Alvin cried. "We choose to talk! Everybody start blabbin'!"

But when V and I didn't immediately say anything, Diego let out a high-pitched whistle, and before anyone could say anything else, the ground beneath our feet began to tremble. A rumble of stamping feet, of creaking, cracking bones, suddenly filled the air, and the tunnel shook so violently that I was ninety-nine-point-nine (*nine-nine-nine-NINE*) percent positive that it was gonna collapse on our heads.

A moment later, the two skeleton soldiers in the elaborate headdresses stepped into view, spears clutched, marching straight for us. Which, on its own, was more than enough to change the color of your undies.

Only they hadn't come alone. They'd come leading a literal *army* of spear-wielding undeads!

I heard myself swallow, felt Alvin sway beside me, saw Sam and Violet pale, and heard Raúl begin to growl deep in his throat.

The calaca army filled the narrow tunnel from wall to wall and probably two hundred yards deep: a sea of bony, grinning faces and staring, soulless eyes.

Suddenly it was beginning to feel *awfully* claustrophobic down here.

CHAPTER FORTY-TWO

ehold the ancient Bone Guard!" cried coronel Diego. "The dreadliest guerreros in all the worlds . . . Warriors of Lady Death herself, with hearts as black as the grave and their very bones sharpened into deadly weapons. Merciless. *Death*less. Will you dare stand before them, Morphling?"

"*Whoa, whoa, whoa!*" I shouted, making a big time-out sign with both hands. "Dude, what the heck?"

The calaca said, "Will you give me the name of the traitor?"

"We can't."

"Then you die."

"But we don't know it!"

"Then you die."

"Can we please get back to you on this?" I said. "Like, early next week maybe?"

Diego shrugged. "Sure. But first *you die*."

Man, talk about an unhealthy fixation on death.

"Don't you get it?" Violet told him. "Killing us doesn't get you *anywhere*. We're on the *same side*! Which means we can work *together*."

The calaca considered that. At last he said, "Why should I trust you?"

"Because we have no reason to lie!"

He considered some more. "So then you truly do not know the identity of this traitor?"

"No!" we both shouted. "We don't know!"

"But what if you were to discover it?" he asked after a moment. "Will you enter into a solemn oath *here and now* to return to this place and reveal it to me, and me alone?"

"Agreed," Violet said.

I nodded too. "Yeah. Sure."

"And what if you happen to come across other information pertaining to a possible attack on the Dooms or these quakes that so interested you?" continued the calaca. "Do you swear to share it with me first?"

"Yes," answered V. "*But* only if that works both ways."

The keeper of the Golden Dooms took one final dip into the ol' think tank. Then his gleaming jawbone curved up in a wide grin. It was terrifying as far as grins went. "It seems as though you have yourselves un acuerdo," he said softly.

"Does that word mean 'deal'?" Alvin whimpered, with a panicky look between Violet and me. "Please tell me it means 'deal'!"

Suddenly the sea of skeleton soldiers lowered their skeleton spears, turned on their skeleton heels, and began marching again—this time, *out* of the tunnel.

The stamp and clack of their fading footsteps was probably the most beautiful sound I'd *ever* heard.

Up in the main hall, Diego showed us to an elevator that had been built from the rib bones of some ginormous but unlucky prehistoric beast. Then he pulled a lever that looked suspiciously like someone's arm, and about thirty seconds later we emerged out of a deep grave marked by a large headstone with an epitaph reading HE WAS DYING TO GET INTO THE FUNERAL BUSINESS, and breathed fresh, surface air again.

"ALIVE!" Sam shouted, clawing his way out of the grave like a newborn zombie. "We're ALIVE!"

Alvin, however, wasn't quite as thrilled. "NOOOOOO!" he cried, sinking to his knees.

"Al, what happened?" Violet shouted.

He held up his golden phone—er, *not*-so-golden phone. (Apparently, it had *un*-Midas'd itself the moment we'd surfaced.) "I'm poor again!" he screeched.

CHAPTER FORTY-THREE

On the whole, I was pretty happy with how the day had turned out. Sure, the whole earthquake lead had been a total bust, but hey, at least we were aboveground again and still breathing, which, when you'd spent the last hour or so six thousand feet below a cemetery, being threatened by an undead ferrier of the dead, was more than enough to put a smile on your face.

And boy was I smiling. That is, until a pair of hands shot out of the shadows of the cemetery (and *specifically* the shadows of a tall, elaborately carved mausoleum), seizing me not very gently by my shirt.

The hands lifted me off my feet and slammed me—hard enough to pancake the air out of my lungs—against the trunk of a crooked tree. Before I had a chance to react, I felt the icy edge of a knife pressing against my throat.

"Anyone moves," growled the owner of the hands (and,

unfortunately, the knife), "and I cut him a one-way ticket to La Tierra de los Muertos!"

The deadly dude was wearing a tattered black hoodie, and as he said that, the hood fell back, revealing a bony, fleshless face. It was a calaca! Another muerto!

Only this one was probably in his upper teens, with raggedy black jeans and wide golden swirls that looped around the empty sockets of his eyes. And as his blade dug deeper into the soft skin of my throat, I couldn't help wondering why stuff like this never happened to Scooby or Scrappy. Guess I was just special like that. . . .

"Oye, easy there, hermano," said Raúl, holding out his hands like he was trying to calm the guy. "Some of us up here got skin . . . and it tends to cut pretty easy."

"It cuts even easier than you *think!*" the calaca hissed back. His voice was as silky as a roll of *sandpaper.*

"Just so you know," Raúl said, "if my cousin bleeds, you *die.*"

The undead punk glanced over his shoulder at him, grinning. "I've already died, gato."

"Well, maybe a second time will make it more *permanent,*" snarled Raúl.

Right then Alvin and Sam, who'd been walking a few yards ahead of us, suddenly realized what was going down. "Who the heck is that dude?" I heard Alvin gasp.

"Don't think that dude's a dude, dude . . . ," Sam answered.

"*WHO ARE YOU PEOPLE?*" raged the aggro muerto. "*¿QUIÉNES SON?*"

"We're just middle schoolers!" Al cried. "We go to PDL Middle. We don't even got driver's licenses yet!"

The knife-wielding maniac looked at Violet.

"It's true," she said.

The knife-wielding maniac looked at me.

"It's true," I agreed.

The knife-wielding maniac sneered. "THEN WHAT DO YOU WANT WITH MY HERMANA?"

"*Your sister?*" I shouted. "Who the heck's your sister?"

"Do not play *tonto* with me, or it will be the *last* game you play among the living!" Then, tightening his grip on the knife: "I know you've been having secret rendezvous con ella all over Miami! I know about the meeting at your school, and I saw her last night at your house—saw you both *holding hands*! And so I ask you again: ¡¿QUÉ QUIERES CON MI HERMANA?!"

Violet—who had been giving me an *awfully* suspicious look since that bigmouthed, bony *bozo* had mentioned the whole "holding hands" thing—suddenly blinked, recognition flashing deep in her blue eyes. She turned back to the calaca. "You're the one who's been tailing us, aren't you?"

"Bueno, at least *one* of you has a brain," he muttered.

My eyes snapped down to his shoes. Yep, old and crusty high-tops. It was definitely h—

Hold up. Those weren't *just* high-tops.

Those were old and crusty *Converse* high-tops.

Navy-colored too.

Hey, those were . . . "Those are *Esperanza's* shoes!" I shouted. "Why did you steal Esperanza's shoes?"

"I didn't *steal* her shoes!" he shot back. "She steals *mine!* If you didn't know, little sisters can be quite the thieves."

"Hold the guac. YOU'RE Esperanza's brother? I didn't even know she *had* a brother."

"I'm sure there's *a lot* you don't know," he hissed.

Just then the latest Sherlock Holmes movie theme song cried out from Violet's hip pocket, loud and actually kinda appropriate in the cold and misty cementerio.

"¿Quién es?" snapped the calaca.

"His mom," Violet said, nodding to me.

The undead's eye sockets narrowed on mine—well, on my eyes, anyway. "¿Tu máma?"

I shrugged. "She can be a little . . . overprotective. You should probably answer that," I told V.

She tapped the screen. "Hello . . . ? Oh, hi, Mrs. Hernández!" she said brightly. "Yep, a lot of fun . . . *tons.* Yes, he's safe. *Very.* Yes, I swear. Not sure why you feel that way, but I'm looking right at him, and he's currently *completely* unharmed. I—I think his phone might've run out of battery, yeah. Oh, just watching a movie . . . *Which one?* Uh—" V glanced at me, I whispered, "*Night of the Living Dead,*" and she repeated it into the phone.

The calaca punk made a face. "Never seen that one."

"You should," I suggested. "It's right up your alley . . . well, more like down your grave, but you know what I mean."

He glared at me. I shrugged.

"I will," Violet said, still talking to my mom. Then she held out the phone: "Say bye to Mrs. Hernández, everyone."

"Bye, Mrs. Hernández!" we all shouted in happy unison (including Esperanza's psycho hermano).

When Violet had put her phone away, the calaca said, "Ahora, ¿donde estábamos?"

"I think you were asking what we wanted with your sister," I reminded him.

"Ah, sí. Gracias . . ." His bony fingers tightened around the knife again. My heart climbed back into my throat.

Meanwhile, behind skeleton boy, Raúl was flapping his arms like some panicky ostrich, trying to catch my attention.

I raised my eyebrows, *What?* But he kept waving—more frantically now—pointing at his mouth and then back at me.

I snapped my hands open at my sides like, *Dude, kinda in the middle of something here,* and finally he burst out with: "GREEN! Your whole lower face is turning GREEN!"

I opened my mouth to shout, "*Green?*" But it wasn't words that came out. It was tongue!

It whipped out like a spring-loaded trap, smacking the calaca in the eye—literally IN his eye socket!—and knocking him off-balance. He went down on his butt, and both his hands popped off.

"Sick!" Sam shouted. "You just lick-punched that freak in the EYE!"

"¿ESTÁS LOCO?" Esperanza's brother roared up at me. "YOU COULD HAVE TAKEN MY EYE OUT WITH THAT THING!"

Raúl immediately jumped on top of him, pinning him to the ground. "You don't HAVE an eye!" he pointed out.

"Sí, I'm aware of that, *tonto!* I'm jess pointing out the fact that his filthy tongue is an *ocular* HAZARD!"

Confused, I stared down at el esqueleto. Had I seriously just given that dude the world's gnarliest tongue-lashing? Certainly seemed that way. But . . . *how?*

Then, as I stuck my tongue out again and examined the pinkish, sticky-looking surface (not to mention the *foot and a half* or so of length!), I realized how—

¡Santo cielo! I'd morphed a frog tongue!

And to say that these things were frogging' AWE-SOME (yeah, pun totally intended) was the understatement of the century!

Thanks to my dad, I knew that a frog could snatch prey with its tongue faster than humans could *blink*. And even though these things were roughly ten times softer than human tongues (which is what gave them their stretchy, bungee-cord-like characteristics), they were also über-strong, able to pull about 1.4 times a frog's body weight.

I wagged it a little, reeled it back in, shot it back out again—quick, quick, like a striking cobra. Frenchflies, anyone? How about some Croak-a-Cola?

Man, how'd I ever live without one?

The only downside to having a reptilian flavor taster? Their taste buds were on a whole *'nother* level, and right now I was tasting all KINDS of nasty.

"What's wrong?" Violet asked as I began wiping it with the sleeve of my T-shirt.

"Think I taste *eye socket*," I said. Or maybe it was just old calaca brains. Either way, *YUCKO!*

"That's so sick!" whispered Alvin.

But already I could feel the manifestation beginning to wear off and was almost grateful, too, because that stale, bony, brainy taste was beginning to wear off along with it.

Turning back to the undead dude, I said, "We're not

your enemies, man. . . . This whole time we've been trying to *help* Esperanza . . . trying to help her help your *other* sister."

The spots where his eyebrows would have been drew up in confusion. "What other *sister?*"

"Magdalena! Who else?"

"*Magdalena?!* I don't know a *single* person named Magdalena! And we don't have a sister! Well, *I* have a sister. *Esperanza.* But she only has a brother. *Me!*"

"You mean it's just the two of you . . . ?"

"Didn't I just explain that? Maybe next time try morphing *a brain,* tonto."

"I had a feeling . . . ," Violet murmured.

My eyes snapped to hers. "You *had a feeling?* What do you mean, *you had a feeling?*"

V shook her head, like, *Sleuth instincts. I'll tell ya later.*

I was so confused I didn't even know what to say. I mean, this guy—er, muerto, whatever—was claiming that Esperanza didn't have another sister. If that was true, then what was the point of the whole loco story she'd fed me?

"Are we cool?" V asked the calaca, and when he nodded, Raúl climbed off him.

"Give me a hand," said the skeleton dude, scowling up at me.

"Oh. Sure." I held out a hand to help him up.

"Not *your* hand," he growled. "M Y hand! It's by your foot."

Ah, right.

I kicked it over, and after Humpty had put himself back together again, he pushed angrily to his feet, angrily picked up his knife, and stuffed it—angrily—back into his hoodie pocket. "And for the record," he spat, "even if I *had* another sister—which I don't—she wouldn't be the one in need of help. That would be Esperanza. *Herself.*"

I gaped at him. "Esperanza's in trouble?"

He sighed. It was a drawn-out, tired sound. "My sister has never quite felt at home among the old and lonely graveyards. She has always been a . . . *free spirit.* Always on the move, constantly telling me of her dream to live among the living. When we were little, she'd make me do the most unnatural things with the spoons she'd steal from the older graves."

Uh-oh. That all sounded *pretty* familiar. "You mean like help her dig tunnels up to the surface?" I asked.

His bone-white jaw nearly unhinged. (As a matter of fact, one side literally *did.*) "How did you know that?" he whispered.

"Lucky guess."

"Hold on," Violet cut in. "So you're saying it's Esperanza who's really in trouble?"

The hollows of his eyes glared around at us. "You

upworlders know *nothing*, do you? You don't have the vaguest notion of what stirs in the shadows." His gaze slid sideways to me. "I bet you don't even know how my sister feels about you."

"What do you mean, how she *feels* about him?" V asked, sounding suspicious.

"Look, we've just been trying to help her, okay?" I said. "That's all we know."

"And we've been risking our *skin* to do it," added Raúl, glaring right back at the skeleton. "Not that you muertos would have the *vaguest notion* of what that's like."

The muerto was silent for a moment. "If you weren't all so oblivious and incompetentes, I might not believe you. But you are, so I do. I believe you really are trying to help my sister."

I threw my hands up. "Well, *duh*, man ... I mean, whatdya think we're even doing here?"

"The problem is, you are totally blind to what is happening right beneath your own *fleshy* noses!"

"So tell us, then! Tell us what's really going on!"

"I will. But not here ..." His gaze slipped suspiciously around the misty tombs. Then he leaned toward me and, in the raspiest voice you can imagine, whispered, *"Meet me at the Venetian Pool. You know this place, sí?"*

I nodded, almost said, *Duh, it's where Mr. Caiman*

kidnapped your other sister, but stopped myself, remembering that he probably didn't even *have* another sister.

"Meet me there in exactly twenty minutes," he continued. "By the pool. If you truly want to help mi hermana, that is where you will get your chance." Then, somehow making his voice even more hollow-sounding, he said the oddest thing: "I have discovered the source of the whistling and have unearthed its *true* malice. I know what unholy thing now possesses the map of the Golden Dooms, and I will draw it out!"

"Wait," Violet said. "What do you mean, *you have discovered the source of the whistling?*"

But his only answer was "What I mean is, I may have found the only way to save my sister's life."

CHAPTER FORTY-FOUR

At this point, I honestly didn't know *what* to think. One second Esperanza was telling us that her sister needed help, the next she'd given me this huge telenovela-caliber story about Magdalena having fallen in love with some bride-sacrificing potioner, and now her brother (whom she'd never even *mentioned* before) was telling us that it was actually *Esperanza* who was in trouble!

There was only one thing I was absolutely sure of at the moment: that family had some *serious* issues. (And that was aside from being dead.)

The Venetian Pool—aka the coolest public pool on the entire planet—was located in the heart of Coral Gables, not too far from La Rosa. It was basically this beautiful oasis spread out over four acres of swaying palm trees and wild-growing bougainvillea. The pool itself was a work of art, with two waterfalls, multiple cavelike grottos, and more corral rock formations than you could shake a snorkel at.

The main grounds were surrounded by a low brambly hedge, which we jumped, and a tall limestone wall, which we climbed. (And by *we*, I mean Violet, Raúl, and me. Alvin and Sam had taken the "Dos-Patas Express" (i.e., their own two feet) back home. They'd already had more than enough "fun" for one night. Plus, I really didn't want them around just in case our little rendezvous with Esperanza's brother took an unexpected—or *not-so-pleasant*—turn.)

Anyway, the three of us made our way to a shadowy archway between two of the Venetian-style buildings nestled maybe thirty yards from the lifeguard tower.

"I thought Esperanza's brother told us to meet him *by* the pool," I whispered to Violet.

She nodded. "He did."

"Then why are we hiding all the way over here?"

"Because he won't *expect* us to be hiding here."

"Uh . . . ¿qué?"

"We have to make sure everything's on the up-and-up, Charlie. We don't even know if we can trust him yet."

She had a point. He could've been lying to us about being Esperanza's brother. Unlikely. But possible. And it's always better safe than sorry, right?

"Tan ingeniosa," purred Raúl, flashing those annoying dimples. "So brilliant . . ."

I groaned.

V's phone began to beep.

She dug it out of her pocket.

"Is it my mom again?" I asked. It wouldn't have surprised me.

But Violet shook her head. "No, it's my uncle."

"The one who works for the FBI?"

"That's the one. I asked him to look into the missing pe— *Oh my gosh, Charlie . . .*"

"What?"

She held up her phone. The text message on the screen read I can confirm 12.

And now I was shaking my head. "Twelve *what*? What's he confirming?"

Violet's voice sorta caught in her throat as her eyes found mine again and she said, "*Twelve missing people* in Little Havana."

I heard myself gulp. Then I heard Raúl hiss, "¡Mira! ¡Ahí está!"

And there he was, Esperanza's brother, melting out of the shadows by a stack of plastic pool chairs, six feet of bony skeleton dressed in a dark hoodie and darker jeans. His crusty sneakers made no sound as he walked slowly, carefully along the edge of the glimmering water and paused, looking around, near a grotto. Something long and silverish flashed in his hand, and I realized he was no longer carrying that bony little pocketknife. He'd upgraded. *BIG-TIME.*

He was now carrying a sword—a huge bony *sword!*

"Well, that can't be good," I said.

"Looks like he's planning to do more than talk," whispered Raúl.

Then the calaca was moving again, stepping into a column of pale moonlight, his head turning this way and that, the wind tugging on his baggy clothes.

"What are we waiting for?" I asked V. "Him to get bored and go home?"

"We're waiting to see if he brought any *friends,*" she explained.

"Ay, I love the way you think," whispered Raúl. "Such a potent combination of brains, beauty, and suspiciousness."

"Would you shut up with all that already?" I growled, and my cousin's lips drooped into a confused frown.

"What's wrong with saying something nice about someone?"

"You wanna say something nice about someone, say it about *me.*"

"Okay. You have nice ears."

I blinked, surprised. "Really? You think so?"

Raúl scowled at me. "No." Then the scowl melted into a dimply grin. "Okay, maybe a little. I like the way they stick out just a bit but not too much."

Violet turned, giving us a funny look. "Are you two seriously having this conversation right now?"

"You're right," I said. "We'll shut up. Sorry."

A moment later my lovely ears—which stuck out *just a bit* but not too much—were straight-up assaulted by a *terrible* sound: that awful, brain-scratching, spine-tingling, *skin-crawling* whistling we'd heard back at Mr. Miller's house: *Do, re, mi, fa, so, la, ti.* It seemed to be coming from everywhere and nowhere all at once. My eyes began to water. My eardrums squirmed uneasily in their ear holes.

Just when I didn't think I could take it anymore, the whistling began fading . . . fading . . . quickly fading until— sweet relief—there was only silence.

"It's that *whistling* again," Raúl hissed, and I nodded, my eyes searching the dark piscina area.

An eerie gray mist hung over the pool and around the palms and between the bougainvillea, obscuring everything. And as we watched, a strange figure—hunched and carrying something heavy over one shoulder (a sack, maybe?)—coalesced out of the misty tendrils like a suddenly summoned spirit.

"Looks like our friend might've brought another friend," Violet whispered, which was exactly what I was thinking too. Except . . . the longer we watched, the less those two looked like besties.

Esperanza's brother had begun an unsteady retreat, slowly lowering his head but gradually raising his sword, its edge catching the moonlight, throwing it back in pale glints. Call me capitán Obvious, but it didn't seem like the friendliest conversation of all time.

Suddenly, like a flash, the figure lunged. Its movement was so quick, so unnaturally *sudden* that it seemed to blur before our eyes, and a thick darkness fell over Esperanza's brother like a huge black bedsheet sweeping through the night—

And then they vanished.

Both of them!

I blinked, rubbing my eyes and thinking, *Where the heck did they go?* But before I could turn those thoughts into words, different thoughts—from a totally different thinker—spoke up behind us.

"Hey, lookie, lookie . . . if it isn't Sir Pokes-a-Lot."

I knew that voice.

We whirled.

A buncha reptile-looking goons, not very unlike the ones we'd run into behind Caiman's shop and inside Mr.

Miller's house, were crowded around behind us. Maybe a dozen or so bipedal crocs, all thick, scaly necks and jacket-busting shoulders. Two of them cracked their knuckles, and it was like the crack of cannon fire in that quiet little archway.

I gulped.

Mr. Sospechoso, who, by the way, looked even *less* crocodilian than the last time we'd seen him—he looked completely *human* now, as a matter of fact!—curved his lips into an evil grin. "Still haven't found your quills, huh, Porky?"

I gulped again.

Then a huge, meaty fist was flying straight at my face.

I felt a solid *thwap!* heard a sharp *crack!* saw a burst of glittery lights, and then went nappy-nap.

CHAPTER FORTY-FIVE

When I came to, I tried rubbing my bleary aching eyes, but could hardly move my arms. I tried to stand up but couldn't feel anything underneath me to stand up *on*. For a dizzy second, I wondered if I was still asleep and floating somewhere between Calle Ocho and Never-Never Land, but the dull throbbing pain in my face made it pretty clear I wasn't.

I groaned.

"Have a nice nap?" whispered a voice close by.

Violet's voice.

Twisting, I glanced sideways to see her hanging out right next to me. *Literally.* Both of us strung up by our wrists, our sneakered feet dangling over a shallow, watery pit! Which explained why I couldn't move. *And* why I hadn't felt anything under my feet.

Immediately my brain scrambled into full-on MacGyver

mode, looking for some ingenious way to free ourselves, calculating the possibility of not breaking something if we managed to wiggle out of the ropes and drop the fifteen or so feet down into the pit.

But as my eye fog cleared and my vision steadied and the world around me swam slowly into focus, and the pit below more sharply into view, I realized that if we *did* manage to wiggle free, it would be *the last* bit of wiggling we'd ever do, because that muddy, watery pit just so happened to be crawling with a horde of hissing, snapping, hungry *CROCODILES!*

"Please tell me this a nightmare," I squeaked.

"It is," Violet answered. "Except it's happening in real life."

¡Magnífico!

The rusty metal hook we were both dangling from creaked and groaned as we spun in a lazy circle.

"Where the heck are we?" I whispered. Only . . . I sorta already knew. I recognized this place. Or at least *the style* of it. The fresco ceilings. Cuban limestone. The carved mantels and gilded golden columns. The stained-glass doors . . . glittering chandeliers. I'd been here before. On a field trip, maybe. Wait—*yeah!* On a field trip! This was Vizcaya!

This was that famous mansion/museum in the middle of Miami's tropical hardwood hammock!

Except . . . it *couldn't* be the mansion proper.

For starters, a giant *crocodile pit* had been dug into the middle of the sleek marble floors. Also, there was a huge rectangular cutout in one wall, through which I could see moonlight glimmering off a bay—Biscayne Bay, maybe?

And the real Vizcaya didn't *have* any huge cutouts in its walls.

At any rate, the place was enormous, divided into three levels, all of which we could clearly see because it was all wide open, like one of those dollhouses split right down the middle.

A spiral staircase led up to a third-floor landing, which basically looked like some top secret research laboratory right off the set of *Jurassic Park*. Bunsen burners, beakers, and fancy microscopes were arranged along the tabletops. Gallons of colorful liquids bubbled inside test tubes and in clear containers, and toward the back, stacks of triangular-shaped vials labeled EXPLOSIVE/EXPLOSIVO were piled high on a shelf labeled NO TOCAR—DO NOT TOUCH—¡NO MOVER!—DO NOT MOVE!

I shook my head. "This can't be Vizcaya . . . *can it?*"

"¡Ah, sí!" exclaimed a deep, hissing voice. "A very sharp eye you have, mi niño!"

The voice had spoken out of the shadows on the third level. From behind a wide wooden desk tucked into a shadowy corner by a row of high-tech computer monitors. "This indeed is—or rather *was*—part of the famous Vizcaya mansion. The boathouse, to be exact. I'm sure you know it was said to have been lost during the Great Hurricane of 1926—yet I assure you it was *not*. See, I so fell in love with the architecture and design of Mr. Chalfin that I used the cover of that natural disaster to steal this boathouse away, taking it as my own and transporting it all the way here, to my native land, where I, of course, have made several upgrades over the years. ¿Te gusta?"

"Actually, I do kinda like it," I admitted. "Pretty sure you could've done without the pit of crocodiles, though."

The figure sitting behind the desk chuckled at that—a low, throaty, hissing chuckle. But stayed hidden in shadows, supervillain style.

As the rusty hook continued to slowly spin, we got a look at some kind of Wild West–looking parlor down on the first level. There were about half a dozen or so large wooden tables and about five dozen or so bulky goons in heavy leather jackets sitting around them on chairs and shuffling cards or playing dominoes. Beyond the tables stood a high wooden bar with rows of colored bottles gleaming on a mirrored shelf, and at the foot of the bar was none other than my cousin—*Raúl!*

He was bound hand and foot, lying unconscious a

few feet from a stack of ginormous limestone rocks. On the other side of the rocks, also sleeping and also tied up (chained to a wall by metal links big enough to stick *your head* through) was what looked like a mapinguari! A huge one, too, with a massive slothlike body, humanish features, and a single cyclopean eyes smack-dab in the middle of its reddish furry face! Its second mouth, down by its belly— yeah, these things had not one but *two* mouths—was snoring, just like the one on its face, and *drooling*, also like the one on its face. These things were known (and *feared*) all over South America, from Brazil to Bolivia, for their incredible strength and their incredible *stink*. Not to mention their incredible appetite. For Raúl's sake, I just hoped that chain was even stronger than it looked. . . .

Behind us the figure said, "It was quite the expense to transport the boathouse all the way here, seeing as we are a ways off the beaten path. But I've always *prized* privacy."

I said, "So screaming for help probably wouldn't do us much good, huh?"

"That depends on how loud you can scream," he replied coolly, and I thought I could hear a vicious smile in his deep, rattlesnake-like voice. "We are currently in a rather rural region of northern Colombia, not too far from the Amazon, near a shallower section of the Magdalena River."

"That's a lie," Violet said. "Your goons carried us less

than *two miles* into the Everglades. We're still in South Florida."

"Are you positivo?"

"*Positively* positivo. Let's just say I have a way with blindfolds."

"I'm sure you do. And granted, had my men carried you into ordinary woods, you would indeed very much still be in South Florida. But those woods, señorita, were *not* regular woods. Those were *sombra wood.*"

The sound of my gulp echoed in my ears like a bomb. Yeah, that was just about the *last* thing I wanted to hear. Violet and I were pretty familiar with sombra wood. We'd actually run into some on our little trip through Central and South America, and besides *crawling* with mythological monsters, they were also sort of like wormholes, meaning they made it possible to travel incredibly long distances in impossibly short amounts of time.

With our backs still turned to "Mister Mysterio," V whispered, "*We need to stall! Maybe three, four minutes tops.*"

So I whispered, "*What's the plan?*" But we were already coming back around, so we left it at that.

"By the way, do either of you know who I am?" asked the figure, now rising behind his desk.

"Apart from someone who hangs kids over pits crawling with crocodiles?" I said.

"Those are, in point of fact, caiman. *Black* caiman—not crocodiles, not alligators . . . a common error. You can tell by the color of their gums, orangish in hue as opposed to tan or beige. Also by their *teeth*, long and sharp in contrast to the conical variety found in gators."

"You sure know your order Crocodilia," I said.

"If anyone should, I think it'd be me. After all, they don't call me Mr. Caiman out of irony."

Honestly, I don't know what I expected to see when the owner of Pierre d'Exquis finally stepped out of the inky shadows, but it certainly wasn't what I *did* see.

First off, the guy or thing or *whatever* wasn't even human! At least not fully. Sure, if you squinted real hard when you looked at him, he kinda sorta might've *maybe* been able to pass for human. He had a humanish torso and humanish arms, humanish legs and a brutish squarish humanish head, but his skin was all scaly and green, the nails growing out of the ends of his stubby little fingers long and curving, clawlike. His ears were weird too—sort of sucked into his skull and pushed up close to his eyes, just like a croc's. But it was his face that really put the cherry on the tres leches. Squashed down, mushed narrow, and stretched out a good six or seven inches, it wasn't quite croc and it wasn't quite not—just some weird something in between.

He wore a bright pink business suit with matching hat and tie and white dress shoes polished to a mirror gleam. And even though you'd think that color combo might not work with his scaly greenish complexion, it really kinda did. I mean, you had to hand it to him—er, *claw* it to him—the reptile had style.

"*What the croc?*" I heard Violet whisper.

And that's when it suddenly dawned on me.

"Oh my gosh," I breathed. "You're Saúl Montenegro!"

CHAPTER FORTY-SIX

M r. Caiman—no big surprise—flashed us a reptilian grin. "So you have heard of me, then?"

"Duh! You're the world-famous Peeping Tom!" I shouted.

Violet made a face. "He is?"

"Yeah, he's el Hombre Caimán—the Alligator Man—the famous Colombian myth! Legend claims he turned himself into a caiman so he could spy on girls!"

"¡MENTIRAS!" Caiman snapped, hissing at me through his fangs. "Those stories are all LIES! ¡CUENTOS! I wasn't trying to *spy* on the girls bathing near the river. I simply wanted to *scare them off*! See, I was a fisherman in those days, and quite a prosperous one—that is, until that flock of pavas turned my favorite río into a *bathtub*, scaring away all the most delicious fish! So, one day, in my anger, I sought out a local sorcerer and begged him for a potion that would turn me into a caiman, so I could swim near the water's edge and scare the girls off once and for all. But the old fool, like you, thought I was some hormonal teenager—a peeper!—and so, to teach me a lesson, he gave me the potion I sought but failed to provide a counter potion to change me back."

"*Yeah*, that's not what I heard."

"I DON'T CARE WHAT YOU HEARD! ¡NO ME IMPORTA EN *LO MÁS MÍNIMO!*" He took a second to compose himself, the subject obviously a touchy one for him. Then he said, "Now allow me to tell you the rest of my little tale, for I doubt you've ever heard this part. See, once I learned of the brujo's treachery, I begged him to take pity on me and teach me his craft, and he did, knowing that after what he'd done to me I could no longer return to fishing. I trained under him for six years, and then one afternoon I asked him for a kindness: I asked him for the counter potion. But el old brujo calmly explained that there wasn't one. That he'd made the first potion too strong. This, of course, sent me into a wild rage, and the next morning I slipped my *own* potion into the great potioner's breakfast tortillas, turning him into a rat—¡*una rata*! Then I picked him up by his tail and flung him into the woods, leaving him to spend the rest of his life as an animal, just like he'd left me. The next several years I slaved and toiled, trying to undo the effects of the potion, but I could never manage to fully break its hold. I became what you see me as now. And so finally I gave up and decided to embrace my inner *crocodrilo.*"

"It's a good look for you," I told him, because—well, what did we have to lose, right?

"Cool story," Violet said. "And now that we all kinda know each better, any chance you'd let us go?"

"About as much as I have of ever becoming fully human again," answered Caiman.

"And may I ask what exactly you want with us?" I said.

"I with you? Nothing. But you seem to have *quite* the unhealthy fascination with *me.* Usually, in these types of situations, I'd let you go after a bit of a scare—maybe dangle you a little closer to the snapping, hungry jaws of my extended family down there. However, an associate of mine very recently informed me that there happens to be a rather large, rather *generous* bounty on your heads over in the Land of the Dead—a bounty I'd very much like to collect."

"Planning on croaking sometime soon, Caiman?" I asked.

A hiss of laughter escaped from between his fanged teeth. "¡Ah, muy bien! You do have a quick tongue! As quick as your legends say! But did you know that a black caiman has an average lifespan of between fifty and eighty years? And that's living out in the wild, in jungles crawling with jaguars! On the *other* hand, the life expectancy of two snooping *mocosos* dangling from a fraying rope over a pit of hungry prehistoric predators—well, that tends to be *significantly* shorter. And *speaking* of your rapidly approaching demises, allow me to introduce my sweet aunt Gabriella and all my little cousins. A rowdy bunch, aren't they?"

Below us, the caimans hissed and snapped, thrashing their tails in the muddy water. Looking down at their hungry, ugly grins, I said, "I can see the family resemblance. Can smell it too."

Caiman hissed. Or maybe laughed again. It was hard to tell with this guy. "¡Muy bien! You are quick—no doubt about it! I owe you both for the good belly laughs."

"How about you let us go and we call it even?" Violet offered.

"¡Ah, sí! Go on, go on! You're both *eating* me up inside! Though not quite as literally as my dearest Gabriella will be eating *your* insides."

With an evil (and let's be honest—*hideous*) smirk, Mr. Caiman strolled over to the edge of the third floor, where he could look straight down into the pit of ravenous reptiles.

"Black caimans are fascinating creatures, aren't they?

Do either of you how they hunt? It's really quite fascinating. See, a caiman will first stalk its prey, usually near the water's edge. Then its jaws will clamp down on a leg or a paw or perhaps an antler, and it will drag its prey into the water as it performs what is known as a crocodile death roll. The objective is to drown its victim, and since a caiman can hold its breath for nearly two hours, this makes for a simple yet most *lethal* combination.

The drowning can take several seconds, sometimes several minutes. But this, of course, is all a formality. The truth is that once a caiman has closed its jaws on you, death is all but assured, for the jaw pressure of an Amazonian black caiman exceeds over six thousand pounds per square inch. That's nearly *fifty* percent stronger than a great white's. However, the ferociousness of its jaws is second only to the ferociousness of its digestive system. The acidity of a caiman's stomach allows us to digest anything—vertebrae, bones, hooves, even turtles' shells, without the *slightest* burp, hiccup, or indigestion. In other words, what we swallow *stays* swallowed. So do feel free to try all your many tricks, little Morphling . . . though I have a feeling they won't be *nearly* enough."

CHAPTER FORTY-SEVEN

So death by death roll," I said. "That's cold-blooded, Caiman. Even for something like you."

The walking, talking croc snorted as if he'd really enjoyed that one. "I ask that you think me not a villain; I'm just a humble crocodilian trying to earn a peso."

"Well, before you earn that peso," Violet said, "there's something you might've overlooked. . . . Just how are you gonna collect our bounty if we're rotting away in the belly of your auntie and cousins down there?"

"I'm afraid that's strictly *your* problem. See, the bounty you speak of is to be paid DOA—that is, dead *or* alive. I figure the former will be easier for all parties involved— perhaps even *preferred*." He showed us his teeth. There were a lot of them and not one was Listerine commercial worthy. "Now, to introduce you to mi tía Gabriella! She's feeling particularly chatty today. I have a feeling she's going to talk your ear off—well, *bite* it off, more than likely."

Then, grinning cruelly, Mr. Caiman sashayed to the opposite side of the room, where several silver levers were sticking out of the marble wall. He was just reaching for the longest of these (which unfortunately probably controlled the hook/pulley system we were currently precariously dangling from) when Violet said, "Just one more thing before dinner."

Caiman's reaching hand halted as he glanced back at us. "Yes?"

"What do you want with the calaca map?" asked V. "The map of the Golden Dooms?"

"Oh, so you know about that! An impressive duo you two make. Muy impresionante, indeed!"

"It's useless to you," I said. "You'll never be able to destroy the Dooms."

"Of course not! Fortunately, I do not *intend* to."

"It's not cool to play with your food, Caiman. Didn't your mother ever teach you that?"

The croc's wide, flat jaws opened in a sort of snarling smirk. "She, as a matter of fact, taught me just the opposite. But in any case, I'm not playing with you. It's the truth. The map wasn't for *me*. I acquired it for a client of mine. You see, I'm what you might call a fence. I get for people what most cannot, and I sell for others what *they* cannot."

"So who's the client?" asked Violet.

"Ha! As if I would ever be *bruto* enough to answer such a ridiculous question! In my business it is not *good* business to have a loose tongue. However, in this particular case, even if I *wanted* to tell you—which I don't—I couldn't, for I do not know his name or even what he looks like. I've only met him in shadow and in darkness." An uneasy tone crept into Caiman's voice as he said, "Such an *odd* fellow, too . . . such strange requests. Did you know he had me acquire *thirteen* red roosters? No easy task, mind you. Cursed roosters are quite prized among the bruja clans and thus quite expensive and hard to steal. I had to send my men all the way to Galatia to find them. But since he pays in ancient bolívares, I don't complain."

And suddenly it hit me. The whole shebang! I realized who the thieves were, the ones El Cadejo and the curupiras had been hunting for. They were Caiman's goons! I also realized why Mr. Sospechoso had looked less and less croc-like every time we saw him: because he'd never actually *been* a croc in the first place! None of them had! It was all Caiman's doing. He must've brewed up a potion that temporarily transformed his gang of goons *into* crocs. Which explained why my abuelita had never told me any stories centering around a race of crocodile people. Because there had never *been* any. And that also explained why El Cadejo and the curupira hadn't been able to find the thieves. Because they'd been looking for sombras and not animals—*especially* not caimans.

They stole the cursed red roosters from the witch market and escaped into el río . . . the river the curupira mentioned. The one crawling with caimans.

A pretty brilliant scheme, actually.

"And how much is he paying you for the kidnappings?" Violet asked.

"*Kidnappings?*" Caiman looked insulted. "What *kid-nappings?* You two are *trespassers.*"

"She's not talking about *us*, capitán Scaly. She's talking about all the missing people around Little Havana."

"I know *nothing* of missing people!"

"Oh, c'mon, Caiman. We saw the truck full of kid-napped pets behind your shop. Pets that just so happened to belong to missing people. And we saw your goons at another missing person's house collecting *their* pet. We know you're involved."

"What you *saw* is both the breadth and the *extent* of my involvement. In those specific cases, we were paid only to pick up animals. Not at all a difficult or *illegal* task, seeing as all the houses we were told to collect the animals from had been *completely* abandoned. No, my hatchlings are basically playing the role of animal control. The worst I can be accused of is rescuing lonely animalitos." He shrugged. "Granted, I don't understand it all either. But then again, I'm not paid for my curiosity, rather my lack of. Anyway, enough of this talk. I'll be honest with you: This particular client of mine sets my fangs on edge for some reason, and I don't very much like to discuss him. There's simply something not *right* about him . . . a pestilential darkness that I cannot quite put my claw on. Of course, I realize that it is a strange thing for a caiman to say, seeing as we are cold-blooded and fearless by nature, but it is the truth. Simply standing in his presence is insoportable—*unbearable*—that is to say nothing of his wretched *whistling*. In fact, consider it a courtesy that I'm feeding you to my family, because if you ever fell into his hands—well, something tells me you'd be begging for a short drop into Auntie Gabriella's waiting *maw*."

As we spun slowly around again, I hissed, "How much longer do we gotta stall this *freak*?" and Violet whispered, "*Not very*."

So I whispered, "You STILL haven't told me the plan, by the way!"

Her eyes flicked to the parlor on the first floor. "It's sort of obvious, isn't it?"

I glanced that way too but didn't see anything even

remotely resembling a plan. "If it were, I wouldn't be asking!"

"I'm guessing you forgot to check your lunar calendar today."

"Of course I did," I told her. "Because I don't HAVE a lunar calendar!"

"For your information, today is December fourth. Lunae."

"Is that—*Latin?*"

"Uh-huh."

"Well, since I'm just kinda hangin' out right now and can't use Google Translate, would you mind telling me WHAT IN THE *FRIJOLES* THAT EVEN MEANS?"

"Means there's gonna be a crescent moon tonight," she said.

"And exactly *how*, may I ask, is a crescent moon supposed to help us not get eaten alive by Auntie G?!"

"Not up-to-date on your Mesoamerican mythology, are ya?"

I opened my mouth to snap, "Mesoamerican *mythology?*" But I didn't even make it past the first *O* before the answer finally dawned on me. Or rather, *dusked* on me.

My eyes slid to the huge skylight in the ceiling, where a slice of bright ascending moon was now climbing steadily into view.

Caiman, meanwhile, was messing with the levers on

the walls, stabbing at the stubby buttons with his stubbier fingers. "Anyway, ¡chao, niños! Or should I say, *chow!*"

But just before he could send us plummeting to meet his lovely aunt and cousins, the moon rose fully into view, and a flood of ghostly light came pouring in through the glass ceiling of the boathouse.

It was a crescent moon. Just like Violet had said. And just like that—I suddenly remembered something: According to ancient Aztec legend, crescent moons were to nahuales what full moons were to werewolves; they basically transformed the werebeasts to their wildest and most powerful forms! (Aztec warriors would even carve the shape of the crescent moon onto their shields in preparation for battle!)

Now a fat, glittering column of moonlight splashed the floor near where Raúl was lying, still unconscious, and then—well, and then it was on like *Donkey Kong.*

CHAPTER FORTY-EIGHT

Ever seen a werejaguar transform? Yeah, me neither. And just so ya know, it wasn't pretty.

Raúl's eyes bulged until they looked like they were going to pop. His spine arched until it looked like it was going to snap. His muscles rippled and swelled until they looked like they were going to burst. A spine-tingling howl erupted from his mouth (well, it was actually starting to look more like a muzzle now) an instant before a wave of dark fur slid down his back and arms, his face and legs.

And the instant after *that*, the thick ropes tied around his wrists and ankles snapped like cheap dental floss as he sprang into a crouch, snarling and showing off massive white fangs. (Oh, and dimples, too. . . . The guy always had to show off those freakin' dimples.)

That's when we got a pretty good idea of the overall intelligence of Caiman's goons.

Half of them were sort of smart.

They ran away.

The other half were plain old stupid.

They ran at Raúl.

The smart ones got away. *Mostly.*

The stupid ones got punched and clawed and kicked and slammed and mauled and thrashed and suplexed and power-bombed and flung through walls and through boxes and doors and into one another (not to mention into the pit crawling with Caiman's hungry fam) until most of the ones who were left standing decided to join the ones who had gone running, and the dumbest ones tried to throw a big fishing net over Raúl and got kicked and bashed and pile-driven into the plank floors until there were enough half-dead half-croc goons lying around that we could've started our own line of croc-skin luggage.

"DID NO ONE THINK TO CLOSE THE BLINDS?" Caiman cried as he vanished into a doorway behind his desk. "WHERE ARE MY SILVER FLECHAS? HAS ANYONE SEEN MY BOW AND ARROW?"

"And that's our cue," Violet said. "Start swinging!"

So we swung—first our feet, then our hips, and then all the rest of us, while the rusty old hook creaked and groaned and bent a little, and I prayed it wouldn't *snap.*

Once we'd gathered enough momentum, V shouted,

"Now!" and we jumped our wrists up and over the lip of the hook and launched ourselves up and over the edge of the little pier.

We landed hard on our hands and knees (it hurt, sure—but nowhere near as much as landing in Auntie Gabriella's snapping maw), and had just wiggled ourselves free from the ropes when a goon in an alligator-skin jacket—ironic, I know—came out of nowhere.

He grabbed Violet from behind, in a big bear hug, but she whirled in his arms, karate-chopping him in the throat. The impact sent him spinning toward me, so I karate-chopped him too, which ping-ponged him back to Violet. This time she socked him square on the nose, and when he spun my away again, I socked him too, and he finally went down in a heap.

"C'mon!" V shouted.

A broad, fancy-schmancy staircase brought us to a pair of equally fancy-schmancy doors on the second level. "Door número uno or número dos?" I said.

"It's always number two."

I flung it open, saw about fifty goons wielding bats and pipes and shiny silver bike chains charging straight toward us, and nearly *went* number two.

"Not this time!" I said. Then, trying door número uno and seeing a lot more of the same, "And it ain't number one, either!"

Hightailing it back down the stairs, we came out on the lower level, where Raúl was still doing his "were-thing," body-slamming henchmen and flipping tables, pausing every now and then to roar up at the moon. The guy honestly made Dr. Jekyll and Mr. Hyde look like your average, well-adjusted English chap.

Frantically, Violet and I searched for another way out. Only there wasn't any—not behind the walls of boxes or the piles of scientific supplies or even behind the stacks of massive limestone rocks.

"WHAT ARE WE GONNA DO?" I shouted as the sound of chasing footsteps echoed everywhere.

Then our eyes fell on the answer: a shiny new speedboat bobbing quietly at the end of the little strip of pier. Painted Ferrari red, it had curves that would make a *cheetah* look slow.

At that point there really wasn't anything left to say.

Our sneakers pounded the damp planks as we sprinted down the pier and hopped into the boat, which rocked and swayed underneath us. Violet squatted by the ignition. Her talented fingers pushed at buttons, plucked at wires. Suddenly, the huge propeller engine growled to life.

I gaped. "DID YOU JUST HOT-WIRE THIS THING?"

"It was either that or ask Caiman for the keys," Violet

said. Then she began wagging the beam of a laser pointer (her key-chain laser pointer) on the walls and floor of the parlor. She also began clapping her hands and smacking the tops of her thighs and calling to Raúl, who was still going all WWE on Caiman's goons.

"*Gooood* boy!" she shouted. "Now come *here*! Over *here*! ¡Rápido, rápido!"

She clapped some more and snapped some more, and finally I just couldn't take it anymore.

"Violet, he's not some Meow Mix–eating *house cat*!" I screamed. "That's not gonna work!"

Then, like he was *purposely* trying to make me look silly, Raúl wheeled around on all fours, like a house cat, and tilted his head inquisitively to one side, like a house cat, then came hurrying over, all big flashing eyes and high furry tail.

Just.

Like.

A.

House cat.

Bah! I guess when it came right down to it, my cousin *was* basically just an overgrown Kitty Purry!

"*Come* on! *Gooood*, boy!" Violet said, waving him in, and in he jumped, nearly *capsizing* us in the process. "That's a *very* good boy! Now, let's roll!"

Slamming the throttle, she steered us out through the open doors of the boathouse as a hundred or so goons rushed up the pier, shouting and pelting us with bottles and sticks.

We zoomed out into a narrow bay, following the curve of the shore into a river flanked by thick, dark jungle.

"We're definitely not in Miami!" Violet shouted, feeding the boat a little more speed.

"Definitely not!"

"Whatta we do?"

"Keep going! Caiman said it was sombra wood, so maybe if we follow it long enough we'll—"

Suddenly I felt the hum and sizzle of ancient magia: We'd entered sombra wood. And just as suddenly, we'd passed *through* the sombra wood to the other side!

No joke—it was like we'd straight-up teleported out the back of the Vizcaya mansion in South Florida, because that's exactly where we came out! Right where the boathouse used to be!

To our left, the famous Miami skyline rose above the glittering bay like the fingers of some steel-and-concrete gigante, and to our right spread about three thousand miles of wide-open water also known as the Atlantic Ocean.

"This is awesome!" I screamed as the cool air washed over us, swirling our hair and whipping our clothes.

And I guess, agreeing with me, Raúl swung his face up toward the moon and belted out a huge, kitty-cat roar: *RRRRAAAAWWWWAAARRRRRR!*

"By the way, where'd you learn to drive a speedboat?" I asked V. I knew she could handle a dingy with one of those hand-tiller thingies—she'd proven that off the coast of Chile—but a high-end, souped-up speedboat was a completely different animal.

"My parents bought one last year."

"And they let you drive it?!"

"*Let me?* That would be totally irresponsible of them. I'm don't even have my driver's license yet. No, I usually just take it for joyrides when they're sleeping."

Yep, that definitely sounded like Violet.

A low growl tickled my ears. I turned to see the crouching form of Raúl sorta perched at the rear of the boat, just behind the engine. His dark eyes were staring back toward Vizcaya, his ears pinned tightly along the furry dome of his head.

I had no idea what he was looking at. I couldn't see anything! But then I *heard* it: the high-pitched scream of several small, supercharged engines.

Uh-oh.

All of a sudden a gang of Jet Skis exploded out of darkness—out of thin, freakin' AIR!—then hit the water, screaming straight for us.

And even from more than thirty yards away, I could make out the twinkle of metal weapons and the sheen of leather jackets. *Caiman's goons.* No doubt about it.

"We got company!" I shouted.

Up ahead, a maze of old, seaworn pylons were sticking out of the sea like the poles of some aquatic slalom course.

Violet steered us right for them, shouting, "Hold on!" Then she began zigging and zagging between the old crusty things while the Jet Skis zigged and zagged along behind us, trying to catch up. But one of the goons must've zigged a little too hard, or maybe didn't quite zag enough, because his Jet Ski went slamming into one. The massive hunk of algae and barnacle-encrusted wood stopped the Jet Ski dead in its watery tracks, crushing its nose and sending the driver skipping across the surface of the bay like a flung stone.

"You got one!" I cheered, pumping my fist.

"*U hua!*" howled Raúl. And next thing, he tackled me onto the half bench and started licking my face, just slobbering all over me!

"Aw, man, dude—CONTROL yourself!"

The floor tilted beneath us as the speedboat surged forward, slicing through the water like a sword.

An instant later, the high-pitched whine of engines split the air again. Pushing to my feet, I looked around and saw the Jet Skis closing in. And fast!

In the pale moonlight, I could see that Caiman's henchmen were wielding chains. Long, silvery ones. Twirling them above their heads like cowboys twirling lassos. I wasn't sure what they were planning, but I *was* sure I wasn't going to like it. *At all.*

"They got cadenas!" I shouted.

Violet glanced back. "They're gonna try to tangle our propeller!"

See? Told ya I wasn't gonna like it.

"Keep them away from the engine!" she yelled. "Fight 'em off if you have to!"

"Fight 'em off with *WHAT?*"

"*HELLO?*" Her eyes pointed at the long plastic pole clipped on to the sidewall of the boat.

Oh. Right.

The Jet Skis screamed up behind us—two on my left, three on my right. I lashed out at the nearest one, swinging the pole like a giant, floppy baseball bat, and nearly went man overboard!

Raúl, who was crouched next to me, gave me a look like, *Dude, is that seriously the best you got?*

"Fine! You do it, then!" I shouted, shoving the pole into his fur-covered (but fortunately still humanish) hands.

Thankfully, there was still enough *Raúl* in that three-hundred-pound fur-covered manimal to get what I was saying, and as another goon roared up behind us, he swung the pole in a wide, flat arc, clobbering the croc across the side of his scaly head and sending him for a late-night swim.

"¡ESO! Good boy!" I shouted, and really had to fight the urge to pet the guy.

Raúl's muzzle parted in a fierce feline grin. The bright full moon reflected in his eyes like a pair of shining silver dollars. Arching back, he roared, "GOO BOOOOOI!" Dude sounded just like Scooby! I definitely lol'd. Caiman's goons, on the other hand, didn't find it nearly as funny. They immediately backed off.

Which, by the way, didn't surprise me, because I wouldn't want to be anywhere near an angry pole-wielding werejaguar, either, unless he happened to be related to me. The cowardly crocs swung out wide, both left and right, then gunned their engines, charging past us and into the dark sea ahead.

"Ha! That's right!" I screamed, watching them scurry off with their proverbial tails between their legs. (Actually, in these guys' cases, it wasn't so proverbial.) "You can't mess with us! That's my cuz, man! He'll whack all of you into *next week*! He's basically Babe Ruth—only furrier!"

"Where are they going?" Violet yelled, her long blond curls whipping around her face.

"Probably to the chicken coop!" I said. "Because that's

exactly what they are—a buncha *GALLINAS!*"

I'd just started to high-five my cousin when a muffled *BOOM!* rocked the boat. An enormous blast of water erupted off to our right, starboard side, and I had to crouch down real low, steadying myself against the sidewall.

¡Dios mío!

"THE HECK WAS THAT?" I shouted.

And then—*SPLASH!*

A geyser of water exploded just up ahead, completely drenching us. Another explosion reverberated through the bay, and I stumbled sideways, tripped, fell on my butt, and smacked my head hard on a seat as a third blast sent a massive plume of water arching over us like we were surfing tubes on a speedboat.

The boat bounced and banged and skipped over the water as Violet whipped the wheel this way and that, swerving to avoid the random (and obviously deadly) detonations.

"Is someone lobbing *GRENADES* at us?" I shrieked.

"See for yourself!" Violet suggested, nodding over her shoulder.

And what did I see? The potion-brewing crocodilian himself leaning over the prow of another speedboat—this one painted battleship gray—and grinning maniacally as he shouted at the driver, "*¡Rápido, rápido! ¡Dale!*"

In his scaly right hand was something like a vial of bright pinkish liquid (the same stuff I remembered seeing back in his lab, on the shelf labeled ¡EXPLOSIVO!). A piece of burning rag was dangling out of the mouth of the vial, and as I watched, the cranky killer croc reared back and let it fly.

My heart went *KA-THUNK!* as the little vial bomb whispered through the air, arcing toward us to land, bobbing and bouncing in the water only a foot or two to our left.

I had time to think, *¡LECHE FRITA!* Then there was a blinding flash, and the bay exploded. Like, *literally.*

Salty seawater sprayed everywhere, and the boat rocked on some serious waveage, but the blast hadn't stopped us. Hadn't damaged the boat. That was the good news. The bad news was that Mr. Caiman probably had a lot more where those had come from, and it really only took *one.* Violet must've been thinking pretty much the same thing because she quickly slammed the throttle, sending us skipping along the bay, with Caiman hot on our tail, gleefully lobbing bomba after bomba.

But the more vials o' death he lobbed and the easier Violet was able to dodge them, the more I got the feeling that he wasn't *actually* trying to hit us. No, he was trying to *corral* us . . . to funnel us into some kind of trap!

Only I never got a chance to tell anyone, because the

next thing I knew, we were hurtling straight toward what looked like the sandy, shallow banks of a sand flat!

Violet veered sharply, whipping the boat around just moments before we would've run aground. And it worked, too. But it was too little too late.

The Jet Ski goons had already surrounded us. Completely. Like, *360 degrees* surrounded! Their long metal chains trailing in the water, just waiting for us to speed by to tangle our propellers. The sandbank was at our back, Caiman's boat was floating dead ahead, and the glittering coastline of Key Biscayne loomed high and beautiful (and totally unreachable) to our left.

There was nowhere to go.

Nowhere to hide.

You know that old expression "sitting ducks"? Yeah, well, we were getting an up-close and *waaay*-too-personal introduction to what that actually felt like in real life.

And let me tell ya, it wasn't any fun.

CHAPTER FORTY-NINE

O verhead, the clouds had thickened, veiling the moon and blanketing the entire bay in darkness. I wasn't sure how long it had been that way, but apparently it had been a while because Raúl, I suddenly realized, had changed back. My no-longer-furry-and-fangy primo pushed unsteadily to his feet, rubbing his face, and mumbled, "What'd I miss?"

"Oh, not too much," I said. "Violet's hot-wiring skills. Our daring escape. A bomb-dodging boat chase. But we're dead now, so no biggie."

Raúl looked around at the coastline and the ring of Jet Skis and Mr. Caiman floating maybe fifty yards away, a twinkling little vial bomb in each hand.

"Bummer," he said. "How'd I do?"

"Not bad, actually. You were good."

"Yeah, you were really good," Violet agreed.

Ryan Calejo

My cousin looked a tad bit embarrassed. "I shoulda warned you guys. . . . I go a little wild under a crescent moon. Sorta lose myself."

"We figured," I said, patting him encouragingly on the back. You know, the whole "were" in werejaguar . . . Then, turning to Violet, "We're gonna need a plan. And pretty fast."

"Already got one," she said, and for some reason that didn't surprise me. Though I'm not gonna lie, it did *kinda* worry me.

"What is it?" asked Raúl.

Violet's fingers tightened around the chrome steering wheel. "Either of you ever seen the scene in the *Starsky and Hutch* movie when Ben Stiller and Owen Wilson try to jump a car onto a moving boat?"

We both shook our heads.

"Good," she said.

I frowned. "Wait. Whattaya mean, *good?* Why would that be *good?*"

"Doesn't matter," V answered coolly. "We ride together, we die together."

"*What?* Now you're just quoting *Bad Boys.* Why are you quoting *Bad Boys?!*"

"*Hold on,*" Violet said.

Then she slammed the throttle straight down while

Raúl and I screamed, "NOOOOOOOOOO!" The speed-boat suddenly lunged forward, practically leaping out of the water as she swerved us around in a tight semicircle.

Fighting the g-forces and the wheel, V steered us straight for the Biscayne shoreline and the Jet Ski goons floating there in the twinkling dark.

Up until that point I'd been worried about Violet's plan without any *specific* reason to be worried. Well, besides, of course, for the fact that it was *Violet's* plan, and sometimes those could get pretty dangerous. But then I found a reason. A good one too. About a hundred yards straight ahead and maybe fifteen yards offshore, the fuzzy, moss-covered remains of some old, half-sunken pier jutted out of the bay like a broken thumb. Its flat face stuck out of the water at about a forty-five-degree angle, and its high side was aiming toward solid, dry land, which just about made it the *perfect* bike ramp.

Except we didn't *need* a bike ramp. We couldn't *use* a bike ramp. And that's because we weren't on a friggin' bike—we were on a friggin' *speedboat*! (Hint: Boats and bike ramps don't mix.)

"IS THAT YOUR PLAN?!" I shrieked, but Violet didn't answer. Only fed the boat even *more* speed. "But that isn't going to WORK!"

"WHY NOT?" she shouted.

"Because this isn't a movie! This is REAL. FREAKIN'. LIFE!"

But our maniacal boat captain only grinned. "The world's a stage, Charlie. We're all just players!"

The instant we hit the ramp, the nose of the boat rocketed up out of the water and onto the rickety, wobbly hunk of half-sunken wood, and then—well, we just stopped . . . *dead.*

The massive silvery propeller sliced into the soggy planks and bit down like massive metal teeth. The engine screamed, first redlining, then popping and sputtering to a stall. Totally anticlimactic, I know. But hey, it was still better than the alternative.

"*Can't believe that didn't work,*" Violet whispered to herself, sounding pretty disappointed.

"*REALLY?* Because I don't see Ben Stiller or Owen Wilson *anywhere* on this boat, do you?!"

"Is now a bad time to say he told you so?" asked Raúl.

Violet glared at him. Even *I* glared at him. This wasn't one of those times I was happy to be right.

Meanwhile, from every direction, Caiman and his goons were already making a beeline for us.

I shot Raúl a panicked look. "They're coming. DO SOMETHING!"

"Hey, don't look at me," he said. "I'm part cat, not *fish*!"

Then suddenly everybody was shooting *me* panicky looks, so I threw up my hands like, *WHAT?*

"Charlie, you're part EVERYTHING!" Violet shouted. "*YOU* DO SOMETHING!"

"LIKE WHAT?" I shrieked.

"Think wings, Charlie! WINGS!"

"He can do that?" whispered Raúl, looking sorta impressed.

V grinned, broadly and proudly. "You should see his plumage."

CHAPTER FIFTY

I glanced back at the oncoming army of hissing, spraying Jet Skis.

At Mr. Caiman's sleek gray speedboat.

At the even sleeker, liquidy, pink vial bombs clutched loosely in his scaly hands.

At the curly tail of rag that one of his goons was now lighting.

And I gulped.

Wings.

Right!

Shutting my eyes, I concentrated, imagining every winged animal I could think of. I pictured bats and eagles. And owls and seagulls. And geese. And cranes. And ducks. And doves. And puffins. And pigeons. And penguins. Then I quickly right-click-deleted the penguins, because those have wings but can't fly, which basically made them useless to my "Keep Charlie and friends from being blown off the face of the Earth" plan, and kept on picturing herons and ravens and storks and quails and parrots. But for all my concentrating, all my high-level mental gymnastics, I didn't *feel* any different. There was no tingle of a coming manifestation.

No prickle.

No tickle.

Not even an *itch*!

"Uh, primo," I heard Raúl say anxiously.

"One minute, *por favor*."

"*Charlie* . . ." Violet now, sounding even more anxious.

"*Shush!* Kinda need to concentrate here."

"I know, but kinda don't want to get *blown up* here."

And who could blame her? Still, she wasn't helping.

Panicking a little—okay, *a lot*—I ditched my original strategy and tried a new one. I picked a single winged animal. A hawk—a broad-winged hawk, to be exact—and concentrated on it. I imagined the majestic bird of prey in flight, soaring high above mountains and valleys, hills and streams and rivers. I imagined its wings as mine, imagined my face on its body, imagined its face on my body, stopped myself because that one was sort of counterproductive, and went back to picturing its wings: I saw them long and strong, extending out of my back, growing, twisting, unfurling—sticking out like a pair of flapping feathery flags.

But they still wouldn't come.

Houston, we have a manifestation problem!

My heart squeezed. My Panic-o-Meter shot into the stratosphere (*without me,* which wasn't *exactly* the plan), and even though I did my best to just keep myself completely focused on morphing, I quickly realized that was gonna be basically impossible. All I could hear was Violet and Raúl arguing back and forth. All I could feel was the rear end of the speedboat rocking and swaying underneath me even as the high-pitched screams of the Jet Skis grew louder and louder, piercing the humid night.

We're so dead, I thought. *Dead, dead, dead!*

And it was totally MY fault!

Because I couldn't manifest a stupid pair of wings!

Because I couldn't manifest *ANYTHING!*

But no sooner had the thought crossed my mind than I felt it. Felt what I'd been waiting to feel. That familiar tingle. That familiar itch.

It was happening.

The animal inside of me was finally waking up.

CHAPTER FIFTY-ONE

My whole body started to tingle.

I could feel the muscles along my back beginning to bunch and flex. The skin there rippled. It burned. I had a second to think, *I feel the need—the need for WINGS!* And then wings—beautiful, feathery, *MAGNIFICENT* wings!—exploded out the back of my T-shirt, tearing it to bits.

I almost couldn't believe it. I really couldn't! But that still didn't stop me from puffing my chest out real proud-like, lifting my chin high, and flapping my wings like some strutting, *I'm-the-king-of-the-yard* rooster.

Raúl's eyes bugged. "Are those real WINGS?"

"Well, they aren't toes," said Violet. "Grab on!"

So they did. They grabbed on to me—Violet on my right, Raúl on my left—and I sort of hooked an arm around each of them.

Then I began flapping, and flapping, and flapping, and suddenly—*finally!*—we had liftoff! My wings caught on a gust of breezy bay wind. All six sneakered feet lost contact with the boat, and we surged up, up, up into the pitch-dark sky and through the low-hanging clouds.

JUST KEEP THINKING HAPPY THOUGHTS! I told myself—laughing on the inside, the outside, pretty much every side.

"YYYYEEEEAAAAAHHHHHH!" shouted Violet, turning her face into the wind, her long strawberry-scented hair swirling, her blue eyes sparkling in the glow of a thousand and one stars.

"YOU GO, PRIMO!" roared Raúl. "YOU GO, CUZ!"

Way down below us, floating on the bay like a horde of wingless sea-stranded *reptiles*, I could see Caiman and his buncha silly half-crocs staring up at us with a bad case of *wing envy*.

Pays to have feathers, boys! I thought. I must've said it out loud, too, because Raúl gave me a funny look.

"I'M LOIS LANE!" Violet screamed. "THIS. IS. AWWWWWWESOME!"

And it was, too—for about sixty glorious seconds.

Then the awe*some* turned to aw*ful* as my muscles began to spasm—spasm *hard*—and a shrinking, twisting feeling rose in my belly. Suddenly, I realized two very important things.

One, my wings had vanished. Like, *poof!*

And two, gravity (like an annoying hall monitor) had noticed.

There was a long, awful moment of falling—of shriveling insides and screaming passengers.

Then—¡ay, caramba!—we hit something.

Hard.

And that something cracked.

Softly. Kinda like ice.

It happened to be the rooftop skylight of one of the bayside buildings.

Our bodies met glass. They didn't get along.

The panes first sagged, then cracked some more, and then finally shattered, dropping away underneath us like a trapdoor in a Spielberg movie. And all three of us screamed and dropped right along with them.

We crashed through what felt like a table, squashing what felt like Jell-O and dinner rolls, and landed in a heap, with our arms and legs splayed out all over the place.

My arms ached.

My back ached.

Even my ears and eyebrows ached.

Then I realized that just about *every* part of me was aching and decided to stop taking inventory and save myself the pain.

What came next were several yelps—and a few peeps and shrieks—and the sound of chairs scuffing on tile.

Someone screamed. A tasty-looking shrimp cocktail bounced along the checkerboard floors and came to a jiggling stop about an inch from my smooshed-feeling nose.

For some reason that seemed like the weirdest thing that had happened to us all night.

A little curious (and a lotta worried), I pushed to my knees and peered slowly around and—*well*, pretty much saw what I'd expected.

We'd landed in the middle of a restaurant. One of those ritzy steak and lobster joints overlooking the bay. People in fancy dinner jackets stared at us. A chef in a tall white chef's hat also stared. Then one flour-dusted hand removed his hat, holding it lightly against his apron for a second before his eyes rolled to whites and he promptly passed out.

With about a hundred sets of gaping eyes on us and the local police department just three little numbers away, I knew there was only one way to play this.

And that was *cool.*

So when one of the waiters came rushing over to see if we were all right, I snatched a menu out of his hand and said, "Table for three, please!"

CHAPTER FIFTY-TWO

You've probably heard of dine-and-dash before, but I don't think anyone's ever tried to pull a dine-after-you-crash, so we decided it was probably a good idea to dash instead of dine and just hauled nalgas outta there the first chance we got. Police sirens were already blaring on the next block by the time we piled into a taxi, but fortunately we were able to make it out of Key Biscayne and back to South Miami without any issues. We had the driver drop us off about a twenty-minute walk from my house (that way he wouldn't know where any of us lived and couldn't rat us out if he happened to see us on the news or something). As we walked, we tried to unravel this whole twisted mess with the new bits of info we'd suckered off Caiman.

Shifting the puzzle pieces around in our brains, we tried to put together the thirteen red roosters, the twelve missing people, the earthquakes, and the stolen calaca map, but we really couldn't make it all fit in any kind of way that made a lick of sense. Even our resident Sherlock was starting to get frustrated. What we needed were some comfy chairs, some peace and quiet, and a couple of cups of cafecito to sip on while we did our sitting and thinking.

Only we'd barely walked in through the door to my room when we got yet *another* surprise:

Esperanza de los Huesos was waiting for us, standing by the window and gazing out. Her hands were clasped quietly in front of her, the pale skin of her glamoured face washed even paler by the moonlight.

I blinked. "Esperanza . . . ? Wha-what are you doing here?"

"I was going to wait outside," she said softly, "but didn't want to risk being seen."

"That's *Esperanza?*" Violet asked, saying it like her name tasted awful, like cafeteria broccoli.

The calaca smiled at her. "Nice to meet you."

V didn't smile back. In fact, the look she gave her could've frozen *the Sahara* over. "Yeah, maybe . . . if that's even your real name."

Esperanza's dark eyes found mine. "¿De qué está hablando? What is she talking about?"

I shrugged, feeling pretty embarrassed about the whole

situation. "We ran into your hermano at La Rosa."

Esperanza's glamoured expression hardly changed, but it couldn't hide her shock. "You . . . *did*? Did he mention me?"

"That's practically *all* he mentioned. We know you lied to us, Esperanza."

"Actually," Violet jumped in, "we know a lot more than that. We know that your sister never had any problems hanging around cemeteries, and we know she was never really engaged to a potion-brewing half-croc *psychopath*, and—oh yeah—we know that you don't even *HAVE* a sister!"

Esperanza didn't say anything. Didn't deny a *single* word of it. And Violet didn't let up.

"You're a *liar*," she told her. "You tried to play us. You sent us into harm's way, again and again, each time under a totally fabricated story, and didn't think *twice* about it. You were using us. You were using Charlie!"

"*Using?*" Esperanza echoed in surprise. "All I did was alert you to the presence of a crime syndicate hardly ten miles from here! Those are *bad* sombras doing *bad* things. *Villains!*"

"No one's arguing that," said V. "And I'm sure you probably have an *excellent* reason for putting us on their case. Not that we're ever gonna get the truth out of you. But if we did, I'd be willing to bet a big ol' bag of Reese's Pieces that it would have a lot more to do with you wanting to help *yourself* than anything even *remotely* resembling a good deed. You're a *liar,* and you almost got us *killed.* You're as much a villain as anyone."

Esperanza said nothing; just stood there silently shaking her head. Then she raised a hand as if to wipe a tear away, and Violet said, "Why even fake it? Sombras like you don't *have* feelings. And you certainly don't have tear ducts."

The calaca flinched. The words had stung her—stung her bad. And next moment, she was scrambling past me, scrambling out the door and down the stairs.

Honestly, I had no clue what would've been the best way to handle all that. But I *was* pretty sure that Violet's approach wasn't it.

"Did you have to be so . . . *blunt?*" I said.

V shrugged. "She lied to us. And she didn't even have the decency to tell us *why* she lied."

"Maybe if you would've given her a chance?"

"Why? So she could lie to us some more? I don't think so. Anyway, nothing she can tell us matters right now. What we need to figure out is who's that whistling guy Caiman seems to be so scared of, and how do the roosters, the missing people, and the map of the Golden Dooms all fit together."

"Yeah, but you didn't have to be so *mean,*" said Raúl.

"I wasn't being *mean,*" Violet snapped. "And why are

CHARLIE HERNÁNDEZ & the GOLDEN DOOMS

both of you taking *her* side? Thanks to that walking cadaver, we were almost *croc chow!*"

"I'm not taking anyone's side," I said. "In fact, I'm pretty sure we're all on the *same* side."

Then I went after Esperanza, hoping I could still catch her.

CHAPTER FIFTY-THREE

Esperanza hadn't gone far. She was down in my back-yard, hanging out on the swing set. Her expression was blank, but her glamour was still up, and I could see streaks of fresh tears shining on her pale-pink cheeks. "You okay?" I asked, sitting down on the swing next to her.

The not-so-honest calaca nodded, but she wouldn't look at me.

"So, is it . . . *true?*"

Her slim shoulders went up and down. "Is what true?"

"That you made all that stuff up. That you lied to us—to *me.*"

"You already know the answer to that."

"But—*why?*"

Taking a deep breath, then letting it out slowly, she said, "Because I was scared. And I lie when I'm scared. Actually, I lie all the time. Even when I'm not."

"So what's the truth?"

Esperanza shook her head, staring silently up at the dark trees, the dark sky. "It's late," she said. "I should probably go."

"Afraid you'll turn into a pumpkin?" I teased.

She tried to fight back a laugh but couldn't. It slipped right out of her as she stood to her feet. She had a nice laugh. She said, "A strawberry, maybe."

"Maybe not. Sit down." I smiled at her, and she sat back down. "If you wanted to go, you would've already gone. But you chose to stay, which tells me you wanna talk. So, *talk*."

Her shoulders went up and down again. "I'm not sure what to say."

"Knowing you, you'll think of something. But here's an idea—how about the truth? It's usually simpler that way." When she still didn't say anything, I tried: "Look, either you tell me or I'm gonna have to go see Caiman again. And hopefully he's changed his mind about feeding me to his aunt Gabriella. I don't usually like being invited to dinner when I'm the main course."

With a snort, Esperanza wiped her cheeks. Her skin looked soft and pink and very real, and her eyes were very green. Glamour was an amazing thing. "You really want to know?"

"I really do."

"It's . . . *my parents*," she said, forcing the words out. "Well, my *mother*. *She's* the Puesha! She's the one who revealed the map to Caiman! Unknowingly, of course. That old croc tricked her, Charlie! His henchmen had probably been watching her for *months*. But she'll still be sentenced for this. La Sociedad will sentence my mother to *the Second Death*!" Her voice was a terrified child's. And almost convincing, too.

I sighed. Man, this girl's stories made Paul Bunyan's tall tales seem like *small* tales. "So, first it was your sister. Now it's your mother. Who's next? Your great-uncle?" I shook my head, trying to believe her. *Wanting* to. Even while I knew it was all just another lie. "So how much of that stuff about your mom was actually true?"

Esperanza averted her eyes, looking off into the night. "Muy poquito." Then she turned earnest, childlike eyes on me: "But I do have a mother."

"I bet you do. Is she involved?"

"Not really, no."

"Sure you're not related to Pinocchio?"

"You don't mean that."

"Actually, I do. That's the difference between you and me."

That second jab got through. I saw the flash of hurt in her eyes. It was in her voice, too. "You think I like this?" she whispered after a moment. "You think I *like* to lie?

You think I like *having* to lie? Well, I don't." A small sigh crawled its way up out of the deepest parts of her. It was an exhausted sound. "I give up," she said finally. "I won't lie to you anymore. How's that?"

"Okay, so you're done lying, but when are you going to start telling the truth?"

"What do you mean?"

"How did Caiman really get his hands on that map? Who gave it to him?"

"I don't know."

"Oh, but you do know. Because *I* know."

"Who—who was it, then? I'd certainly like to know."

"I'm sure you would. Because it was *you*."

Her mouth opened a little too wide, and her breath caught a little too sharply—a little too *forced*. And *the Academy Award for best overacting performance by an undead goes to* . . . "Why—why would you say something like that?" Esperanza whispered.

"You mean aside from it being the truth?" I shut my eyes, hating to say it but knowing that it had to be said. "It was you, Esperanza. As much as it hurts me to admit it to myself, and as much as it might hurt you to hear me say it, it was *you* . . . just *you* and only *you*, from the very beginning."

She put her hands on my arm. They were surprisingly

warm against my skin. "Charlie, listen to me. You have it all al revés—*upside down*! I don't have the *slightest* idea how Caiman got his hands on that map! One of his henchmen probably snuck into the underworld through an abandoned graveyard. Then they found a copy and stole it. It's probably that simple!"

"Oh, c'mon, Esperanza! ¿Más mentiras? Yeah, Caiman may have *wanted* to try something like that. But even *he* isn't dense enough to think that any of his scaly-skinned goons would make it more than *ten steps* into the underworld before some spear-wielding watchmen spotted them and made gator soup out of their leftovers! No, he'd know that the only way to steal that map would be with an *insider*...a calaca...a calaca he could *turn*. Even better, a calaca whose father was the Puesha in charge of keeping the map of the Golden Dooms. Am I getting warm?"

Twenty seconds ago, the idea of coronel Diego and Esperanza being father and daughter had been nothing more than a sneaking suspicion. A possibility. I mean, how else could she have gotten close enough to him to steal the secret he'd been charged to keep? Sure, she could've been his niece, or a goddaughter, maybe. But when I saw the flicker of shock in her eyes—*genuine* shock, this time—and heard its tremble in her voice, all my suspicions were instantly confirmed.

"You . . . you spoke to my father?" she whispered.

"Yeah, and he tried to kill me too. Kinda like your brother. Must run in the family."

"But . . . Charlie, think about what you're *accusing me of!*" she said suddenly. "Why would I betray my own father, steal the map for Caiman, and then turn around and turn him in?"

So I told her. "Because you got cold feet, that's why. You were *scared.* Scared what Caiman might do with the map. Who he might sell it to. You had a change of heart. That happens. But it was too late by then. Caiman wasn't about to give it back. So you came to me. And you *specifically* told me not to go to the League of Shadows. *Why?* Because you knew Joanna would've started asking questions. She would've witched you out in a *second.* And you couldn't go to La Sociedad, either, because they would've seen through your lies even faster.

No, you needed to find someone who wouldn't know any better. Someone you could lie to—someone dopey enough to *believe* those lies. And when you realized your first lie wasn't big enough, that it didn't give me enough to go on, you spiced it up a bit, added more layers. And what was the point? What it always was. You wanted us to start sniffing around Caiman and bring you back any evidence you could use against him. Anything that would get him locked up. And you didn't care how far into the croc's mouth we had to stick our heads to get it. As long as it never got back to *you*. You even included that little bit about Caiman love potioning your sister because you assumed, correctly, that I'd know his legend, that he was into potions and stuff, and it would make your lie even more credible. A nice touch, I gotta admit."

Esperanza, meanwhile, just sat there with twin tears tumbling down her cheeks. She didn't look up at me as I said, "You probably figured that with the Morphling poking around, that greedy gator might start feelin' a little *less* greedy. Maybe wouldn't sell the map on, after all. Might even give it back, if I asked him nicely enough."

"Now *you're* the one who's lying," she said in a low, resigned voice. "I never thought any of that."

"¡Por Dios, Esperanza, enough with the lies already!" I shouted. "La Mano Peluda's armies are preparing for an invasion less than *twenty miles* away! And the moment the Golden Dooms are destroyed, those armies are coming. *Here.* To this world! And most likely to *my* backyard!"

She looked hurt now. Genuinely hurt. "Why are you talking to me like this?"

"Because there isn't time for me to talk any other way! Innocent people are going to *die*. Everything we know and love about the Land of the Living is going to be overrun and destroyed by everything we fear and hate from the Land of the Dead! Now it's your turn to talk. ¡Háblame! What's *really* going on?! Why didn't you just tell me the truth from the beginning?"

"Because I didn't think you'd want to help a villain!" she suddenly burst out. And then very softly: "And that's *all* I am. You're right about everything . . . todo. Every single thing you said. It was *me.*"

Breathing hard now, shaking my head, I said, "But why'd you do it, huh? Why'd you give the map to Caiman?"

"Because he offered me the one thing I've always wanted back," she whispered. "*My humanity.*"

CHAPTER FIFTY-FOUR

ot everything I told you was a lie," Esperanza explained. "Caiman *is* a master potioner. And in exchange for the map, he promised to brew me an elixir that would turn me human again."

The surprise in my voice was probably pretty obvious. "That's . . . actually *possible?*"

"In a way. But few potions are ever permanent. And therein lies their thorn."

"How long would it give you?"

"A day. Veinticuatro horas. That was his promise."

"But it wasn't true. I mean, he lied to you?"

"No, he didn't lie. Caiman may be many things, but a liar he is not."

"So he gave you the potion?"

"He gave and I drank."

"And?"

"And here I am . . . flesh and blood." Her hands reached out again, and they touched my arm again, and again I was shocked by their warmth.

Staring at her trembling lips, her tear-streaked cheeks, those sad green eyes, I suddenly realized that it wasn't a glamour, after all. It was just . . . *her*. "You—you're . . . *human* right now?" I whispered, dazed.

"As human as you are. Well, maybe *a little* more." She gave me a watery smile. Then old shame—or regret, maybe—twisted that smile into a bitter frown. "Don't judge me, Charlie. You don't know what it's like not to be able to taste or to feel warmth or cold, or even to see color. You don't have the vaguest idea of what it's like to be cut off from the Land of the Living, knowing that the whole world is dead to you and you to the world. You don't know the bitter sting of death." Her voice broke. All of her seemed to break. "When you've been dead for a hundred years, you'll give anything to live for a day."

Silence fell around us like the night and hung there like a curtain.

At last she gave a bitter laugh and said, "You wanna hear the funniest part? I had all these fantasies about how I'd spend my one day, each and every one of my precious seconds, minutes, and hours. I had all these *extravagant* plans for where I'd go, what I'd taste, what I'd do. But it all seems so . . . so *trivial* now."

"Because you feel guilty?" I said, hardly knowing what to say. This was, like, the saddest thing I'd ever heard. . . .

Esperanza shook her head. Her hair fell across her fleshy, rosy cheeks. Her warm fingers brushed it away. "No. I mean, I *do* feel guilty, and sorry, and scared. But that's not it."

"Then what *is* it?"

"That I forgot the most beautiful thing about being human: the ability to feel *love*." Fresh tears now spilled down her face, and her hands shook a little as she looked at the ground again. "And now there's something on my mind . . . something that I can't get *off* my mind no matter how hard I try, and I know that if I don't do something about it, it will *stay* on my mind for as long as I have a mind, and just the thought of that is driving me *out* of my mind."

"Wha-what is it?" I whispered, and suddenly her dark eyes found mine again and she whispered, "*This*."

Then she kissed me.

CHAPTER FIFTY-FIVE

Ever been pegged in the face in gym class by an over-inflated, badly balding soccer ball while sipping on a Capri Sun and talking to your best friend about last night's episode of *Dragon Ball Super*? Well, I have. And let me tell ya, it's quite the surprise. But it wasn't even *half* as surprising as Esperanza's super-DUPER, super surprising, surprise kiss. No, *that*, my friends, was on a whole 'nother level of surprise—a whole 'nother *planet*! But as the old saying goes: *When it rains, it pours.* And just three seconds later, here came the *deluge*.

"I finally figured it out!" shouted a voice. "Diego is her FATHER!"

And yep, you guessed it—that was *Violet's* voice.

Uh-huh.

Violet's.

Guess I'm just lucky that way.

Whirling, I spun around to face her and saw that she was already standing there, already frozen, her mouth already forming a little O of shock.

I had time to think, *Oh man, oh man. NOT cool!* Then, without a word—without a single word—Violet turned and disappeared back into the house.

I'd just started after her when Esperanza's hand closed around my wrist. Her eyes, large and shining, stared deeply into mine as she whispered, "I fell for you in your stories. And . . . I'm sorry. I'm sorry for *everything.*"

For a split second, all I could do was stare at her, pretty much speechless.

But then my feet were moving and I was gone.

It was super rude, I know. Esperanza had kissed me, and I'd run off after another girl. Now, did I *like* Esperanza? Sure, I did. I mean, she wasn't like any other girl I'd ever met. She was unique. *Different.* And different in the same way that *I* was different. She knew exactly what it was like having to hide your real self from the rest of the world. Exactly what it felt like to be thought of as a "freak," an "outsider." And yeah, she'd lied to me and manipulated me and almost gotten me killed (on *several* occasions). But once you knew *why* she'd done all that, it was kinda hard not to feel for her. Plus, she was, like, a *huge* Morphling fan, and how could you possibly hate on that?

Thing was, I didn't exactly *like*, like her. Not in that way. Then there was Violet. *Ultra Violet*. The biggest, sweetest crush I'd ever had and would probably *ever* have in my entire life. But would Violet ever feel the same way about me that Esperanza did? The same way I felt about *her*? I didn't know. It's one of those things you just don't know until you do. But my abuelita always said that the part of your body most connected to your heart is your feet. And mine chased right after V.

My mom was in the kitchen, whipping up a batch of flan for tomorrow with Raúl lurking nearby, watching her work and salivating when I came in. He glanced my way like, *What's up?* and I whispered, "Gimme a sec," and then caught up with Violet in my room.

She was standing by my bed, staring up at the ceiling, at the loaf of bread my mom had glued up there.

"V, I can explain," I said.

She shrugged. "I don't care about the bread."

"No, I meant about—what you *saw* . . ."

"What's there to explain? The mechanics of kissing are pretty straightforward. I'm not in kindergarten, you know."

"It's not what it looked like."

"It never is."

"What I'm trying to tell you is that she kissed *me*. I wasn't the one who star—hold up. Are you . . . *crying?*"

"No, I'm not *crying*. I'm *angry*! These are *angry* tears! There's a HUGE difference, you know!"

"But—what are you so angry about?"

"That you broke the *number one* rule of investigative journalism, Charlie Hernández!" she erupted. "Never— NEVER *EVER*—fall for *your source*!"

"Wow . . . Didn't know you took that rule so personally," I said.

Violet looked away. Her arms were crossed, her lips pressed into a rigid line. Finally, she said, "She's very pretty."

"Only if you notice that type of thing."

"What type of thing?"

"Pretty . . . *ness?*"

V looked confused. "Is that a question?"

"I don't know. Is it?" Yeah, I was babbling. What can I say? I'd never exactly been what you'd call "smooth."

Violet didn't find it amusing, though. She gave me a real *sharpish* look.

So I tried again. "Listen, all I'm saying is that I haven't really noticed her quote-unquote *prettiness*, okay?"

"Oh? Were your *faces* too close?"

"Hey, I already told you: *She* kissed *me.*"

"Did you kiss her back?"

"I did not."

"Did you consider kissing her back?"

"I did not."

"Did you *want* to kiss her back?"

"I did not." I knew to answer quickly. I'd watched my mom grill my dad in somewhat similar situations (though nothing as serious as kissing someone) and had learned pretty fast that speed was paramount. Honesty was a close second.

Violet said, "Why not?"

And I said, "Why do you care?"

To which she shrugged and looked away again. "Because I just *do*, okay?"

"But . . . it's not like you're my *girlfriend* or anything." And just so ya know, I nearly passed out on that "girlfriend" part. Something about saying that word in front of Violet, and especially *to* Violet, got me feeling all woozy. (I know . . . I get super weird around her.)

"Well, maybe I *wanna* be," she said, and now I SERI-OUSLY almost hit the deck.

"You *huh?* I mean, you *do?*"

She gave another little shrug, still not looking at me. "Maybe."

"Well?"

"Well, *what?*"

"Do you or don't you?"

Her left foot began tapping anxiously on the floor. "Why don't you ask me?"

"I—I think I just did, no?"

"I mean, ask me . . . *nicely.*"

"You mean, like, ask you to go *steady?*"

Her left foot went *tap-tap-tap.*

Her mouth went, "I don't know . . . I guess."

"*Wait.* If I ask, are you *positive* you're gonna say yes? Because I don't wanna ask unless you're gonna say yes. I've been in love with you for *waaay* too long to hear a no, and I don't think I can handle that kind of rejection right now."

Dude, did you SERIOUSLY just say all that out loud? I thought. *And to VIOLET REY of all people?*

My guess was probably yes, because my face was burning so bad, it felt like I'd just visited Hawaii's Mauna Loa volcano for a molten-lava *facial.*

Violet blinked. Her lips barely formed the words as she said, "You . . . *love me?*"

I decided to be honest with her about my feelings. For once. "I—I think so. Can't pinky-swear to it or anything. But, baby, if this ain't love, I don't know what is."

"Those sound like Barry White lyrics."

"Yeah, probably." (My mom's a big fan.)

"It's also arguably the sweetest thing anyone's ever said to me. Think you just beat your own top score, Pac-Man."

Then, summoning all the inner courage I could muster (and I do mean ALL of it), I whispered in a teeny-*tiny* voice, "Hold up, so, do you . . . wanna be my . . . *girlfriend?*"

What came next out of Violet's mouth was only one word. Just one little word. But somehow it seemed to make the entire world around me explode into 8-D Technicolor:

"Uh, *duh.*"

CHAPTER FIFTY-SIX

A t that point, I think I actually passed out. Or at least momentarily *blacked* out. I think I might've said something like "Really?"

And Violet said, "Want me to reconsider?"

And of course I said, "*NO!* No, no, no. Don't *ever* reconsider! Always go with your gut! I hear nine out of ten dentists recommend it." Yeah, I was babbling again.

Then V—or shall I say, *my girlfriend*—frowned. (Ooh, *man*, that sounded good, didn't it?) So I was all like, "What's wrong?"

"I just realized something," she whispered.

"What?"

"I'm not gonna be your first kiss."

Huh. Yeah, that kinda sucked. Except . . . "No, but you can still be my *best*," I said, hoping, praying, fingers crossed, toes crossed, *eyes* crossed—

But suddenly they *uncrossed.*

Suddenly they focused on something.

Something on the floor.

Between my bed and the dresser.

A wrinkly something.

A *scaly* something.

A strip of dried-out snakeskin!

Like the one my mom mentioned having found a couple of days ago behind the fridge.

And just like that, everything clicked together.

The red roosters.

The missing people.

The giant feather we'd found outside one of the houses in Little Havana and the snake tracks and bit of skin we'd found inside the other.

Just like that, the whole sick, twisted scheme made perfect and terrifying sense.

"*Oh my gosh,*" I breathed.

Violet's brows puckered into the shape of a question mark. "Don't people usually wait until *after* the kiss to say that?"

"I know what they're planning."

"Who?"

"Caiman, or whoever he's working for. I know how they're going to destroy the Golden Dooms!"

"How?"

"It's the roosters. The red roosters we keep seeing everywhere!"

"*Roosters*, Charlie? I mean, *c'mon*, if you don't wanna kiss me, you can just say so."

"It's not that. I'm *serious*. It's the roosters!"

Violet stared at me like I had the IQ of a pet rock. "You *honestly* believe that someone is planning to attack the magical equivalent of *Fort Knox* with a bunch of red-feathered *roosters?*"

"It's not the roosters themselves," I explained. "It's what they *lay*."

"Charlie, *roosters* don't lay *anything*. Think you might've missed a biology class or two."

"You mean, *regular* roosters don't lay anything. But cursed *red roosters* do! At least, according to the old myths they do. And according to those myths, it ain't no average chicken eggs they lay either. It's *basilisco* eggs. *Basilisco Chilote!*"

"Basilisco? What's a basilisco?"

"They're monsters. Half serpent, half chicken. According to legend, they burrow deep beneath the houses of their victims and come out super late at night when their victims are fast asleep and feed on their saliva, slowly dehydrating them, until they're big enough—and their victims are weak enough—to just gobble them alive."

V's face went suddenly pale. "Charlie, the boxes of soda we saw stacked in front of Mrs. Sifle's house!"

I nodded. *Uh-huh.* "And all the empty milk cartons and water bottles and soda cans we found inside the other one."

Violet's bright blue eyes locked on mine. "*Twelve* Golden Dooms. *Twelve* missing people. And all *twelve* of their houses are within a couple miles of *La Rosa*. They must've been built *directly* above the spots where the Dooms are buried! The tremors must be the result of those monsters burrowing into the earth, trying to reach the Dooms!"

Arrow meet bull's-eye. She was exactly on target. Whoever Caiman's client was, whoever had sent him after the roosters and the map of the Golden Dooms, was planning a simultaneous attack on the ancient calaca watchmen, mostly because that was the only kind of attack that would work. So they'd had the basiliscos eat the missing people to build up their strength and now had them burrowing deep into the earth, on their way to destroy the Dooms and bring down the great veil between the worlds.

"That's also why Caiman's goons were hired to collect all the missing people's animals!" Violet said. "So that they wouldn't draw any attention to the fact that their owners had gone *missing*. So the basiliscos could burrow without being discovered!"

"Exactly!" See? I was smarter than your average bear—er, *Morphling*.

V blinked. "But how are they going to get past the magical force fields protecting the Dooms?"

Then it hit me.

"Easy. Basiliscos are invulnerable to anything except fire! The magic probably can't even hurt them!"

V hesitated again, but only for a moment. "Wait. So let's assume all that is true, all of it—why thirteen roosters? Caiman said he'd been asked by his mysterious client to get him thirteen, but there're only *twelve* Dooms. So what's the last egg for? Where's it buried?"

And *that*, my friends, was when we got our answer.

Suddenly the floor began to roll, the walls began to moan, the ceiling fan flickered and clicked, and my heart began to pound out a panicky SOS in my chest.

My eyes slid to Violet. "I *think* we just found it."

CHAPTER FIFTY-SEVEN

I got that far, and not another word, before the house *EXPLODED!*

Okay, so maybe "exploded" wasn't exactly the right word. Exploded kind of implies an *explosion.* You know, like a big, fiery *BOOM!*

Well, there wasn't a boom. But the sound of the floor bursting apart—I mean, literally just *erupting* in a cloud of broken tiles and splintery wood—wasn't that much more pleasant.

Then something feathery and scaly and absolutely *TERRIFYING* reared up through the floor, its huge chickenlike head rising on an impossibly long, impossibly serpentlike neck.

A basilisco Chilote!

There it was, in all its plumy, serpentine glory.

Or more like *gory.*

I mean that thing was U-G-L-Y. It *definitely* didn't have no alibi—it was *ugly*! And it was big, too. Ever come face-to-face with a velociraptor? Yeah, me neither. But this thing looked about the size of the ones in *Jurassic Park*, only about three times meaner.

Wings flapping, it leapt up into my room, hissing and crowing, bearing samurai-sword-length fangs, which dripped a sizzly, venomous, greenish liquid. A row of jagged spikes stuck out from its bright-red rooster comb and ran down its leathery, feathery back until they reached the end of its scaly, slithery, scute-covered tail.

The monster looked like a horrible cross between an overgrown rooster and a giant sea serpent. Which, as a matter of fact, was *exactly* what this thing was!

The basilisco Chilote hissed at me. A shiny forked tongue flicked out the side of its serrated yellow beak, and I immediately snatched up the closest weapon: my stack of next week's pre-algebra homework. Hoping to distract the thing—even if just for a split second—I flung the papers sidearm, like a dodgeball, but the monster pecked them right out of the air!

¡Dios mío! I thought. *A basilisco just ate my homework!* Then: *I wonder if any of my teachers would actually buy that.*

At the very least, I was hoping the math problems I'd been working on for Ms. Galvan would give it some indigestion. I knew they sure gave *me* plenty.

Suddenly, Mr. Huge, Scaly, and Ugly lunged. I tried dodging left, but the monster had anticipated that. Its scaly tail sliced around like a whip, catching me square across the chest. Bright pain lit up my entire body. I was flung back against my dresser and smacked my head hard enough to see stars. (And a few planets, too.)

The world teetered. My ribs screamed. Then I heard *Violet* scream, "Charlie, watch out!"

Scrambling up, I dove for my bed even as a giant yellow chicken foot smashed through the spot where I'd been just a split second before.

Deadly talons dug into the tiles, pulverizing them. Had I been even half a heartbeat slower, I would've now resembled one of my all-time favorite side dishes: tostones, aka *squashed* green bananas.

I shouted: "DON'T LOOK INTO ITS OJOS, V! WHATEVER YOU DO, DON'T LOOK INTO ITS EYES!" (Because looking into the eyes of a basilisco meant death—I'm talking Medusa-style *insta*-death.)

The gigantic rooster-serpent let out a hiss of fury. Its ginormous red and yellow wings fanned out wide, and its huge, scaly chest swelled up like a balloon as it strutted toward me like an angry mama bird defending its nest.

And even though my eyes were locked on its deadly tail and its deadly feet, I could still feel its even deadlier eyes—eyes like a *rattlesnake's*—boring a hole in me.

It was clearly *yours truly* it wanted. *Yours truly* that it had been sent to kill. And that didn't exactly make me feel all warm and fuzzy on the inside.

But even less warm and fuzzy making? A heartbeat later, the saliva-slurping abomination lunged, half slithering, half running, but altogether too fast!

I rolled to my right, but I might as well have stood perfectly still. A leathery claw swiped in a blur, snatching me up like some little kid's plaything. Breath like vapory death blasted my face as its massive beak opened wide, revealing row upon row of gleaming fangs.

Right at that moment I found myself in complete, total, and 100 percent agreement with the Chick-fil-A *EAT MOR CHIKIN* cows.

Suddenly something sailed through the air, clunking off the side of the monster's feathery head.

El basilisco hesitated, got ready to strike again, and—*clunk!*—was hit again. Harder this time. And this time it let out a hissing crow of pain.

As the murderous mongrel staggered sideways, slithering and beating its gigantic wings, I wiggled free of its talon, landing on my bed, and looked across the room to see Violet flinging my mom's potted cactuses at the thing. If I hadn't just been staring death in the face just two seconds ago—or, more specifically, in the *beak*—I probably would've burst out laughing. See, in a lot of Latinx cultures, cactuses are believed to protect against evil. And Violet—or shall I once again say, *my girlfriend* (yeah, I was liking that more and more) had basically just proved that old superstition true!

El basilisco, meanwhile, was none too pleased. It hissed at her, crowed at her, its taloned feet stamped the floor, ripping up chunks of tile and wood.

Then, before I could yell, "V, WATCH OUT!" its tail whipped around, quick as a cobra, and slammed into her.

She was flung sideways across the room and crashed through the closet doors, disappearing into a forest of hanging jeans and guayaberas.

At the same moment, the creature's giant chicken head swiveled in my direction. I could feel its serpentine eyes burning into me again but didn't dare look. Instead, I watched its giant chicken feet . . . and they were already strutting this way.

The feathered people-eater came on, slithering and clucking, pecking angrily at the air.

"V, YOU OKAY?" I shouted. But no answer came. Not even an "Uh-huh."

And just as I was about to call out to her again, our diabolical and very much unwelcome house guest lunged, wings beating with the force of a Cat-4 hurricane.

It barreled straight into me—about two thousand pounds of free-range, underground-raised killer chicken-serpent.

The impact knocked me off my feet and punched the air out of my lungs. I could only lie there, pinned beneath its razor-sharp talons, squirming and wriggling like a dying earthworm.

There was honestly nothing I could do. I couldn't even *scream!*

But I *could* smell "the end" coming (or at least the stink of its serpenty breath), and in my head all I could hear were Porky Pig's famous final words, "Th-th-th-that's all, folks!"

All of a sudden the door to my room banged opened, and Raúl shouted, "WHAT THE HECK WAS THAT?" Then, probably spotting the not-so-inconspicuous, HUMONGOUS, scaly soil spawn bearing down on me: "AND WHAT THE HECK IS THAT?"

"HELP ME!" I choked out. My primo didn't hesitate. He leapt forward, and the change from human to werebeast was so fast that I would've missed it if I'd blinked. Claws the size of butcher's knives extended from his fingertips. A mass of shaggy black fur exploded out all over his body like *cha-cha-cha-chia!* growth on super fast-forward.

One second a boy was leaping through the air, and the next a three-hundred-pound werejaguar was lunging for its prey, bared fangs gleaming.

Basilisco and werejaguar clashed in a whirlwind of teeth and talons. My cuz was fast and strong and extremely well trained. I'm talking MMA-fighter-level trained. He hit the monster with a Wolverine-esque combination that should've turned the sucker into a side of snake-flavored McNuggets.

But the basilisco wasn't quite ready to be added to the dollar menu. Plus, the thing was pretty much invulnerable. Not to mention *crafty*. It faked like it was hurt, then counterattacked, lashing out with its terrible tail and catching Raúl right across the stomach.

He was flung backward off his feet. His head banged hard off the wall—leaving a dent in the middle of my Cristiano Ronaldo poster—and he sank to the floor in a cloud of plaster dust, already changing back from kitty-cat to teenage heartthrob.

El monstruo immediately moved in for the kill. Its wide shadow fell over Raúl. Stalactite-like fangs reached for him.

But a split second before it could strike, a figure appeared in the doorway, silhouetted in light.

There was a click. A *twang!* Then something long

and silvery went whistling through the air.

It thudded into el basilisco's scaly end, and a hiss of pain and shock erupted from its roostery end.

Another flash of silver and another something—a dart? An *arrow?*—buried itself in the monster's side, just below a wing.

The creature tottered sideways, talons scrabbling over tile, and then toppled onto its side, hissing and crowing.

My eyes already bugging Looney Tunes style, I turned toward the door and thought: *¡Ay, caramba!*

My mom was standing in the doorway, clutching a . . . a CROSSBOW? The sight was so outta-this-world, so off-the-wall loco *BONKERS* that I found myself rubbing my eyes again and again, just trying to make sure I wasn't hallucinating.

But each and every time my vision cleared and her image swam back into focus, there she was: crossbow raised, eyes slitted, staring down the iron sights like a Cuban Katniss Everdeen.

"MOM, YOU KNOW HOW TO SHOOT A CROSSBOW?" I screeched.

"Baby, if I can teach a roomful of rowdy fourth graders to conjugate Spanish verbs," she said, loading another arrow, "I can teach myself how to handle a crossbow."

CHAPTER FIFTY-EIGHT

In my mom's left hand was a strip of damp-looking cloth, which smelled strongly of alcohol. She wound it carefully around the end of her next arrow. Blasted it with a couple of sprays of Raúl's extra-stench—er, *strength*—cologne. Then brought a long-neck lighter from the pocket of her favorite BESE AL COCINERO apron and—breaking her number one house rule: no fire in the bedrooms—set the rag ablaze. Once the flames had gotten all big and sizzly, making the steel arrowhead glow molten red, she leveled the bow, growled, "Hasta la vista, *basilisco*," then let the burning arrow fly. And with a catch-phrase that cool, how could she miss?

Hint: She couldn't. The arrow found a home above one of the rooster-serpent's brightly feathered wings, and the monster let out a bloodcurdling shriek—a sound somewhere between a terrified billy goat and Sam when he found out that the latest *Guitar Hero* game had been delayed a week. Then its body began to shudder and shiver, its feathers and scaly flesh rapidly melting away, until there was nothing left but a stinking, simmering pile of soot-gray ash.

"Smells like someone ordered KFC," said Violet, rubbing her head as she came limping out of the closet.

Mrs. Van Helsing—er, my mom—smiled. "Yeah, now I just have to add the eleven secret herbs and spices." She turned to me, holding up the sleek crossbow. "Figured a flaming arrow would be easier than burning down the entire house."

Oh, man, that's right! I thought. According to the legends, fire was the only way to kill a basilisco! You had to burn your house down!

"Mom, you know the legends too?" I said, surprised, and my mother gave me one of her looks.

"Charlie, before Nana was your grandmother, she was *my* mother. Of course I know the stories."

Eh. Fair point. "Well, we gotta hurry," I said, pulling on my Zoo Miami Henley. "We have to warn the calacas! There's twelve more of these things!"

"In that case, let me go grab some extra arrows."

"But, tía," said Raúl, "it's probably gonna be dangerous,

and besides for being a pretty good shot, you don't got any real . . . *superpowers*, you know?"

My mom said, "I'm a mother, Raúl. That *is* my superpower." Then she slung the crossbow over her shoulder and started out of the room.

CHAPTER FIFTY-NINE

La Rosa Cemetery was dead quiet (no pun) when we arrived. It loomed out of the night like something old and gray and buried (*ba-da-bump-ching!*) in the ground.

The wind whistled through the spindly trees and the high weedy grass as we slipped inside and began searching the boneyard for the grave that marked the entrance into the world between worlds—the calaca world.

It wasn't hard to find. Graves, like the people in them, are usually pretty stationary. *Usually.* And we found that one right where we'd left it: across from the giant statue of the angel.

However, there was a *teeny little* problem—and by teeny little, I mean gigantic and quite probably *IMMOVABLE*: a five-foot-tall, ten-foot-around, two-ton *mammoth* limestone boulder that someone must've "accidentally" dropped was blocking the entrance.

Violet got there first. "That's one of the boulders we saw inside Caiman's boathouse!"

She was right, of course. It *was* one of those boulders. But even more concerning, it wasn't the *only* one. Scattered about the cemetery, wreathed in mist and shadows, were dozens and dozens more—some as big as doghouses, others as big as *people* houses.

"They're trying to block off the entrances and exits," Violet breathed. "Trying to keep the calacas trapped underground so they can't come up to fight the basiliscos!"

She was right. Again. The question was, seeing as I'd left the keys to my forklift in my *other* shorts, what the heck were we supposed to do about it?

Another thing. Something just didn't *feel* right. Which isn't to say that *anything* feels right when you're standing in the middle of a misty, spooky cemetery at nearly the stroke of midnight surrounded by about five thousand slowly rotting corpses and your mom's waving a Van Helsing–style crossbow around at anything that moves, but you know what I mean.

"C'mon, we're gonna have to push it," said Raúl, waving me over.

Only I couldn't make myself move. There was a silent, eerie vibe in the air—a vibe that had put a quiver in my bones and a chill in my heart.

"Charlie, help us!" shouted my mom.

But still I didn't move. My Spidey-sense was tingling. Okay, fine. Not my "Spidey" sense, per se ... I obviously wasn't part *insect* or anything like that. But the little hairs on the back of my neck *were* up and on their tippy-toes. I could almost sense something prowling among the graves, in shadow. Like secret eyes watching us through peepholes in a painting. Something vague and lurking ... and *close*—

And that's when I heard it. The sound. *That* sound. It came to me on a gust of wind—that awful, unmistakable whistling, faint and far away, like a half-remembered dream.

Or rather, a half-remembered *nightmare*. *Do, re, mi, fa, so, la, ti.*

"GET AWAY FROM THAT BOULDER!" I shouted.

Too late.

Shadows stirred. A blur of movement swept across the front of the limestone rock, sweeping past Violet and past Raúl and past my mom.

Except it didn't simply *sweep* past. It SCREAMED past, with a sound like tearing shadows—and the next moment, the three of them were gone. *Poof!* As if they'd been swallowed up by the night!

Then, suddenly, the blur began to, well, *unblur* ... slowly at first, until I saw that it was more *solid* than *ghostly* and more giant leathery sack than anything else.

It reminded me of something Santa Claus might carry over his shoulder on his way down someone's chimney. But it was a whole lot bigger and whole lot *uglier*, spotted with dark, blotchy stains, crisscrossed with stitches like old scars.

Then I saw something even *uglier* than the sack—a figure, melting out of the shadows of the boulder: very tall and very, very thin, wearing a long black scarf around its bony neck and a tattered, raggedy tunic over its bony frame. Its clawlike fingers were clutched tightly around the neck of the sack, its hollow, glowing eyes peering out of a face of the deepest darkness, and from within that darkness, below the wide, curving brim of an old sombrero, I heard that venomous whistling again: *Do, re, mi, fa, so, la, ti.* Only now it sounded farther away than ever.

In a flash everything clicked for me. Those burning eyes. That awful whistling. The bulging, writhing, blood-stained sack.

That was El Silbón—aka the Whistler! The legendary (and bloodcurdlingly TERRIFYING) Latin American anti-Claus! What I mean is, the guy didn't go around the world handing out presents to good boys and girls—no, he went around the world snatching them up and throwing them into his sack!

I couldn't believe it had taken me *this* long to sniff him

out! How many times had we heard the whistling? I mean, we'd even *seen* the dude! He was the one who'd vanished with Esperanza's brother—scratch that, the one who'd *kidnapped* Esperanza's brother!

¡Si fuera perro me muerde!

But there was no time to get all down on myself. I roared, "Let them go!" and knowing my request had about a snowball's chance in the Everglades of being granted, I charged, intending to rip the sack out of his hand, intending to rip his friggin' *arm* off if necessary.

As it turned out, though, my charge and that snowball had about the same chances of success. See, to say the Whistler was *fast* would be like saying an elephant is *big*. He basically sidestepped me without even trying, driving his pointy, bony elbow directly into the back of my neck. Which, by the way, felt like getting karate-chopped by a *lightning bolt*. And it all happened lightning quick, too.

I barely had time to do more than scream and fold my arms over my head before—*WHAMMM!*—I came crashing back down to Earth like a pigeon shot out of outer space. Pain played a symphony along my back. The agony orchestra cued up the percussion section in my head. My legs felt suddenly weak. My ego felt suddenly small. Doing my best to ignore all that, I pushed slowly, painfully, to my feet and turned to face El Silbón.

The whistling creep was already stalking toward me—
you guessed it—whistling, his dark eyes blazing. "No te
preocupes," he said, hefting the sack over one shoulder,
"your friends aren't dead . . . *yet*." There was a malicious
glee in his hollow voice as he added, "It usually takes a few
weeks before they starve to death. And then many, many
days before I hear the final hollow rattling of *my prize*."

And that was all *I* needed to hear. Just the idea of my
mom, and Violet, and Raúl wasting and rotting away at the
bottom of some disgusting sack of bones made my blood
boil, made rage well up in my heart like a dark, rising tidal
wave.

My pulse began to beat painfully behind my eyes. And
in my chest. And in my hands and feet. Electricity sizzled
over my skin, humming and tingling through every cell in
my body. And then, well, and then it was on. . . .

I could feel the change coming on like a final exam,
strong and savage and completely unavoidable. The animal
inside me had woken up. My blood was on fire. Scratch
that—my blood *was* fire. Superhuman strength surged
into all my muscles.

For a moment the incredible power went silent, still.
Then it just EXPLODED out of me, and I cried out as
that familiar tingle rippled through every part of me.

Pinpricks of heat flared at my temples. They grew

hotter and hotter until a pair of horns, dark and twisted, like an ibex's, pushed out through my skin, curving upward and outward.

Teeth clenched, I curled my hands into fists even as the fingers of my left hand hardened and fused, reddened and then calcified, becoming pincers, claws—a great big *lobster* claw!

But the morphing wasn't over yet.

Suddenly my spine arched, my joints coiled like springs, and a cascade of fluffy white feathers slid over my arms and neck an instant before the back of my Henley shirt instantly blew open as wings—massive, feathery wings!—flapped free.

"Ah, sí! Sí!" cried El Silbón, laughing maniacally. "The legendary horns and feathers of a Morphling! How long it's been since I've seen those!"

My burning-hot eyes fixed on his blazing ones. "I would say it's morphin' time, but we're a little past that now, huh?"

The Whistler grinned. Or at least he seemed to. It was hard to tell with his face looking like nothing more than a pit of shadows. "Did you know that it was I who killed the third of your kind? Oh, sí. I still have the bones to prove it. You will see them soon, te lo prometo. Y no te voy a mentir—I've looked forward to our meeting for *quite* some time now. But the fact is, you are so young and weak. Will you truly be a worthwhile adversary? Or just another *flapping* disappointment?"

"Only one way to find out, whistly."

"*¡Correcto!* And so, I'd like you to meet a few of mis amigos. . . ."

A moment later Caiman's leather-jacket-wearing goons emerged from behind the tombs. Only this time they were all potioned up—more scaly and crocodiley than ever, with massive fanged jaws and skin so dense and thick that even Excalibur would've had a tough time leaving so much as a scratch. Their scales—black and oily—glimmered in the pale moonlight. One of them was holding a chain so thick you could've towed a jumbo jet with it. And attached to the other end of that chain was a gigantic, snarling, two-mouthed monster, the mapinguari!

I gulped. Yeah, that was a whole lotta baddies for one cemetery. I guess you could say that the "scales" had suddenly tipped against me. (See what I did there? Scales?)

Anyway, as they say, the more the merrier.

El Silbón tipped his straw sombrero. His haughty, hollow voice reverberated through el cementerio. "Prove yourself, Cambiador! Usher these along to the Land of the Dead, and so show yourself worthy of battling *me*!"

"Oh, he's quite worthy," said a new voice. "But *we* will be the ones ushering your friends to the other side."

CHAPTER SIXTY

ehind me, two glowing orbs shone out of the darkness. They glowed brighter and greener until they'd resolved themselves into burning emerald-colored eyes, and until a face had materialized itself around them. Joanna's face—Queen Joanna's! The Witch Queen of Toledo!

And she wasn't alone. A figure about as tall as a house (and nearly as wide) emerged from the shadows to join her, and now I was staring up—and I do mean *up*—at the hard, leathery face of Juan the basajaun. His thin lips split into a friendly grin as his eyes met mine; then they pulled back in a fierce, fang-lined snarl as his gaze fixed sharply, darkly on the Whistler.

Around Juan—but, like, *waaay* down low, at around knee height—was what looked like an entire battalion of armed duendes. Usually the little castle elves wore Spanish breeches, pointy hats, and clogs made of rock. But today they were outfitted in steel breeches and steel helmets, glittery chain-mail vests and glittery chain mail-covered shoes. They looked like a bunch of medieval knights on their way to slay some infamous dragon. The only thing they were missing was horses. Oh, and about four feet worth of legs and torso.

At any rate, we now had ourselves a full-on battle royale.

Crew versus crew.

A fair fight.

Maybe.

Probably.

But I hoped not. I hoped we were about to kick some serious gator butt. (Or tail . . . whatever you wanted to call what they had going on back there.)

The gang of gators hissed and snapped their jaws, while the gang of duendes blew their tongues at them and made funny faces, rattling their swords and shields and spears.

"¡ATAQUEN!" cried the Witch Queen, and the duendes instantly leapt into battle. The mischievous pint-size elves and the malicious linebacker-size gators collided in an explosion of ringing steel and flashing fangs.

Next came the big guy, our enforcer. Juan charged.

His massive, furry hands closed around the mapinguari's

huge head, and he slammed it into the trunk of a nearby tree, once, twice, *THREE* times. Like he was playing a game of Smash los Cocos!—and followed that up by flinging the unlucky sloth thing, headfirst, into an equally unlucky group of croc-monstruos, sending them all crashing through about half a dozen different unfortunately placed gravestones on their way to Sleepsville.

Then he grabbed the nearest goon (Mr. Sospechoso, I'm pretty sure), flipped him upside down, and proceeded to Hulk-smash! him into an unmarked grave, burying the hater gator to his waist in the rocky earth.

Now it was Joanna's turn. With a loud shriek, she flung out both hands. Red lightning burst from the tips of her ringed fingers in sizzling arcs. The bolts slammed, simultaneously, into about a dozen different gator guys, hitting them square in the chest, incinerating them on the spot. A charred, tangy smell filled the air. Embarrassingly, my stomach began to grumble. (*What?* Deep-fried gator is totally yums.)

"Someone order a platter of charbroiled reptile?" I said, and then lol'd at my own funny.

Anyway, now it was *my* turn. And I was itchin' to get a-kickin'! So I sprang at the nearest baddie and in my best Bugs Bunny impersonation said, "What's up, croc?" then whacked him clean across the side of the head with my crustacean sensation (aka my giant lobster claw).

There was a satisfying *crack!* and the leather-headed punk went down just as another leather-headed punk came at me from the side. I whirled, ducking and spinning at the same time, and roundhouse-kicked him in the face, scoring an instant KO.

This time I shouted, "FLAWLESS VICTORY!" and told the unconscious croc that he could thank Trini from the Power Rangers for that move. (Truth was, I'd learned some of my best moves from watching the Rangers do work.)

Beside me, the Witch Queen turned to Juan and said, "El saco, por favor."

The basajaun nodded. "Con placer, mi reina."

El Silbón, meanwhile, had just been standing there, watching all this, unbothered to lift so much as a crooked, crusty finger. Now his hollow voice turned mocking as he held out his sack. "Come and take it," he said to Juan.

And Juan—ever the giant gentleman—obliged. A ginormous furry fist flew straight at the Whistler's face. The punch was *fast*. Like, blink-and-you-woulda-missed-it fast. But it wasn't fast enough, because his fist swung through nothing but empty misty air as El Silbón flickered and vanished, reappearing a few feet away.

With a mighty roar, our Basque bigfoot charged once

again. Fangs and claws flashed. Juan leaped and lunged and swiped and the Whistler dipped and ducked and dodged his attacks.

Twice Juan's kicks struck a tombstone, obliterating it. Another time he plowed straight through a huge mausoleum like a diesel-powered bulldozer plowing through a sandcastle.

Then, when the Whistler reappeared a few yards to his left, the basajaun flung himself at him headlong. His massive furry arms had just started to close around the sack-lugging villain's skinny shoulders when, suddenly, El Silbón *poofed* out of sight as though he'd poofed off the face of the Earth . . .

. . . only to reappear again directly behind Juan!

His huge black sack came sweeping down. The opening stretched wide—*impossibly* wide—like the mouth of a greedy python.

And my heart seized up as the sack swallowed Juan WHOLE!

For a moment the basajaun's arms and legs pushed frantically against its sides, trying to tear his way out. But even as the strange, gruesome-looking fabric stretched and strained, it simply wouldn't tear. It *couldn't*! At least according to several of the legends.

Instead, el saco wriggled and wormed, working like a busy small intestine. Like it was *digesting* him! Then the wriggling stopped, and the bag went still, and the basajaun was . . . *gone.*

For several seconds nothing happened. No one moved. Joanna and I stood there in total *I-CAN'T-BELIEVE-MY-FRIGGIN'-EYES* silence, looking on in both terror and shock.

Then, somehow, things got even *worse.* El Silbón began to change. His body stretched. His stick-thin arms and legs thickened. Bony shoulders hunched, broadened, then began to swell and swell until they threatened to tear his tunic. I watched the shadows around him darken. I watched them deepen. I watched them transform into pits of swirling, lightless black.

I didn't think—just charged toward him screaming, "JUAN!" But even before I could raise my claw—*¡Dios mío!*—the Whistler vanished again!

Panting, my eyes frantically searching the misty tombs, I yelled, "Where'd he go?"

And that's when I heard the queen cry, "¡CHARLIE, DETRÁS DE TI!"

I blinked, and Joanna was right on top of me. Shoving me sideways. A blur of darkness swept through the spot where I'd just been standing.

The Whistler's sack! I realized. And if Jo hadn't shoved me out of the way, it would've gobbled me up!

As it was, the sack only gobbled *her* up.

"JOANNA!" I screamed. But it was too late. El saco was already wriggling, already squirming, and El Silbón's form was already changing—changing yet again!

Clawlike daggers curled out of his fingers. He grew taller. His raggedy tunic ripped in two as his body seemed to double in thickness. The shadows of his face became even deeper, darker, and flames—yeah, legit *flames*—spat from the sunken holes of his eyes, sending up curls of thick black smoke.

Magia was pouring off him in waves. In *tsunamis*. And finally I began to understand the type of power I was dealing with here. It was a power like I'd never felt before—a power as vast as space, as old as time. It sizzled and burned. It crackled and churned. Waiting. Just waiting to destroy.

As if that weren't bad enough, I was suddenly struck by a horrible realization: the sack-wielding freak was somehow absorbing everyone's power! Somehow feeding off the life force of every single person he captured in his sack!

And if I'd had roughly a *one* percent chance of beating this dude before, back in his old shrively form, that percentage had just taken a rather *sharp* nosedive. I wondered if there was an algebraic formula specifically designed to calculate numbers that ridiculously small. If there was, I figured Ms. Galvan would probably know it. Maybe I'd ask her one day. In another life, of course, because this one looked like it was about to come to a very abrupt, very *violent* end.

El Silbón let out a peal of wicked laughter, which boomed through the cemetery, rattling the tombs and graves and thundering against my bones. "¡Sí!" he cried. "¡Sí! Now, this—*this* is POWER!"

CHAPTER SIXTY-ONE

There were about five or six duendes still standing and no one from Team Whistler (except the Whistler himself, of course). But that lasted, oh, about two seconds as the bone-collecting creep went blurring between the graves so fast that he made the Flash look like the Sloth, gobbling up all the little castle fairies with his nightmarish saco. Then twin columns of black smoke curled up from his blazing eyes as the ghoul stalked toward me, his footsteps making the ground tremble.

Now, *usually*, when faced with the most terrifying thing you've ever encountered in your whole entire life, the smartest strategy is to turn tail and head for the highest hill. But South Florida didn't really have any hills, and no one had ever accused me of being smart. That was Violet's thing. Mine, I guess, was courage. Not courage *instead* of fear, because I was usually pretty afraid—heck, I was *ter-*

rified right now!—but courage *in spite* of fear. The courage to act. And that's really the only thing anyone can ask of themselves.

At any rate, I wasn't about to run. Pretty much everyone I knew in this world—everyone I *cared* about—was inside that freak's saco. Not to mention our only hope of stopping the basiliscos. Because without Joanna, I didn't see how in the world we were supposed to stop *twelve* of those things. So instead of running away from El Silbón, I did just the opposite: I ran *toward* him. I charged!

And then I quickly learned why charging terrifying, leveled-up, infamous supervillains isn't usually the best move. El Silbón hit me. Well, that doesn't *really* describe what happened, so let me try that again. His arm rose. His left hand came up in an arc, sort of like an uppercut, and connected with my face—right below my chin. And just like that, every last scrap of momentum I'd built up over the course of my charge was *instantaneously* reversed. It was as if someone had hit x10 rewind. On THE WORLD!

My body hurtled backward through the dark. Wind screamed in my ears. My head bounced off a boulder, my back smashed through a gravestone, my butt banged off the ground, and the rest of me thudded painfully off a rectangularish tombstone that was sticking up, half-crooked, out of the stony ground.

Honestly, it felt like I'd been whacked by a giant fly-swatter. Or like someone had dropped a house on top of me. A very *big* house. Suddenly I felt very sorry for the Wicked Witch of the East.

Grimacing, clenching my teeth against a wave of dizziness, I rolled over and spat something up. It felt like a lung. Fortunately, I think it was only my bottom left molar.

My head spun and my legs nearly gave out as I struggled to my feet, turning to face El Silbón again.

The indestructible boogeyman was already marching this way, slipping through the shadows like a predator hunting its prey. His voice made the graves quake: "I have broken La Liga de Sombras, and now I will *break* the line of Morphlings. You have failed, Carlito. Just like the four before you. And just like the four, you too shall be swallowed up in *DEATH!*"

Lowering myself into a crouch, I said, "Maybe. But not before *you* swallow *my fist!*" And suddenly I flung myself at him again.

Now, I know ... I know. What's the definition of insanity? Doing the same thing over and over and expecting a different result. Which is true. But I wasn't *planning* on doing the same thing again. I only wanted to make it *look* like I was. See, this time I wasn't gonna try to outfight him. This time I was simply gonna out*smart* him. My target was no longer El Silbón. It was his sack. If I could just get in real close like, close enough to drag my claw along its coarse, bloody side, then maybe—*maybe*—I could tear it open and free everyone inside. It was a long shot, sure. Like, Pinky and the Brain's plans-for-world-domination type of long shot. But hey, even they'd sort of gotten close on a couple of episodes, right?

With a great thrust of wings, I hurled myself through the dark, zooming between the graves and running even as I flew. About five yards away, I kicked my right leg out, in sort of a baseball slide, hoping to slide by the sack real nice and low.

But next thing I knew, the Whistler's bare and dirty foot came straight up in a massive soccer kick that would've made Lionel Messi jealous. The impact was ridiculous. It hit me so solidly and so *brutally* that at first, I didn't even feel any pain. I didn't feel anything at all, in fact. All I knew was that one second I was zooming through the air, and the next I was doing my best crash-test-dummy impersonation, arms and legs flapping, body flopping, head banging and bouncing and crashing through every tombstone in sight.

When I finally—*mercifully*—rolled to a stop, I saw about three Silbóns stalking toward me. And I was pretty sure it wasn't some kind of super sombra power.

"Even as we speak," said the legendary ghoul, "my basiliscos are tunneling ever deeper underground. Soon they will reach the Golden Dooms and destroy them, opening the veil to the Land of the Dead, where our armies stand ready. The Land of the Living will fall. The dead will once again reign. And you, little Morphling, can do *nothing* to stop that." Santa's evil anti-twin was looming over me now, looking about a hundred feet tall and as dark as death. "La Mano Peluda sent me to kill you," he murmured, "and though great glory awaits me with the completion of my mission, I still find myself un *poquito* disappointed. I'd hoped the last of your line would have put up a better pelea. But I cannot say I'm surprised. In the end, your kind always dies. Que tengas dulces sueños," he whispered evilly, raising his sack. "Sweet dreams."

The sight of its saggy, sinister mouth was like a shot of fear straight to the heart. I could practically see a jumble of falling arcade letters spelling out: GAME OVER.

Too hurt to move, too scared to scream, I did the only thing I could: I waited—just held my breath and waited for the long, fast fall into a deep, dark sack, thinking, *Somebody cue the ominous scary movie music.*

CHAPTER SIXTY-TWO

This is gonna sound really silly. But some dim and dazed part of me *actually* expected to hear some of that scary movie music. (What can I say? Maybe I'd watched too many scary movies.)

Fortunately, though, the music never played. And not *just* because this was real life. But *also* because El Silbón never got me. See, an instant before he could sweep his sack o' death down to swallow me up—a *split second*, really— something flashed behind him, and he let out a startled, stinging cry and stumbled sideways.

And that's when I saw it. Or rather, *them*. A figure, standing behind him, silent in the silent night. Hooded, clutching a gleaming saber, it didn't say anything—not a single word as it circled slowly, cautiously, until it had put itself directly between me and El Silbón, forcing the ghoul back at sword point.

Then, in a flash, that sword arched upward, a glimmering whitish blur, and a cry erupted from the Whistler's unseen lips.

The bone-collecting fiend fumbled backward. His bare, crusty feet tangled underneath him, and he went down in a heap, collapsing onto his sack before finding his balance again and pushing slowly to one knee.

At the same moment, the figure turned to face me. And at that moment, a shimmering column of moonlight pierced the clouds, lighting up familiar hazel eyes.

Honestly, if my eyeballs hadn't been firmly secured to the inside of my head, they would've popped right out—because the figure was *Esperanza!*

"¿Estás bien?" she asked me. "Are you all right?"

Grinning—partly in shock, partly in overwhelming, unspeakable *RELIEF*—I shook my head. "No . . . But I'm definitely starting to feel better."

Esperanza grinned back, moonlight glinting off the deadly edge of her big sword as she held it up. "Calaca blades are formed from the tusks of the elder mammoths and forged with the most ancient magia. There's nothing in this world they cannot cut."

She faced the Whistler again. Her sword flashed again. This time the blade screamed—I mean literally *screamed*—through the air, and the scream that tore from El Silbón's lips shook the cemetery. Probably shook *the world*.

Then, with Olympic-level fencing form, Esperanza lunged forward, burying the sword deep in his chest and twisting the hilt. Black liquid, thick as tar, oozed around the sunken blade.

A cold wind moaned through the lonely graveyard. The grass rustled and swayed around the forgotten tombs.

I saw El Silbón's flaming eyes dim. I watched his shoulders sag and his head bow low like some giant robot who'd just gotten its batteries yanked out.

Then he began to weep.

Or at least it *sounded* like he was weeping. At first, anyway. But soon the weeping sound became a huffing sound, and then a chuckling sound, and finally a gust of maniacal supervillain laughter that sent a haunting chill through every cell of my body.

"You truly believed your silly bone blade could kill me?" he sneered at Esperanza. "You'll need more than the trinkets of the undead to still this dark heart."

The Whistler rose now, towering over Esperanza. His taloned fingers curled around the handle of the sword still buried in him and he yanked it free, tossing it back over her head in a lazy arc.

The calaca sword flashed and bounced along the ground, clanking off a granite gravestone about five yards away. Then El Silbón's burning gaze met hers. His eyes were no longer dim, but blazing—like exploding miniature suns!

And an instant before I could scream, "Esperanza, LOOK OUT!" a column of boiling hellfire erupted out of his mouth—a beam of such concentrated and destructive energy that it made Superman's heat vision look like a squirt of cold water from a Super Soaker.

Esperanza flew backward, struck full-blast by the force of it. Her body smacked off a nearby tree so hard it made a shower of dead leaves rain down from the high branches.

A soft moan escaped her as she slumped lifelessly to the ground, and I immediately rushed over. Taking her wrist, I felt for a pulse—

And almost cried out in relief when I felt one!

She was still alive. If only barely.

"I'm sorry," she murmured, squeezing my fingers.

"*Shhh* . . . It's all right," I said. "You don't have to be sorry."

"But I am . . . I'm sorry about everything. For lying to you. And to your friends. For getting all of you involved in this twisted mess. There's only one thing I'm not sorry about."

"What?"

"Meeting *you*." Her eyes were closed, but her trembling

fingers groped in the grass until they found what they were searching for. Then her hand closed around the sword's leather-wrapped handle, and she dragged it painfully over as if it weighed a thousand pounds.

Pressing it into my hands, she breathed, "Take it. It can cut through anything. Free your friends."

"That's not enough," I whispered. "He's too strong now." But Esperanza never heard it. She was out before I could utter another word.

CHAPTER SIXTY-THREE

I t was all I could do not to shut my eyes and lie down in the weedy grass beside her, counting the seconds to the inevitable—that is, the Whistler coming over and shoving us both into the deep dark belly of his sack.

And I was still staring down at that ancient weapon of the undead (and still pretty much ready to give up) when a voice spoke up inside me. It was a strong voice. A familiar voice.

It was my *grandmother's* voice.

My abuelita's.

The voice that was always with me, ever since I was little—every time I got into trouble, felt weak or sad, or just needed someone to talk to.

It wasn't magic or anything like that. It was just the memory of her. But when you love someone enough, that bond can become stronger than any magic, and even their memory can give you strength.

And that's exactly what her memory gave me. *Strength.* I could feel it rising in me even now, like a fountain of water, fresh, bubbling, life-giving water, right there in the desert of my fear.

And suddenly I wasn't so afraid anymore. Because suddenly I didn't feel so alone anymore.

Think back to las leyendas, Carlito, my abuelita's voice urged me. *Remember . . . remember the Legend of El Silbón!*

So I tried. I closed my eyes and traveled back through time, back to when I was a little kid, back to the living room of my old house, to lazy Saturday afternoons hanging out with my grandmother and my coloring books—all the way back, back, back to when the only things that really mattered were her stories and her smile, and the way her eyes lit up and her brown and wrinkled hands painted pictures on my heart. The pictures of myths that I would never forget, the very stories that would forever fascinate me. That would one day *save* me.

And then I remembered. I remembered *his* story. El Silbón's. The legend of a spoiled young brat. Un mocoso. A guy who always whined and complained until he got what he wanted. And I remembered how, one day, he craved deer meat for dinner, so he sent his father out to hunt for some. But when his father returned empty-handed, the young man went into a wild rage, and in his rage, he murdered his father. When his mother found out about it, she had the boy's grandfather punish him for this great evil. The grandfather whipped the boy and rubbed hot peppers in his wounds and even sent a pack of vicious hunting dogs after him. So the boy fled from home, scarred and forever terrified of whips and dogs; and the curse his mother had pronounced over him changed him into something between human and ghoul—no longer among the living but not exactly a muerto, either. He was condemned to roam the plains for all time, carrying a sack of his father's old bones.

That story had been passed down through the generations as a cautionary tale. And it was never my abuela's favorite to share. But boy was I glad she'd shared it, because just like that, I knew what I had to do.

And, just like that, I knew *exactly* how to do it!

An echo of her words came back to me then, a saying of hers: *Monsters are the biggest cowards of all,* she would remind me after telling me a scary story. *That's why they're always hiding in the dark!*

I smiled at the memory. Smiled on the inside.

I know, Abuelita. I remember now.

Brushing a soggy green leaf from Esperanza's face, I whispered, "I'll finish this."

Then I turned to face El Silbón. He was still striding menacingly toward us, maybe ten yards away now. I shouted, "Hey, I feel sorry for you, dude! I really do!"

"¿*Qué?*" he sneered, shouldering his heavy sack.

"I said I feel sorry for you! I know your story. It's pretty horrible, man. . . . Tragic even."

That stopped him—stopped him dead in his tracks. "You know NOTHING about me!" he roared, smoke and hellfire boiling up around his face, wreathing his head like some volcanic crown.

"Oh, but I do!" I shouted. "The truth is that some of the worst people in the world have the most tragic backstories." But then I thought about Esperanza and everything my grandma had gone through, and even Queen Joanna and Saci Pererê, one of my best friends in the entire world, and I said, "But so do some of the *best* people. What I'm saying is that it's *your* choice. Good or evil, dude. It's just a choice. And the best part? You get to make it. So I'm gonna give you one more chance. Una más. One chance to change, but that's the best I can offer you, and I'm only gonna offer it once."

"¿CREES QUE PUEDES NEGOCIAR CON-MIGO?" he raged, making the entire cemetery quake. "I'VE ALREADY *DEFEATED* YOU! ¡Y AHORA I WILL *FINISH* YOU!"

"Como quieras," I said. *However you want it.* Then I squeezed my eyes shut, took a deep breath—and began to bark.

CHAPTER SIXTY-FOUR

Yeah, I know. I probably looked like a total *goof*. A super goof. But barking was one of the things that I knew from his stories he was most terrified of, and it was the one thing I knew just might be able to rattle him.

And rattled was *precisely* how I needed him.

Anyway, at first my barks were—well, *weak sauce*. They had no punch. No *bite* (no pun). They sounded like a regular ol' human trying to *imitate* a dog. Which, of course, was pretty much the case.

But then I felt that familiar tingle of an oncoming manifestation. And then it was morphin' time—or shall I say Morph*ling* time.

My nose flattened, squished, turning sort of black and rubbery. Next it started to lengthen, right along with my jaw and mouth, and together they stretched and stretched until they'd formed a sleek, furry, doglike snout! Kookiest part, though? In the span of ten or eleven barks, my voice had completely changed too, dropping several octaves, becoming more throaty, more snarly, more feral and vicious—as authentic a doggy bark as had ever been barked by any doggy. *Ever!* And that was because it was my awesome new doggy face doing the barking!

Man, I just *LOVED* being a Morphling sometimes!

El Silbón, on the other hand, wasn't quite as impressed. His body had tightened with panic. With fear. He clamped the black shadows of his hands against the sides of his shadowy head and cried, "¡CÁLLATE! ¡CÁLLATE, NIÑO INSOLENTE! ¡CÁLLATE YA!"

But I wasn't about to stop. In fact, I did just the opposite—barking harder, louder, *meaner.* And suddenly the ol' bone snatcher couldn't take it anymore. A horrible, unearthly shriek of mingled fear and fury exploded from his unseen lips, and he charged me—headlong, blindly, without even bothering to turn into his vapory, ghostly self.

Which was a mistake.

And not only a mistake, but the *exact* mistake I'd been hoping for!

So I waited—just holding my ground and watching him charge until he was practically right on top of me, bearing down like a runaway train, the black mouth of his sinister sack gaping open to gobble me up, to swallow me alive.

Then I made my move. Ducking down, I snatched up Esperanza's calaca sword and swung it sidearm, clean across the belly of his sack, even as I dove out of the way. The serrated edge bit into the coarse fabric like a mouthful of hungry teeth. But for a heart-stopping moment nothing happened. And I couldn't help thinking that the blade had simply slid harmlessly off the sack! Only, that wasn't what happened at all. What *happened*—or rather, what I *heard*—was a roar of tearing cloth, followed by a sound like the Earth itself being ripped violently apart. And every grave within two hundred yards rolled—rolled like an ocean wave—as an incredible shock wave of energy, of black magia, exploded outward, ripping through the cemetery like a tornado and sweeping me off my feet.

I sailed almost thirty yards through the air before crash-landing against the cold, unforgiving block of a tombstone. My head smacked hard against the stony edge. Grass and dirt and bits of brownish fabric showered over me. The world teetered, tottered. Bright spots danced in front of my eyes even as I watched El Silbón's sack rip and sag, shredding like a piece of fraying rope, spilling out bodies and bones like guts. A rotten, putrid smell choked the air. The sack's contents came pouring out in a mighty avalanche. They piled up, up, up, nearly sky-high, massing into a mound that might've given Mount Kilimanjaro a run for its money. (Maybe we could call it Mount Deathaman-jaro?) And among the bones and raggedy strips of clothes, I saw Violet and my mom, I saw Raúl, I saw Queen Joanna and Juan, and all the little duendes. Oh, and Esperanza's brother, too. (He was the hardest to spot, being pretty much just bones himself.)

Every single one of them looked dazed and confused and completely disoriented, but they were alive—alive and kicking—struggling out of the mountain of ancient bones, and the sight sent an equally massive avalanche of relief crashing over me.

El Silbón, meanwhile, was looking on in utter dismay. He screamed, an awful, wailing shriek (*DO, RE, MI, FA, SO, LA, TI!*) that stabbed my eardrums and made me wish I could morph a pair of Bose noise-canceling headphones.

A moment later, he began to change again. His skin shriveled and his body thinned. His fingers and toes curled back on themselves, the tendons and joints swelling into lumps even as liver spots bloomed on his arms like ink splotches. His back hunched. His bones drooped. The once-fiery eyes dimmed, darkened, and then whiffed out, like dying candles, leaving only the empty, hollow sockets of eyes. I blinked, watching as every ounce of muscle on his body, every ounce of fat, rapidly dissolved until all that was left was a ragged, withered, wasted skeleton-man. Not quite a calaca, but not quite human, either.

Watching all this go down, I couldn't help grinning like I'd just won the latest special edition Xbox or something! I mean, I'd done it! I'd defeated El Silbón! The Whistler would never again imprison another living thing in that nasty old saco of his!

And the next moment the ghoul was on the run, sackless and frail-looking, stumbling away on twig-thin legs, and Juan was already after him.

I grinned some more. Served the punk right. More than right, actually. Because that tune-whistling supervillain had been terrorizing people for longer than I'd been *alive*.

But this wasn't over yet, I realized with a pang of panic.

The basiliscos were still tunneling toward the Dooms. Still on their way to destroy them! And if those monstruos succeeded, La Mano Peluda's invasion was on.

CHAPTER SIXTY-FIVE

My plan was simple: Stop los basiliscos. And stat! But in order to stop those scaly, overgrown, almost unkillable killer chickens, we needed the locations of the Golden Dooms.

And there was only one group of sombras on the entire planet that knew where all twelve were buried.

"Joanna!" I cried. "The boulders! They're blocking the graves! Trapping the calacas underground!"

She got me pretty quick. With a nod, she flung both hands out in front of her, palms up. Then, as she raised them above her head, muttering some secret spell, the boulders went with them, levitating right off the ground like someone had flipped the reverse switch on gravity!

Trailing weeds and bits of smashed headstones, the massive limestone rocks shivered into the air and then just hovered there for a sec, like some floating alien planets, before la bruja, letting out a single earsplitting cry, sent them screaming off into the night.

A heartbeat later, the ground began to tremble. Then the now unblocked graves suddenly came alive, *Thriller* music video style, and clumps of earth and grass and rock sprayed up as a literal swarm of calacas started clawing their way out of the world between worlds like a colony of very angry, very *large* zombie ants.

There must've been thousands of them. No, *tens* of thousands! All sporting elaborate feathered headdresses and bony spears. Which made it pretty obvious that these weren't your regular ol' calacas, either. No, these were the warriors of Lady Death herself, the ancient Bone Guard!

At that point I expected to see them form battle lines—y'know, like you see in all the old war movies—as they began marching toward the basilisco's burrows.

But that wasn't what happened. Not at all. What *actually* happened was way more unexpected. And WAAAAY cooler!

Dropping their headgear and spears, the calacas began pulling themselves apart—arms and legs and ribs and feet. Then they began to fit themselves together. Only not *back* together, mind you, but ALL together—as in, to *one another*, so that a thousand shin bones now formed a single shin and a thousand spines now formed a single spine. They clicked and clacked and fused, like the world's largest (and *freakiest*) puzzle, until they'd formed giant walking skeleton things! Almost a dozen of them! And when I say giant, I'm not talking André the Giant giant (even though he *was*, obviously, pretty big), I'm talking King Kong kinda giant. Like, five hundred feet tall and fifty feet wide kinda giant!

The graveyard trembled and headstones rattled as the squad of bony skyscrapers began to march, fanning out in every direction. I watched the closest one travel maybe three hundred yards south (which took it all of *three* steps), and then it bent and squatted, reaching a ginormous bony arm deep into the earth, and a moment later came up with a hissing, squawking, flapping basilisco! Not too far away, another giant skeleton-man ripped a massive oak tree, roots and all, right out of the ground with about as much trouble as plucking a blade of grass. It set the leafy top ablaze by dragging it across its thigh bone like a mammoth matchstick, then tossed the flaming tree over to its buddy (the one holding the basilisco by its scaly tail), who used the tree like a titanic torch, touching the crackling greenish flames to the rooster-serpent and instantly incinerating it.

All around La Rosa, the other giant skeletons were doing the exact same thing, digging the monsters out of their burrows and charbroiling the things like it was fish-fry Friday or something. The smell was awwwful, though. Think dumpster barbecue.

Trying not to hurl on myself, I looked slowly around and spotted Violet. She was lying near a headstone, sorta pushing to her knees, sorta swaying in dizzy little circles. "V!" I burst out, and had just started toward her when I felt the strangest thing: something like a big, icy fist squeezing my insides.

The pain was so sharp, so sudden, and so incredibly HUGE that I didn't even have time to scream. I just sank straight to my knees, clutching my chest, as the world began to wobble again.

The night seemed to be growing quieter, darker, and I could feel myself growing quieter and darker along with it.

The last thing I remember was seeing Joanna rushing toward me, her long silky gown fluttering in the night, shouting something, and Raúl running with her.

Then everything went black.

CHAPTER SIXTY-SIX

I woke with a start. I was on my back, lying in a . . . a . . . *forest*, it looked like. The air was cool and fragrant, and the ground was soft and dry. Lush green leaves formed something like a ceiling overhead, and the thick, gnarled trunks of ancient trees formed something like walls.

I realized I was sprawled out on a bed of pillowy grasses, shredded coconut husks, and pine cones.

So, not a random forest, then. More like . . . a room.

As I blinked dazedly around, my first thought was: *How in the frijoles did I end up here?* And before I could even get to my second (which I suspected was probably gonna be something in the neighborhood of: *And where in the arroz con pollo WAS here?*) a voice spoke up from nearby:

"Buenos días, Charlie," and I turned to see Queen Joanna, El Cadejo, and the curupira girl I'd met in the woods near the Witch Markets standing there. They were all watching me with small, pleased smiles on their faces. The curupira was clutching her feathered spear.

"Hey, wha—where are we?" I asked, my words coming out like leche condensada—all slow and a little sticky.

"We currently find ourselves in South America," answered la bruja. "Inside an old Provencia in the curupira-controlled lands of the western Amazon basin. We brought you here because you were not doing too well after your battle against El Silbón. The amount of dark magia you absorbed upon releasing us from that cursed saco would have killed nearly any living thing. Perhaps even myself included. But, fortunately, your blood is strong, and you held on long enough for us to bring you here." Her eyes went to a bedside table, where there was an assortment of small wooden bowls. One was filled with mashed sticky leaves. Another with a dried pinkish powder. A third with hissing, bubbling, greenish liquid. The smell was strongly herbaceous, something between Vicks VapoRub (my mom's favorite cure-all) and oregano extract (my dad's favorite). "The curupira know the secrets of La Selva, and their herbs can cure nearly all that ails."

¿Cómo te sientes, Carlito? asked El Cadejo, placing a massive furry paw ever so gently on the center of my chest. Then, dipping his huge, white-maned head, he dragged his big ol' doggy tongue across my nose. (What can I say? The guy was just friendly like that.) He nuzzled my neck, saying—er, thinking, *Luces mucho mejor.*

"Yeah, I feel pretty good," I admitted, stroking his dense, silky fur.

You have your friends to thank for that, he told me. *For hours Violet sat here, just where I stand, feeding you the curupira tinctures.*

Violet. Just her name had me sitting bolt upright in bed. "Is she here?" I breathed. "Is she good? And what about my mom and Raúl? Are they okay?"

Smiling softly, Joanna motioned for me to relax, to lie back. "They are all *fine,* mi niño. . . . Everyone's *fine.*"

"So we won, then, huh? I mean, it's over. The calacas stopped los basiliscos. La Mano Peluda won't be able to come back, right?"

El Cadejo's shining mane appeared to darken for a moment. His large, wise eyes fixed on mine as he said, *I am afraid that there will always be ways for the dead to return, Carlito . . . siempre.*

I didn't like the sound of that. Well, *the thought,* anyway. In fact, I was just about to tell him *how much* I didn't like it when the image of someone's unconscious face sliced into my thoughts like a screaming sword.

I sat bolt upright again. "Esperanza! The calaca girl. Where is she? What happened to her?"

Fear had risen in my throat like a stone, making it hard to breathe. But El Cadejo nuzzled me back against my pillows, pulling the sheets over my shoulders with the tips of his pointy teeth.

She is not hurt, if that's your concern, he thought softly.

La bruja was nodding her head in agreement. "No, but she has committed a high crime against her kind, and for that, there will be consequences. . . ."

"But she didn't *mean* to!" I said. "I mean, she *did* mean to. But she realized that she'd made a mistake. She tried to fix things. Plus, she saved my life. Without her, I wouldn't have been able to beat El Silbón. The calacas need to know that."

"I am not a judge among the dead, Charlie. I do not know what will become of her. But I will certainly make sure La Sociedad knows how you feel." The ageless Spanish Queen looked straight at me now. Those strange emerald-colored eyes appeared to burn. Even in broad daylight. "In my many years, I've learned that the mistakes we make rarely reflect the true character of our hearts. I've also learned that in the end one always gets a chance to prove their true worth."

"Well, Esperanza proved hers," I said. She'd proved it as much as anyone.

El Cadejo's snowy head dipped again. The brightness of his fur and the radiance of his presencia wrapped around me like warm starlight. *The world is a strange place full of creatures making strange decisions that they do not fully understand. But it is not for us to judge those decisions, only to love the creatures.*

After that everyone was silent for a while. At last Joanna said, "There is much more for us to discuss, Charlie. But ahora is neither the time nor the place. We will leave you por un ratico so that you may talk with your friends. They are all eager to see you."

Beside her, the curupira girl's lips suddenly split into a friendlyish grin. It was a wild grin, too. As wild as her fiery orange hair and the streaks of blue and yellow war paint on her beautiful brown skin. "I recognize the face," she said.

"Huh? *Oh.*" I glanced down at my T-shirt. It was one of my Miami Heat championship tees. My mom must've put it on me when I was busy countin' sheep. "That's, uh, D-Wade . . . Dwyane Wade. The basketball player?"

"Not his face. *Your* face." Her grin widened. Her dark, wild eyes smiled into mine, and I couldn't help smiling back. "Tchau," she said, waving at me with her spear.

"See you soon, Charlie." The Witch Queen touched a gentle hand to my cheek. "Nos vemos." Then she pointed at the large bronze door on the other side of the little meadow—er, I mean, *room.* The door appeared to have been built right into the wall of tree trunks. Or maybe the trees had just grown up around it. Either way, it was a pretty cool door. Only I wasn't sure why she'd pointed it out. But when I turned back to ask her, she was gone. And so were El Cadejo and the curupira.

A split second later, the door opened. And through it I saw a familiar sight: the grand sweeping bookshelves of the great library inside La Provencia in North Miami Beach.

Then I saw an *even more* familiar sight: the smiling, happy faces of Sam, Alvin, and my cousin.

"PRIMO!" Raúl shouted, charging toward me. He jumped onto the leafy, coconutty bed, throwing his arms around me and basically squeezing my eyeballs out of my face. I thought I heard something snap. I hoped it was just a pine cone.

"Ay, my bad." Raúl pulled away, giving me a sheepish (or would that be *jaguarish?*) smile. "Ocēlōtl strength."

Then I noticed something odd: shiny tracks of wetness gleaming on his cheeks. "Bro, have you been *crying?*" I asked.

He shrugged like there wasn't a thing in the world he could do to help it. "Was worried about you, primo."

"But weren't you the guy who said real men don't cry?"

He shrugged again, still grinning at me. "I was wrong, cuz. I spent some time thinking about all that stuff you told me and realized you were absoultamente right. I mean, I've heard all your stories; you pretty much cry all the time, and look how strong and courageous you are!"

"Hey, *easy there.* I don't know about *ALL THE TIME* . . . but yeah, I'm not afraid to show my feelings."

"Exactly! You opened my eyes, primo! No more of this *I'm-a-man-I-gotta-be-tougher-than-everybody* attitude. Forget machismo! I'm jess gonna do *me!*"

Huh. Sounded like I'd actually gotten through to the guy. Good job, me.

Alvin, meanwhile, standing behind Raúl, nodded at me and said, "How you doin', dude?"

I smiled, raising my arms, and then dropped them. "Nothing feels too badly broken."

Sam gave me a weak smile. "You look kinda beat-up, hermano."

I laughed. It hurt. "I *feel* kinda beat-up."

"Well, *I* think you've never looked better," said a voice.

My eyes flew to the open doorway. Standing there, leaning against the gnarled tree trunk frame, was Violet.

Honestly, it was like seeing an angel just sorta hanging out on a street corner somewhere. The sunshine streaming in from everywhere soaked her hair with golden light, and the long golden locks that framed her pretty pink lips appeared to be lit from within, lit like Christmas lights.

She smiled at me, and suddenly the world seemed to make perfect sense. It was a strange feeling. Especially when the world so rarely made any sense. But it definitely wasn't a feeling I minded. Honestly, I don't think I'd ever been so happy to see anyone in my entire life.

"Hey, so how many teeth am I missing?" I asked her as she came to sit on the edge of the little bed. "I never got a chance to look."

Smiling, Violet peeked into my mouth. "Oh, just a couple," she said very matter-of-factly.

Which pretty much had me jumping out from underneath the sheets. "*Seriously?*"

V laughed, shaking her head. She had a great laugh. "Your teeth are *fine*, Charlie. Your *ears*, on the other hand . . ."

I rolled my eyes. "Yeah . . . yeah." *Fool me once . . .*

Raúl gave my shoulder a pinch, those catlike eyes of his flashing like black jewels. "So that was a close one, huh, cuz? Even closer than Mexico."

Violet blinked, surprised. "You heard about Mexico?"

He gave her a deadpan look. "*Everybody's* heard 'bout Mexico. The world almost *ended* when you two went down to Mexico."

"Hold up," said Sam with a slightly panicked look. "The world's almost ended before? I mean, besides this last time?"

Violet, Raúl, and I all looked at each other. Then we just burst out laughing.

"Yeah," I said to Sam, "but only like once or twice." And off his even *more* panicked look, the three of us started laughing even harder.

"Oh, Charlie, you forgot this," Violet said, digging around in her pocket.

"Huh?"

"You left it back in your room."

"Left what?"

"*This*," she said, and then her hand came out empty, and she bent forward and closed her eyes and kissed me. Right smack on the lips, too.

Now, I gotta admit, I've experienced some pretty cool things in my short time as a Morphling; I'd brinco'd all the way from Miami, Florida, to Northeast España; I'd been transported via magical funnel cloud courtesy of Saci Pererê; I'd been drowned and sent to the Land of the Dead by a witch queen; I'd even been swallowed alive by an earthworm the size of the Empire State Building. But nothing—not a *single* one of those things—could compare to the rush I felt when Violet kissed me.

Sounding a million miles away and like a chorus of annoying five-year-olds, I heard Raúl, Sam, and Alvin shout, "OOOOOOOHHHHH!" and couldn't help laughing.

Fortunately, it hurt less this time. And probably because I could hardly even feel my face at the moment.

"*C'mon*, I just ate breakfast," grumbled Alvin. Then, slipping his once golden phone out of his pocket, he knelt down beside us and whispered, "By the way, check *this* out!"

He held up his cell. The screen showed a picture Al must've snapped down underneath La Rosa—me, Violet, Sam, and Raúl all with shocked, panicky looks on our faces and a backdrop of walking, talking, laughing skeletons.

I looked a little closer.

Saw that he'd titled it.

Looked a bit closer and saw that he'd put a filter on it.

Looked a *teeny* bit closer and saw that he'd *posted* it—
ONLINE!

"Bro, have you lost your *FRIGGIN'* mind?" I shrieked, nearly jumping out from under the covers.

Alvin grinned proudly. "Dude, I'm almost up to a thousand followers!"

I could've bitten the kid. Seriously! (Probably my cousin rubbing off on me.) And I might've too—but just then, Lynda Eloise Hernández appeared in the doorway.

Our eyes met, and I instantly shouted, "Mom!" expecting for her to come rushing over, to throw her arms around me and start bawling her eyes out, telling me how much she loved me and making me promise never to battle another thrice-cursed, sack-wielding super ghoul—saying that she wouldn't know what she'd do if I ever got hurt.

Except . . . she didn't do any of that.

Instead, she just stood right where she was, her back rigid, her brown eyes glazed. And it didn't take a Sherlock— *or* Violet—to figure out that something was *seriously* wrong.

I felt my mouth turn down into a frown as I whispered, "Mom, what is it?" Then felt it turn down a little deeper when she said, in a tight voice, "A letter came for you today. In the mail."

Clasped between the trembling fingers of her left hand was a rectangle of neatly folded paper. The letter, probably.

I shook my head. "A letter from who?"

My mom didn't say anything. So I said, "Mom, who sent it?"

And finally she told me: "It's from—well, it's from your abuelita. . . ."

I blinked. "But—" (My grandma had *died*. When I was, like, *nine*. There's NO WAY she could have sent that letter.)

And, as if reading my mind, my mom said, "I know."

ABOUT THE AUTHOR

Ryan Calejo was born and raised in South Florida. He graduated from the University of Miami and spends most of his free time coming up with excuses to go hang out at the beach. When he isn't lazing out on the sand or working on his doggy paddle, Ryan can be found purchasing more books than should be legally permitted or sampling artisan olive oils—yes, that's a thing. Having been born into a family of immigrants and growing up in the so-called Capital of Latin America, Ryan knows the importance of diversity in our communities and is passionate about writing books that children of all ethnicities can relate to. Follow Ryan @RyanCalejo on Twitter or Instagram.